MW01634649

This is a work of fiction. Names, characters, places, and incidents either are the product of the author's imagination or are used fictitiously. Any resemblance to actual events, locales, organizations, or persons, living or dead, is entirely coincidental and beyond the intent of either the author or the publisher.

Moon Shadows
TOP SHELF
An imprint of Torquere Press Publishers
PO Box 2545
Round Rock, TX 78680
Copyright 2012 by Neena Jaydon
Cover illustration by Alessia Brio
Published with permission
ISBN: 978-1-61040-362-7
www.torquerepress.com

First Torquere Press Printing: August 2012
Printed in the USA

Neena Jaydon

Moon Shadows

Moon Shadows
by Neena Jaydon

Moon Shadows

To UT, who helps more than she knows.

Moon Shadows

CHAPTER ONE

First Quarter

The dark highway stretched out before Theo, leading from his friend Marnie's family farm back to town. Pleasantly weary, he replayed the evening in his head with a stomach full of junk food and a face stiff from too much laughter. He and his friends had been pen-and-paper role-playing lately, but with a complete lack of reverence for fantasy conventions and a heavy emphasis on dirty jokes. It was these jokes he was smiling over when he saw the tire tracks sliced across the road.

He leaned forward as he slowed his car. Alone on the highway, he had to rely on his own headlights. He saw the black marks clearly head into the dirt and flattened bushes next to the bridge. There was an ominous, red glow touching the bridge's metal railings. Immediately, his mind went clear and his pulse into overdrive. He crushed the brake pedal to the floorboard, bullying the car to a stop. Throwing on the hazard lights, he leapt from the car.

He ran to the railing and leaned over. Below, he could see the rear end of a car. Most of the car appeared to be submerged, wedged up against the rocks jutting out from the bank. Theo stripped off his jacket, then ran across the bridge and vaulted the railing.

His weight took him deep, frighteningly so. He waited

until he lost downward momentum before swimming for the surface. He broke through to discover the car nearly on top of him. Clawing up it, he got onto the trunk and peered through the back window.

Someone's still in there! The dark figure inside sat at an awkward angle across the front seat. Gritting his teeth, Theo kicked at the rear window. On the third stomp, his boot heel turned the glass into pebbles. He lunged headfirst into the car.

There wasn't enough room to move around. He made one false start, running out of air before he could get to the front seat. Cursing mentally, he retreated for a proper breath. Then he went in again. The woman in the driver's seat had her head bowed, her hair floating around it. His fumbling fingers couldn't unfasten her seatbelt. He growled out bubbles as he forced himself between the front seats for a better look.

The car rocked strangely. Taking the seatbelt in both hands, he snapped it free of its mooring. He wrapped an arm around the woman's waist. Her limbs hooked on the headrests and between the seats. Lungs bursting, he brought his feet down and pulled mightily. With one last thrust, he sent them both flying out the rear window.

The mass under him tilted as his feet cleared the window. The car began to tip sideways. Panting, his heart beating so fast he couldn't hear individual beats, Theo found more strength in his thighs and leapt. He twisted in mid-air. The woman's weight crushed his breath from him when he landed on his back. He wrapped his arms and legs around her as they went under. The moment they surfaced he began to kick, swimming backward to shore. When he found support underfoot, he stood, picking her up. She dangled from his arms in a terrible way. The late August breeze felt icy against his wet skin.

Once on land, he put her down on her back. Distant

noise drew his attention to the bridge. A parked semi lit up the highway. He could see someone standing near it.

"Call 911!" Theo roared. He couldn't smell her breath. The first aid Ma had insisted he learn flashed into his mind. He moved automatically. The woman's mouth was cold rubber beneath his. In the faint light of the half-moon she looked washed out and strange. Theo shook his head and kept trying.

"Come on now," he whispered to her as he caught his breath. "I was fast enough. C'mon, lady, I was fast enough. Don't tell me I wasn't." Another breath into her mouth. "Don't tell me I wasn't." Two more breaths, and then he jerked back from the terrible croaking sound she made. "Oh, my god," he whispered. Running footsteps didn't make him look up; he was too intent on her eyes as they opened.

All at once she wasn't strange and unnerving. Her face took on life and expression. She stared at him, eyebrows knit.

"Hey," he said hoarsely. "H-how do you feel?"

"Awesome." Her voice was barely audible. "Who're you?"

"Theo."

Her mouth curved awkwardly.

"Nice to meet you, Theo."

Those words gave him permission to feel relief. He sat back on his heels, letting out a weak laugh. The truck driver arrived, bringing news of an ambulance on the way, and Theo looked up at a half-moon in a charcoal sky.

Thank god it wasn't full.

There was a car parked out front, and he'd clearly heard the doorbell respond when he pressed it, but no one came to the door. Max glanced up and down the street, which was full of old-fashioned stuccoed houses like this one, before facing the ragged screen door and its scratched white partner again. He tapped his fingers on the wrought-iron railing as he tried to decide whether to ring again or just leave. Just as he reached out to the button again, the inner door opened.

A face appeared: pasty, stubbled with dark whiskers, largely hidden by a combination of brown-framed glasses and heavy, black curls. Taken aback, for a moment Max just stared. Presumably the other man was staring back, but Max couldn't see his eyes clearly. He rallied himself.

"Hi, I'm Max Shevchenko. Anastasia's brother."

The face rose as its owner straightened. The man pushed his hair back with one hand, revealing wide, gray eyes behind the glasses. He took a half-step back and glanced around.

What, is he expecting trouble? Max covered his offense with a smile.

"I'm sorry to intrude, but I just wanted to say thanks for what you did for my sister."

"Oh." The voice itself was a sturdy baritone, but spoke softly.

"You are Theo Dimitriadis, right?"

"Yeah. Yeah." Theo cleared his throat. "Sorry. Come in." He gestured for Max to enter.

The little house had a sloped ceiling and small, paned windows. The living room wasn't exactly out of control but clearly fought the reins. Stacks of magazines wobbled on a stool, and DVD and game cases sprawled across the coffee table, while the sofa provided a home to a potato chip bag, a wadded blanket, and a video game controller. The armchair tucked next to the window overflowed with half-heartedly folded laundry. An incongruously new home entertainment center dominated the room.

As he took this scene in from the front hallway, Max carefully kept his expression pleasant. The last thing he was here to do was judge.

"It's a pleasure to meet you, Theo," he said, holding out his hand. Theo shook it; his hand was big and warm, but his grip too careful. After the handshake, Theo rasped his fingernails across his stubbled chin. He wore a black T-shirt, plaid pajama bottoms, and a ratty, gray cardigan.

"You, too."

"I hope you don't mind," Max pushed on, "but I just really wanted to say thanks in person. The police say you saved her life."

"I just did—what anyone would do." Theo took off his glasses and held them in both hands. The eyes that kept avoiding Max's were remarkable. They weren't blue at all, but a stormy gray that paled when light touched them. "Is she doing okay?"

"Yeah. She should be out of the hospital by next week." Max pressed his lips together. "She doesn't remember how the car got into the river."

"It happens," Theo said. "Trauma and all that," he added hastily when Max looked at him.

"Yeah, that's what the doctors think." Running out of steam, Max looked at the floor; for at least a minute silence reigned in the hallway.

"Do you want some coffee?" Theo asked abruptly.

"Sure."

"The kitchen's this way." Theo led the way down the hall. The kitchen was tidier than the living room, but even more outdated. Formica topped the white table, and the fridge was a dark yellow-beige color. The table had space for four chairs but only had two. At Theo's nod, Max took the nearer and sturdier of the two.

"Is that a harvest gold fridge?" Max asked. Theo looked up from pouring coffee and nodded. "I just had to ask, because we had one when I was a kid. My mom said it was a '70s thing."

"Yeah, my grandmother, uh, said that, too." Theo looked at the fridge. "She loved it. Ma hated it."

"My mom wasn't so big on it, either. As soon as we could afford it, we got new appliances." Max noticed that the coffeemaker was an expensive brand and sized to serve more than one. Possibly as many as four.

"How do you take your coffee?"

"I always order double-doubles," Max said sheepishly, and again Theo nodded. He brought Max coffee in a mug decorated with a famous TV spaceship crew. His own mug of clearly black coffee had the initials "FQVII" on it. "Thanks," Max said, trying to work out what the initials meant. "So what do you do, Theo?"

"I'm a game tester," came the reply. Here, for the first time, was a hint of a challenge in his voice.

"Game tester?" Max blinked.

"I test video games for game companies. Freelance."

"That sounds like a fun job to have." *That's a job?*

"It's actually pretty rough sometimes, but, uh, lots of people want to do it." Theo drank from his mug.

"I bet. How'd you get into it?"

"I won some competitions. Passed some tests." Theo quickly drank again. "I've got better reflexes than most people." This was almost inaudible.

"Huh." Max tentatively sipped his own coffee and then paused. "This is really good coffee." Running back and forth from the hospital, he hadn't slept well since the accident, and the caffeine hit him like a slap.

"I drink a lot of coffee," Theo said with a shrug. "I'm willing to send away for good stuff."

"Hm." Max had more of the best coffee he'd ever

tasted. After a false start, Theo spoke.

"What do you do?"

"I'm a dog trainer." He saw those pretty eyes go wide again, and tension lift the broad shoulders hidden in the cardigan. Theo's build was a mystery under the baggy clothes, but he certainly didn't seem to be as soft as Max would expect of a man who played video games for a living. "My family runs a boarding kennel," Max went on. "I grew up around dogs, so it was a natural fit." He leaned forward, trying to gain eye contact. "Look, why don't you drop around for supper next week? Maybe Sunday? My family would love to meet you, and Anastasia should be home by then."

"I really don't need any fuss made over this." Theo stared into his coffee. At this angle, his curly flop of hair cupped his cheekbones, as if trying to draw attention to them. They were worthy of attention, high and finely carved.

"Don't worry about that," Max said. "It'd mean so much to my mom."

"Okay." Theo nodded, offering a smile that did nice things to his well-shaped lips.

"Great," Max said, feeling a warmth inside unrelated to the coffee. *I'm not sure, but I think this guy might actually be really cute.*

Theo hadn't been looking forward to this dinner. Spending time in the homes of strangers didn't count among things he enjoyed. He pulled restlessly at the collar of the button-down shirt he wore under his most respectable sweater. His mind took a straight line to the sudden visit last Saturday.

He caught me one day after a full moon. God. Just too close.

Max, he'd said his name was. He was about Theo's height, and athletic in a jogging-every-day-tennis-on-the-weekends way. With a face on the softer side of square and heavily lidded hazel eyes that matched his dark blond hair's autumn theme, he'd been a type that Theo would never normally talk to: well-dressed, outgoing, handsome, sure of himself.

Never mind out of my league, we're not even talking the same sport here. He grimaced, peering into the rearview to check just how unruly his hair was.

The sign for West Poplar Road pulled his attention back to his driving. Theo turned onto the gravel road and slowed, leaning forward to peer through the windshield. Sure enough, there was a wooden sign for "Northern Excellence Kennels," accented by thick beds of pansies. He drove halfway around the circular driveway and parked.

Getting out, he paused to take a deep breath. This brought not only cool air into his lungs, but a whole symphony of scents as well, set to the key of "kennel." Not a neglected kennel, though; there was no despair in the air here. And the neatly trimmed fingernails and softly perfect hair on Max Shevchenko didn't match a messy kennel.

Theo stalled by looking around. The small acreage was close enough to town to have cost some money even without the two kennel buildings and the large country house. A mobile home lurked beyond a clump of poplar trees, and shadowed by the two kennels were a paddock with a shelter and a small red barn. He detected horse under all the dog.

Theo squared his shoulders and walked into an uneven chorus of barks. The barking grew louder as he approached the first run. The German shepherd in it abruptly went quiet, retreated, then began to growl.

"Oh, hey!"

Theo looked up at the house in time to see Max come out the back door. Max came down the white-painted steps with his hand out, preceded by the odd couple of a pug and a greyhound. Before Theo could respond, the pug was standing in front of him with his wrinkled face contorted in a snarl. His hoarse woofs were completely serious. The greyhound crouched behind Max's legs with his ears flattened. "Delmer!" Max's tone was surprised. "Delmer, come here. Del—" He picked the dog up, giving Theo a baffled look. "Sorry, that's really not like him. Del, enough!" He gave the pug a gentle shake, and the dog's growling turned into a nervous lick of his nose.

"Uh, it's okay," Theo said. "Dogs just don't s-seem to like me."

"Come in," Max said. "I'm glad you could make it." He smiled, and Theo's cheeks grew warm, then warmer still as his own reaction embarrassed him. Fortunately Max moved away without appearing to notice. Turning his head, Theo gave the German shepherd a direct look, putting some weight behind it. The shepherd shot into its kennel.

The interior of the house was just as tidy and country-magazine as the exterior. The walls were a gentle yellow, accented by framed cross-stitched images of horses and dogs and stained wood hooks holding a variety of coats. Theo could smell dinner as he got out of his shoes and jacket: soup, cheese and wine jelly on crackers, a Caesar salad, garlic bread, pasta with a garlicky Alfredo sauce, and cheesecake with raspberry sauce.

Well, I can keep my mouth full enough not to have to talk too much, maybe.

The greyhound bounded up the staircase to the floor above, which earned it a puzzled look from Max as he shut the pug into a dog crate near the front door. Then a petite older woman came through a doorway to his right. Her attractive, windburned face was framed by braided, silver hair; she wore a simple sweater and slacks.

"You must be Mr. Dimitriadis," she said. "I'm so glad you could make it."

"Call me Theo."

"But she's been practicing your last name all day," a female voice said from within the kitchen. It was a voice too young to care about surprising or offending anyone.

"Oh, don't tell him that. Come on in, Theo," the woman said. "Dinner's almost ready."

"Theo, this is my mother Kaitlyn," Max intervened, stepping past into the kitchen.

"Nice to meet you," Theo said.

"I'm so pleased to meet you, too, after all you've done."

"Oh, that was—that was really nothing."

"I think Theo's a pretty modest guy, Mom," Max said. "Maybe keep it low-key, eh? These are my baby sisters, Chrissi and Charli." At a very large dining room table sat two girls of about twelve. They were identically sturdy, freckled, and blonde. They took crackers from a big platter and made no effort to clarify which twin was which. Helpless, he gave them a smile that felt sickly.

"Anastasia's upstairs, resting," Kaitlyn said. "My husband is away on business, unfortunately, so it'll just be six of us tonight."

A surreptitious glance at the waiting dishes on the table and the stove suggested she was expecting far more than that.

"It smells great," he ventured.

"Thank you," she said, sounding pleased. "You can sit down at the table if you like."

"Wine?" Max asked, reaching for a bottle on the counter. "I opened a red, and there's a white chilling."

"Red's fine," said Theo, going for the first option because he knew nothing about wine. He sat down with a quick glance at the twins. He also knew nothing about children, especially at their age. They stared up at him as they munched.

Max helped his mother set food on the table, tugged the noses of the twins to make them stop stealing food, and poured Theo a glass of wine. Theo sat quietly and waited. His mind was lightning-fast at times, but rarely forthcoming with good conversation.

Finally, Max convinced his mother to sit down, then disappeared through the doorway. After a moment, he returned to announce that Anastasia was on her way down. Theo's ears picked up footsteps on the stairs, and his spine stiffened. Max took the seat at the end of the table, next to Theo.

"Oh, let Theo sit at the head of the table," Kaitlyn said.

"I'm fine," Theo said quickly.

"Mom," Max said, making eye contact with her.

Theo lost track of that interaction when a young woman, smelling of lavender soap and freshly laundered clothing, came into the kitchen. When he looked up at Anastasia, he had to blink. For a flash, he hadn't seen an attractive brunette woman in her twenties; he'd seen her pale skin, limp limbs, and soaked hair.

Now, however, she wore a tight smile that told him she also found this strange. Theo's neck prickled, and he glanced over to discover Max gazing at him with hazel eyes gently narrowed. It wasn't an expression he could safely look at for very long. He wondered if Max was straight.

Ashamed, he dragged his attention back to Anastasia.

"H-h-how are you feeling?"

"Good," she said. "Sore, and tired, but good."

"Sit down and eat, Anastasia," Kaitlyn said.

"I will, Mom," Anastasia said patiently.

For Theo, who was on a nodding acquaintance with every delivery person in town, the food was amazing. It helped distract him from his feelings, which were unclear and yet strong enough to make speech even more difficult than usual. Anastasia ate tidily, seated across from him. He glanced at her slender fingers and tried very hard not to remember how they'd looked in weak moonlight.

"Did that magazine call you?" she asked.

"Yeah," he said. "They left a message on my machine. I—need to call them back."

"They called here a few times, apparently. I just talked to them today. It's nice that they want to do a story about this, but I'm just as glad Max wouldn't let reporters in to see me when I was in the hospital."

"You needed your rest," Kaitlyn said primly.

"I'm also just as glad we managed to talk Dad into going to his conference," Anastasia added.

"Oh my god, he was so close to not going," one of the twins said. "We had to practically shove him out the door."

"I didn't have the heart to say that him hovering around worrying wasn't doing either of us any good." Anastasia chuckled.

"I told him that," the other twin said.

"You would."

"Wh-what kind of training do you do here?" Theo tried changing the subject.

"Obedience training, mainly." Max reached out for a piece of garlic toast, shrugging one shoulder. "Problem dogs. Mom breeds and shows Weimaraners, and Anastasia does some show handling, but the boarding's the biggest part of the business."

"My husband sells real estate," Kaitlyn said.

"We couldn't support this entire family on the dogs, unfortunately."

"I'm surprised you don't have more dogs in the house," Theo said, listening to the quiet panting of the greyhound lurking at the top of the stairs.

"We used to do that," Anastasia said. "Now we keep it to See-Bell and Delmer. Our kennels are heated, so the show dogs can live out there, and we don't have Weimaraners underfoot all the time. How's that Border Collie coming along, Max?"

From there the dinner progressed. Theo let the words flow around him as he filled himself up on home-cooked food. The room was warm from all the bodies in it, and the relaxed, comfortable voices bounced off golden walls. Theo's family had been himself, Ma, and Grandmother. Even when Ma had a boyfriend, it was clear that he was not counted as family.

Don't they find it stifling? He gazed down at his cheesecake as if it knew the answer. *Sometimes would be nice, but every day?*

After dinner, Max helped Kaitlyn with the dishes while the twins went into the adjoining living room to watch TV. Anastasia pulled Theo into the hallway.

"Um, I don't know how to talk about this," she said. "Things are all muddy, and I don't remember anything about the accident. I know I was fine, I didn't have anything to drink, and I wasn't tired or anything. I have no idea what happened." She glanced up at him, her hazel eyes darkened in the dim light. "But it wouldn't be right if I didn't thank you."

"You don't have to say anything," he said. "I just reacted. You don't really—owe me anything for that."

"But I want to," she said, grinning. She didn't resemble Max strongly, but her grin was identical to his. "Thank you, Theo, for saving my life." There was a hitch in her voice as she put her arms around him. Startled, he froze; then, hating himself for that reaction, he carefully returned the embrace.

Anastasia left things at that, and Max helped extricate him from Kaitlyn's urgings to stay for coffee and cookies. When Theo got into his car, he saw from the dashboard clock that he'd been there for three hours. It had felt like an eternity.

As he drove away, he glanced back at the pleasant country home with its lively family, and felt very dark, strange, and different.

Louis Wilson had lived his entire life in Fort Rivers. His job had occasionally taken him to other parts of British Columbia, but now that he was retired, he didn't see any need to be anywhere else. The gold leaves were already half off the poplars. That and the slow traveling of the beige river told him that it really had been a dry summer. It made for a disappointingly short fall.

The walk was under doctor's orders. He'd been too sedentary since leaving the ambulance service. His plump little wife had gamely joined him in his exercise plan, but today she was bundled up before the TV, treating a case of the flu with rest and her Monday dancing show. He didn't mind being out of the house when that was on.

The river was a tributary of one of the two major rivers that gave Fort Rivers its name. The path took him out of the trees and along its banks. Almost immediately he felt a peculiar tingling across the back of his neck. He rubbed his nape and looked around, wondering if he was being watched by wildlife. Bears were a distinct possibility. He didn't see any big, black shapes, yet he grew nervous. The building dread stirred some very old memories. Memories of his childhood, of being told by his parents that he mustn't believe what he heard and saw.

Cold sweat sprang up on his forehead. Louis wiped at it, stumbling to a stop.

"What the hell? Am I having a stroke?" All at once his body seized up. He arched into a painful rictus as a place inside him opened up. At first the link, a strange thread connecting him from the inside to somewhere entirely *other*, was barely perceptible. Then it widened, and darkness began to spill through. It filled him insistently, in the back of his mind where he'd once imagined (heard) the voices of the dead, a space immeasurable yet being rapidly occupied.

He could do nothing about any of it. His body was no longer his own. As the darkness grew, it overtook his vision. There was an animal groan that seemed far away, though it vibrated in his body.

All at once, the door slammed shut. The dark peeled away with an acid tear. It was both painful and a relief to have all that space inside emptied out. As the darkness receded, his vision returned. His body came back.

He could feel damp ground under his cheek. When the dark left, it took all his strength with it. He tried to lift his head and managed to raise it only a couple of centimeters. Ahead on the path stood a figure, a pitch-black shadow in full sunlight. It turned, revealing its face had no features.

"What in god's name?" Louis croaked. The thing turned silently away and walked into the trees. Louis slumped to the ground as his consciousness melted away.

CHAPTER TWO

Hey, what are you guys doing up?" Max leaned through Anastasia's door to find all three of his sisters inside. He quietly slipped the paper bag behind the vase on the stand next to Anastasia's door. Chrissi was on her stomach, a binder open in front of her; Charli was sprawled across her sister's back, texting on her cell. At twelve, the twins were still inseparable.

"Chrissi's getting help with her homework," Charli said, not looking at him.

"Yeah, but it is getting late." Anastasia swiveled her chair away from her tiny, wooden desk.

"What do you want?" Chrissi narrowed her eyes at Max.

"I was going to talk to Ana about Theo," he said, returning her challenging look. "Got a problem with that?"

Charli snorted, closing her phone. "Theo?"

"That guy's such a dork," Chrissi said.

"Guys," Anastasia complained. "He's sweet."

"He's a dork," the twins chorused.

"If he went to our school, I'd push him in a locker," Charli added.

"You guys are so judgmental. He's obviously just a little shy."

"No, he's a dork," Max said, making Charli grin and Anastasia glare at him. "Get to bed, guys. It's a weeknight."

Muttering, the twins untangled themselves. Max dodged Chrissi's pinching fingers as they came for his side, giving her a playful push in return. Once he saw that they were in their room, he retrieved the bag and held it up.

"Want a doughnut?"

"Sure." Anastasia stretched and moved to sit on her bed. Her small room was impeccably tidy. He didn't like a mess himself, but even their fastidious mother couldn't find anything to complain about in how Anastasia cleaned. Her bed was a single, making the room seem to belong to a younger person; the patchwork quilt on it didn't argue much with this impression. Her book collection took up most of the wall space. Light from the yard filtered through her pink curtains, warming the color of the sandy carpet.

Max sat down on the other side of her bed and handed her the bag. He supposed most men his age didn't hang out in their sisters' rooms, but he and Anastasia had always been close. They'd been able to see the same things from a young age, so he'd taken it upon himself to teach her how to talk to spirits long before he knew much about it himself. He now realized how important it had been to have a smaller presence in his life when their biological father died. Being the "man of the house" for his mother and little sister had kept him going until their stepfather came along to take over that role.

His family was probably thought of as strange by many. Both adult children still lived on the property, which wasn't uncommon these days but still frowned upon, and both parents preferred to have them there. It had taken a year of arguing before they had let him put his own trailer on the property; Anastasia's occasional suggestions she might be better off closer to town were always immediately dismissed. The kennel operation did need family around at all times to cover for absences like business trips, dog shows, and training clinics. But deep down Max knew the real reason: it was better for them to always have someone around who understood.

It also meant that Max kept his sex life in town as much as possible.

"Why'd you go to Jimmy's? I thought you were staying in tonight." Anastasia fished the doughnut out of the bag.

"The trailer got too small for me." Unlike how he would have treated that question from their mother, he simply told Anastasia the truth. "I needed to see a different space for a couple of hours."

"Jimmy's is a different space?" she asked dubiously. "You go there all the time."

"Well, it's not here." Max sighed. "I don't know, sometimes I just feel like I'm missing something."

"Like a boyfriend?"

"Who are you to talk?"

"Well, I sort of have one." She glanced at her computer as she munched. "It'd be easier if he worked closer to home, though."

"Yeah." Max let himself fall back on the bed. "But things are good with Lawrence?"

"I think so. It's kind of hard to tell, long distance, you know?" She brushed crumbs off her fingers. "So, what about Theo?"

"His sweater. I was wondering if you wanted to take it back to him, or if you wanted me to do it."

"Hm." Anastasia tilted her head.

"What?" he asked, irritated.

"Why did you make it sound like something you want to foist off on me?"

"Look, he's your knight in shining armor, not mine." *I can't quite figure him out. Physically he's got all kinds of things going for him. If he was gay, I'd sure like to try him out in the sack. But then he goes all shy and quiet like a little kid, which he's way too old to do.*

"Max, you know how sometimes you sound like a jerk? This is one of those times." She was gazing narrowly at him. "Especially when he obviously likes you."

"What?" Max laughed in surprise. "Oh, come on."

"I saw how he kept sneaking looks at you." Anastasia's eyes took on an eager glitter.

"Don't let your eyes go all shiny like that. Theo's not even gay."

"How do you know that?"

Max pondered for a moment.

"No, I've never seen him at any of the LGBT events in town. I'd have remembered him."

"Oh-ho." She didn't quite snicker.

"I'm not saying he's not cute." Max turned onto his side, tracing patchwork with his fingertip. "But I think he's straight, and dogs don't like him. Those are turn-offs for me." Anastasia put her hand next to his, leaning down to peer into his face.

"It's weird. You don't usually latch onto stuff, but this still brings back memories?"

"Well." Max felt his cheeks heat a little. "It's not like I remember anything about that. Just running into Deep Murky, then the next thing was me wrapped up in a blanket and Mom pale as a sheet." When he was ten, he'd met a particularly nasty spirit out in the weeds on the edge of their property. He didn't know what it was called, but he'd nicknamed it Deep Murky for how it had felt to him. It had taken possession of him so firmly he'd fainted. He had no memory of it then walking his body out across the highway, probably trying to get to the forest on the other side. A neighbor had recognized him and swept him off the highway before he could get run over. The quilt had been a present from that same neighbor.

Anastasia hadn't responded; her silence startled him out of his reverie. He looked with concern at her drawn face.

"Anastasia?"

"Eh?" Her lashes fluttered, and she straightened up, running her hands over her hair. "Sorry."

"What's up?"

"Nothing."

"Anastasia," he said, over-enunciating each syllable. "What's wrong?"

"I've sort of remembered stuff about the accident." She hunched her shoulders; he abruptly sat up, putting an arm around her. "I remember seeing light. Weird, purple light." She reached up to rub at her chin, her gaze aimed downward. "A feeling of being pulled, really hard, but not in a physical direction. Like connecting to the spirit world but so much rougher." She bit her lip. "It almost felt like possession."

"Do you think that's what happened? Was it—it couldn't have been Deep Murky, could it?" Max squeezed her shoulders, chilled by the very thought.

"I don't know, Max." Anastasia rubbed her elbow, shaking her head. "I really doubt it, though. I didn't get that boggy water feeling you told me about. I didn't get that feeling of greed. Just ... blank determination. Like maybe something was trying to get through." She shuddered. "I'm sorry; can you take the sweater to Theo? I'm still kind of working through this."

"Yeah," Max said. "Of course." He held out his palm, and she put the crumpled paper bag in it.

"Thanks," she said, smiling. "I will be okay, you know."

He smiled back, pretending to be convinced.

Max glanced at the sweater in the passenger seat, then sighed and turned on the turn signal. It really wasn't such a great chore, but he'd been putting it off. He distinctly remembered Theo slipping out of it after dinner, mumbling about feeling too warm, pulling up the hem of his T-shirt at the same time. In that all-too-brief moment, Max had seen the lower cuts of a distinct set of abs and the top of Theo's happy trail. That very pleasant experience had been followed by an awkward time attempting to get more than a few syllables out of Theo's mouth.

So which is he? The hottie or the total nerd?

As Max turned onto Theo's street, a trio of children on bikes shot across in front of him. He gasped loudly, stomping on the brake. Time slowed as he drew closer and closer to the little girl straggling behind the two bigger children. She seemed to shrink as the hood of the car obscured her body. She didn't seem to even be aware of the car. At last Max was thrown forward against the seatbelt. The tires gave a last little screech of protest before everything came to a stop. Except for the kids: they kept pedaling madly, up onto the sidewalk and away.

Max sat staring, his heart battering against his ribcage, while adrenaline surged through his entire body. It drew anger after it, fast and powerful. He slammed his hand against the wheel, then clenched it into a fist and punched the dashboard.

"You little idiots! You trying to get yourselves fucking killed? You trying to turn me into a murderer? Jesus!" He groaned, burying both hands into his hair, and bit down on the rage. After a moment, he heard the soft rush of a car coming up behind him. He moved his foot from brake to gas. He breathed slowly and carefully as he cautiously drove on. As the shock eased, he picked up on the tingling on the back of his neck. Max glanced next to him.

The elderly woman sat primly in the passenger seat,

clutching what might have been a purse. She was nearly colorless to his vision, as well as translucent. He cruised down the street, keeping an eye out for more sudden appearances.

"Hi," he said.

You have a temper. He distinctly sensed her disapproval as her voice entered his head.

"Sorry." He eased his car into a clear space in front of Theo's house, finally letting the traffic behind him move on. "I don't normally lose control like that. I didn't mean to draw you here."

Well. She sniffed. *One can't ignore disturbances these days. They've gotten through twice already.*

"Pardon?" Max turned as he pulled up the emergency brake, and found her already gone. After a moment he shook his head, grabbed the sweater, and got out of the car. He ran his hand through his hair, relieved to find his fingers no longer trembling. *She must be from the neighborhood. Normally spirits don't come* that *fast when I get angry.*

Max hurried up the steps, then blinked in surprise as the door opened before he got to it. A cluster of young men and women looked at him in equal surprise through the screen door as they hitched up purse straps or zipped up jackets.

"Hi. I'm Max. Is Theo here?"

"Yeah," one of the men said, stepping out of the way and holding the door open. "Go on in. Theo's in the kitchen."

"Uh, thanks." He sidled past the four strangers, all of whom sported a college dorm look they were too old for. He smiled reflexively at the two women in the group, who were giving him measuring looks. "Did I interrupt something?"

"Just Worldhammer," one of the women said bluntly.

"No worries. We're all heading out anyways." To his relief, they did, clearing out the cramped hallway. He heard the screen door close, and then some hushed laughter he suspected had to do with him. Max grimaced and swung the main door shut.

What the hell is Worldhammer? "Hello?" Max went down the hall and peered around the corner, feeling the intruder.

Slouched in a computer chair, Theo had his hair tied into a ridiculous little topknot. There were dots of paint and holes in his worn-out T-shirt. He was squinting through his glasses at the very small statue of a chariot in his hand. Then he visibly stiffened, tiny paintbrush hovering in midair.

"Hi," Max said. Amusement and embarrassment warred within him, but he tried to keep his tone normal. "Sorry. You forgot this." He held up the sweater. "Your friends said to come in."

"Oh." Theo set down the miniature chariot. "Thanks. Just, uh—" He pointed with the end of his paintbrush to an empty chair.

Max sat down and saw by the startled flutter of Theo's lashes that the chair had been intended for the sweater, not him. That made him perversely want to stay.

"So, what are you doing?" he asked.

"Worldhammer. It's an RPG. You can use miniatures for it." Theo laid aside the paintbrush and rubbed his hands against his jeans. "D-did you want some coffee?"

"Sure." Max watched Theo get up and move to his coffee maker. Theo's baggy jeans didn't quite hide the length of his legs and the curves of his butt. When Theo turned back to set a mug of coffee in front of him, Max saw the strong column of his neck, how it tapered out to his shoulders, and pressed his lips together. *What a waste.*

Theo began to tidy up, hands deftly putting little glass

bottles of paint into a plastic storage box. They were big hands, yet not clunky, with long, agile fingers.

"You think it's weird." It hadn't been a question, and he almost hadn't heard it.

"What? No." Max handed Theo a stray paintbrush, a laugh escaping him. "Yeah, a little. I'm sorry."

Theo shrugged stiffly. "Not everybody has to be into the same, uh, things."

"That's true. You're right. I shouldn't judge." Max felt something inside him relax. He leaned on the table, looking into his coffee mug. "Most of my friends think I'm just playing around, being a dog trainer. To them it doesn't sound like a real job."

"Yeah," Theo said, dipping paintbrushes into clear liquid. "I get that all the time." Finally turning his head, he looked at Max sidelong. That conspiratorial look made Max's heart beat faster. Then Theo turned away, going to the sink.

Damn. Did we just have a moment? Max gave himself a stern mental slap. *Don't go misreading straight guys.*

"I'd better get going," he said. "Thanks for the coffee."

"No problem." Theo dried his hands on a towel and followed him out to the entryway. "Thanks for dropping off my sweater."

"I'm sorry it took me so long to remember to do it. I've been driving around with it for days now."

"You could've, y'know, uh, called me to pick it up."

"No way," Max said. He tasted his coffee and found it milky and sweet: just as he'd asked for it the last time. "I owe you way more than that." His words sent Theo's gaze downward, hair falling forward over his eyes. "I know that doesn't exactly make you comfortable, Theo, but my family really appreciates everything you've done for us. You ever need a hand with anything, just ask." He bumped Theo's arm with his fist. "Except with Worldhammer. I still have no clue what that is." He laughed, but Theo just nodded solemnly. "See you around."

As he stepped out into the cooling evening air, not looking back, Max shook his head.

I swear there's a really good-looking man in there. I wish he'd let him out.

"I don't know why they even bother. If you're going to make a movie about pouting, scrawny Hollywood drones, don't pretend they're supposed to be superheroes!" His friend Frankie was holding court, as usual. Theo shoved his hands in his coat pockets and snorted amusement at the loud voices of his friends. Marnie and Whitney flanked Frankie, offering their own critiques. Theo walked at the back of the pack so he could measure if he was walking too quickly.

They were cutting through an unpaved alley to get back to Theo's parked car. Theo heard muffled music and frowned; they were two streets over from the nearest bar, and even on Fridays the bars weren't usually that loud. The back door to a nearby building opened and spilled the music into the night. Wincing, Theo turned away from the light escorting the sound. Then he stopped, caught by a new scent: poplar trees and hayfields and dog kennels and tobacco smoke and warmly-spiced aftershave. His eyes widened as he turned in time to see two men head straight past him. They walked very close together, giving Theo and his friends no notice.

Max nuzzled the other man's cheek and murmured something to him, then spotted Theo. His step hitched as he turned to look fully over his shoulder, but although his mouth formed the beginnings of a word, he didn't speak it. Instead, he quickly looked away. When his companion gave him a curious look, Max initiated an aggressive kiss.

Theo's friends had fallen quiet. Whitney glanced back, then came to a stop himself as he looked at Theo in concern. Marnie hastened back to look up into Theo's face, a hand coming to rest on his elbow.

"Hey," she said softly. The streetlights reflected off her thick glasses as her wide, green eyes examined his face.

"I-it's nothing." Theo's voice came out weakly. He still felt like he'd been mule-kicked in the chest.

"Like hell," Frankie said too loudly, making them all wince. "C'mon, what's wrong?"

"You know them?" Whitney, in contrast, tended to speak too quietly. His words occasionally carried a hint of a faded Jamaican accent.

"Just one."

"Is that the guy we ran into at your place?" Marnie asked.

"What did he do to you?" Frankie asked.

"Nothing." Theo shook his head and rubbed his face. "It's really nothing. We just met. It was all ... all on my side." He tried to laugh and failed. "Didn't even know he was gay."

"That's rough." Marnie patted his back. "Come on. Let's go get some coffee and forget about him."

"Y-yeah." It was difficult to put down slow step after slow step, surrounded by his protective friends. His instincts told him to run and run until he was out of breath; until he could no longer smell Max.

What did you expect? His chest ached, and his face felt stiff and tight. He pushed his hair back as he walked, feeling the night breeze against his forehead. The sensation felt naked and lonely. *A normal, preppy guy like Max isn't for you.*

CHAPTER THREE

You're a TV man."

Theo, just about to bite into garlic toast, froze. Seated opposite him, Frankie nearly choked on his cheeseburger. Theo creaked around to look at the small girl peering over top of the booth.

"Ruthie!" The girl's mother sounded mortified.

Feeling his neck grow warm, Theo listened to Frankie start to chortle. He stared into the girl's large, brown eyes. She stuck a finger into the corner of her mouth and apparently waited for him to take the reins of the conversation.

"She must have seen you on the news," Frankie wheezed.

"Oh, so you are the one who saved that woman in the river," her mother said, eyes widening. "I wasn't sure."

"Uh, yeah," Theo said, feeling the heat reach his cheeks.

"That was really heroic of you. Really brave." She picked up her purse and began rummaging. "Would you mind signing this for Ruthie? Honey, pass this to the nice man." Ruthie took the pen and memo pad, then presented them to Theo, who couldn't look at anyone as he signed his name.

"There you go," he said.

Ruthie took pen and pad back, looking at them in bemusement as she slid back out of sight.

"Thank you so much," her mother said. "I think she's

really going to appreciate that when she's older."

"Y-you're welcome," Theo said, before gratefully turning back around. He narrowed his eyes at Frankie, who was bright red behind the hand pressed over his mouth. Rubbing at the back of his hot neck, Theo turned his glare on his plate. Then he took his feelings out on his garlic toast, ripping off a chunk with his teeth. "What's so funny?"

"You, dude." Frankie snorted. "Who else would go tomato-red because someone asked for his autograph? You've got to accept that you're a good guy who did an amazing thing."

"It's not that simple," Theo muttered.

"It kind of is."

"It didn't really feel like me doing it. I just sort of went on automatic. I don't feel like I did something other people wouldn't." *Although maybe they couldn't. I can never tell what normal people can really do.*

"That just proves you're a good guy. It didn't occur to you that you could've *not* jumped in, did it?"

"No," Theo said, "it didn't." It had felt like breathing, like the instinct to chase: something his body did without checking with him first. "Look, I'm not ashamed of what I did, I just ..." *I've spent my whole life trying to avoid getting noticed. Now people here have seen me on TV. What else could they find out about me?*

"Don't like attention." Frankie waggled a disapproving French fry. "Get over it."

"You're probably right." Theo sighed. "I have to call a magazine reporter back this afternoon. Another one."

"It'll be fine."

"Yeah," Theo said, picking up his spoon. "Oh, hey, there's Whitney."

"Where you been? You're never late," Frankie complained as Whitney slid into the booth. "These

Thursday lunches were your idea to begin with."

"I'm sorry, guys." Whitney rubbed at his forehead, his gaze distant. "It's been kind of a rough day."

"What's going on?" Theo lost interest in his chili at the obvious worry on Whitney's lean face. Frankie picked up on it enough to quiet down, too.

"Marnie's sister is in the hospital. In a coma." Whitney waved away the waitress who offered him a menu. The uncharacteristic abruptness of the gesture spoke volumes about his stress level.

"Jesus, what happened?" Frankie set down his cheeseburger, eyes wide.

"Nobody knows. They found her by her car last night. Marnie's freaked out, of course." Whitney twisted up a napkin, shaking his head.

"Is there anything we can do?" Theo asked.

"Marnie's hanging out at the hospital. Maybe go see her? She kicked me out so I could go back to work." Whitney smiled weakly, sheepishly.

"We'll do that for sure," Frankie said.

Theo nodded, stirring his chili aimlessly. He ate chili, hardly noticing that it had cooled. His mind lingered on the topic of healthy young women abruptly driving off of empty highways or falling down in random comas. If it was all related, then something nasty was going on in Fort Rivers.

Theo hated hospitals. Not only were the scents overpowering, but his family had always painted hospitals as fearful places. They featured in childhood nightmares of being locked up and used in sinister experiments. No, a hospital was no place for his kind. He didn't like how grateful he felt that Whitney had come back, meaning

Marnie had support and he could leave. That didn't mean he didn't take advantage of the chance to escape.

Outside, the smoky air seemed delicious in comparison to the antiseptic breath of the hospital. Theo slouched toward his car. A familiar scent stopped him, and he turned.

"Theo?" Anastasia, wrapped in a long coat, hurried across the parking lot toward him.

"Uh, hi." He cleared his throat as she came right up to him. "Are you okay?" There were tension lines around her mouth and she was looking over her shoulder.

"Hm?"

"Are you, y'know, all right?" Theo jerked his head toward the hospital building.

"Oh. Oh, yeah. I'm just here for a couple of follow-up tests." She tucked her hair behind her ears, squeezed her eyes shut for a moment, then looked up at him. "I just had some awful news."

"R-really?" His heart leapt into his throat.

"I just ran into a client. Her husband's Louis Wilson, used to run the ambulance service. Do you know him?"

"No." *I try not to know very many people.*

"Sorry, it's not that small a town." She bit her lip. "They found Louis out on their property, collapsed. He's been slipping in and out of consciousness ever since."

The hairs on Theo's nape lifted. He felt his face stiffen, and Anastasia gave him a startled look.

"What's wrong?"

"N-nothing. Really. You were, uh, saying?"

"Well, that was it, really. I mean, it looks like he's going to be okay, but there was just no warning, I guess." She crossed her arms over her stomach and looked at the ground. "It's strange."

"Yeah. Strange." Theo slowly inhaled through his nose, sampling the air. He got nothing but the usual mix of pulp mill, trucks, and pine trees. Of course, just because he couldn't smell it didn't mean there wasn't a problem.

"Anyways, I'd better go. I'll be late." She touched his elbow lightly. "Come over for dinner again sometime, okay?"

"Uh, yeah. Sure." He watched her make her way across the parking lot, then turned toward his car again. He shook himself, as if that could shake off his unease. *I might not be the weirdest thing in Fort Rivers anymore.*

Work came in spurts, and Theo had just come to the end of a rush. He often got restless after a busy period, but he couldn't remember it being this bad before. He paced continuously, unable to bear even looking at a game. Books or TV didn't help, either.

Some of it was probably due to the hospital visit yesterday, but Theo didn't want to consider how much of it might be Max. To keep himself from replaying the image of Max dressed for clubbing and wrapped around another man, Theo decided to see what he could find out about the other thing bothering him: the people randomly collapsing in town. He started with Louis Wilson.

Louis lived just outside of town, in the same rural area as Max. Theo doubted that qualified as a coincidence, yet he couldn't help but notice how much of the route was the same as he drove down the dark highway. The last thing he wanted to do was disturb the Wilson family, so he parked up the road and walked the rest of the way. He heard dogs barking in the distance.

Idiots. Better try to stay downwind.

Fortunately, the Wilson family dog was indoors. He heard its high-pitched bark as he slid past the house, but it was soon silenced. Theo didn't bother with the house itself; even if he could investigate undiscovered, there'd be too many scent trails inside to do him any good. He didn't know what he was looking for, which meant he needed as little interference as possible.

He did find it behind the house, agonizingly faint and days old. It was a peculiar, inky scent, unfamiliar and metallic around the edges. He crouched down, running his fingertips over the grass to stir up scent. A noseful of fertilizer and lawnmower made him shake his head sharply, his eyes watering. This lush grass, cropped to a uniform height, was likely Louis' baby. It painted a picture of a man probably wholly unremarkable, yet with a distinct life of his own.

Being unremarkable had often been Theo's dearest wish.

He snorted to clear his nostrils and found the dark smell again, leading toward the back of the largely uncleared acreage. The trees provided welcome cover.

The scent led him first to the river, then ended, making him circle back. He picked it up leading away from the house in another direction after wandering nervously behind the Wilson house for some time. Not even the most obsessive gamer could match his concentration and persistence, which kept him on the trail, as well as making him very good at his job. Grandmother had not only told him that their kind were stubborn, she'd demonstrated that on many occasions herself. Even Ma, who could get hard-headed, had often given up when it came to Grandmother. When things got bad at the end, she'd even joked about how Grandmother's stubbornness might have saved her.

Theo hastily forced down such memories. Losing his mother had been the worst thing that had ever happened to him. Grandmother had made it to old age and seemed content to go; Ma had been far too young, the cancer far too sudden. He could think about their deaths clearly now, but never without pain.

"*We don't live that long, Theofanis.*" Grandmother's words. "*The moon, she wears us out.*"

He could always feel the moon. She hadn't waxed large enough to bother him yet; tonight she was just a glowing presence above, no more, no less. After cutting through bush, pasture, and someone's personal car graveyard, Theo found the trail curving south. It led him out into the moon's view.

Theo stopped, inhaling cool air deep into his lungs. The scent had abruptly thickened. It was fresher here, but that wasn't the only thing that he noticed. He was standing on the edge of a shorn hayfield. The road was a few acres away to his right; between him and it lay a yellow house with outbuildings large and small, and kennels he could clearly smell.

"You've got to be freaking kidding me," he whispered.

"Good night, guys," Max said, hitting the switch. The kennels were as quiet as they ever got. He left them full of rustling and scratching and soft groans. "Damn, it's cold tonight." He zipped his coat and started for his trailer.

A glance out across the field brought him to a stop. He saw someone walking onto it from between the trees that formed a casual barrier between properties. From a distance, he could only tell the person was tall.

"What the hell?" Max changed tracks, hurrying out into the field. It had been hayed about a month ago, and the gamely recovering grass crunched softly underfoot. His eyes widened as he recognized the slouching figure.

Theo stopped, then belatedly moved on. He was walking quickly toward the back of the field, and Max had to run to catch up.

"Hey," he said breathlessly. "What are you doing here?"

"Nothing. Looking." Theo finally stopped. His cheeks were dark red. "I didn't realize how close this is to your place."

"How close what is?" Max scratched at his neck. "Wait, what? Looking for what?"

After a pause that was far too long, Theo spoke.

"I'm looking for a place for me and my friends to play paintball. I heard there was a guy here that'd rent us part of his farm. I thought I was on it." All of this came out like Morse code on fast forward.

Max burst out laughing.

"You're a really bad liar, Theo. What, were you buying weed from Leonard?" His neighbors had been known to sell things they weren't supposed to. Theo bowed his head, and Max clapped him on the shoulder. "It's Fort Rivers. Who cares about stuff like that here?"

"Mm." Theo gave him a sidelong glance.

Max sighed, wondering if he imagined the accusation in that look.

"Look, Theo, about the other night ..."

"It's okay." Theo spoke hastily, raising a half-hearted hand in a gesture of dismissal.

"It's just I think I probably freaked you out. I'm not really discreet about it, but I don't advertise what I am, either." Max shrugged. "I never know how people are going to react."

"It's not that." Theo blinked, looking surprised.

Intrigued by that reaction, Max pushed on.

"If you're not used to seeing that kind of thing, I'm sure it's a bit of a shock."

"That's not why—I *am*—" Theo looked at the ground.

What? You're what? Max held his breath, watching

Theo's face intently. He wanted the blush forming on those high cheekbones to mean what he thought it meant.

"I'm the same as you." Theo sniffed and rubbed at the back of his neck, still not making eye contact.

No way. No way. Ana was right? Max frowned despite his elation. "Then why don't you come out—"

"I'm not in the—" Theo started heatedly.

Grinning, Max reached out to take hold of his wrist. The skin under his fingertips was startlingly warm.

"Out to the *dances*. I've never seen you there." *I'd have remembered you. Hell, I'd probably have taken you home.*

"I'm not, y'know, good with crowds. People."

"It's a good group, though. We're nice people there. Well, if you're not into it, I understand that." Max shrugged one shoulder. "It's just too bad." He slowly released Theo's wrist, letting his fingers trail over the back of his hand. He saw Theo's gaze flicker his way and suppressed a grin.

Do I still make him nervous? Am I a jerk because I'm starting to like that I do? He raised his shoulders almost to his ears, then dropped them, pushing his hands deeper into his pockets. Letting out a breath, he saw it in the air.

"It's getting late in the year," he said, turning his head to look at Theo.

Theo was scanning the tree line. Max resisted the urge to look himself, because he'd rather look at Theo. There was an amazing stillness about him, his body held at the ready without tension. The shadows cast by his brow turned his eyes slate-colored.

The house lights created a yellow pool that separated the yard and the field into different spaces. Here the night surrounded them. There wasn't another person in sight; it was just the two of them. Mist rose in little clouds across the raggedly tufted field, a miniature sky they stood above. Max's next thought came without embarrassment.

This is seriously romantic.

He stepped in close, making those black-fringed eyes widen, and reached out with both hands to cup Theo's jaw. Everything was as natural as breathing, and it was breath he felt on his mouth as he came in for the first touch.

Delighting in the softness of Theo's mouth, Max closed his eyes. Theo was a pillar of heat that drew him near, away from the chill, but he didn't quite let their bodies touch. That would take away from the kiss, which was paramount. Theo's inhalation was suction, and then those silken lips parted and he leaned into Max. Max put his fingers around the back of Theo's skull, pressing his palm into thick curls.

It was enough to put him on the precipice. If he went over the edge, this would turn to shoving and nipping and sweating and tugging and all kinds of other things that made him breathe harder just thinking about them. This was starting to look like an exciting place to tumble to the ground together. For a moment, he teetered.

Hell with it. Let's do this. Weird or not, I want him. Max dropped his hands to Theo's hips and jerked him close. At the same time, he shoved his tongue into Theo's mouth.

Making a noise in his throat, Theo groped at Max's jacket, then grabbed it in both hands. Then he held Max in place as he took a big step back. They looked at each other in silence. Max waited for an explanation, but didn't get one.

"Sorry," Max said, trying not to sound disappointed. But that was as far as he got before intense tingling spread across his back. He turned sharply to look toward the back of the property. At exactly the same moment, Theo also turned to look, but Max was too distracted to process that oddity.

If it weren't for his sensitivity to the spirit world, Max doubted he would be able to see the dark figure standing between two trees. He felt its presence as a pressure on the base of his skull. It made him sweat with the strength of its presence. Even though he felt its malevolence, this was an unfamiliar dread. He knew that this wasn't Deep Murky because it had none of the aura of decay and swampy water.

He glanced at Theo, then looked longer, startled by the intent look on his face. Theo seemed to turn into someone else, his expression coolly focused, his posture straight and strong. Then, his eyes never leaving the shadow, Theo began to run.

"Theo?" Max blurted, startled. *Wait, can he see that?* "I don't think you should—" Theo was already halfway to the trees; his speed took Max's breath away. Belatedly he took off after, shocked by how little progress he made in comparison. "Theo! Don't go in there! Wait!" Max could no longer see the peculiar shadow in the trees, which was no comfort. That didn't mean it was gone. He didn't know what the thing intended.

Theo stopped at the edge of the trees. By the time Max caught up, the shadow was gone, its unearthly presence no longer making his skin tingle. Breathless, he looked into Theo's face. Quickly, alertly, Theo probed the trees with his eyes. His breathing, to Max's great annoyance, was nearly normal.

"What's going on?" Max asked. Theo gave him a sharp look.

"You shouldn't be here," he said.

"Theo," Max laughed in exasperation, "this is my property. What are you looking for?"

Abruptly Theo sagged, turning his attention to the ground.

"I'm sorry," he mumbled. "I—I can't."

"Seriously, you can tell me." Max reached out to put his hand on Theo's upper arm. He didn't miss how Theo's gaze landed on his hand. "Did you see something in here?"

"You'd better go inside." Theo abruptly began walking quickly back across the field.

"Theo—" Max found himself, yet again, hurrying after Theo. For some time they walked in silence, Max annoyed to find Theo's stride too brisk. "Was that inappropriate?"

"No," Theo said, his tone miserable. "That's—that's not—"

"You can talk to me. What did you see back there?"

"Nothing," Theo said quickly.

"Nothing? Theo, you took off like a bat out of hell. You were chasing something." *And if you know what it was, I'd really like to know.*

"Hey," Theo snapped. "I'm weird. You know that." He shook his curls back angrily. "You don't know— anything about me. Let's just l-leave it at that." With that he took off at a run, heading for the road. Max stared after him.

No. That's enough running after you for one night. He watched until Theo was out of sight down the road. *But I'm not done chasing you, Theo.*

Theo sat cross-legged in his worn-out computer chair, leaning his cheek on his hand as he stared at his computer screen. He flicked the cursor across the spreadsheet but didn't add anything to it. The familiar ache in his joints and muscles was not what distracted him from his work.

Fingers brushed his cheeks, and lips pressed gently against his own. Theo sat up in his chair so abruptly he nearly tipped it over. He slapped at his cheeks to make those ghostly sensations go away. Firmly resisting the urge to touch his mouth, Theo threw himself out of the chair and stomped upstairs.

Stop thinking about that. That wasn't the biggest thing that happened that night, even.

He poured himself an angry cup of coffee and downed half of it at once. It was hot but not painfully so; it was bitter, but he liked it that way. Other people turned to alcohol when under stress, or smoked something, or jumped on a treadmill. In almost every situation, Theo turned to caffeine.

It was one stupid kiss, two days ago! He gulped down the rest of the coffee and refilled the cup. He hadn't done anything about the mystery thing in the bush, paranoid that Max would show up any time he stepped outside. He peered through the open blinds at the pungent orb in the sky. Mother Moon, sapping his strength. She looked like she was visibly growing fat on his life force. Of course, he knew that wasn't true. He did, however, find it horribly unfair that the more beautiful she was, the sicker he felt.

There was still the matter of the thing near Max's house. Was that coincidence? Did it have anything to do with Anastasia? He pulled out his cell and looked at it. Resistance immediately filled him, dragging him to a standstill until he guiltily put his phone back in his pocket.

I have no idea what I'd even say. On days like this he could barely think, much less talk.

"About two days," he said to himself. By tomorrow he'd need industrial strength coffee to get him through the day. The day after that ... "Of all the times to have a hot guy show interest," he muttered into his mug, leaning his hand on the counter and sighing heavily.

Leaning against the fence, Max looked up at the night sky and coughed. He put the cigarette between his lips and crossed his arms over his chest, wishing he'd put on a heavier coat. It was still early fall, but the nights got cold fast at this time of year. He felt Whiskey, a training client, nose at his thigh.

"This is just between you and me," he told the dog. Whiskey, a large lab-something, gave him a wag.

Max jumped as he heard a voice in the kennel; he'd thought everyone was already in the house. He hastily dipped the cigarette in the rain barrel, stuck the sodden butt in his pocket, and gave his fingertips a sniff. But a muffled scream, followed by an explosion of barking, made him forget about the nicotine smell on his hands. Even as he rushed for the kennel door, he felt the tingle of a spirit's presence.

"Ana?" He looked down an empty corridor as barking and growling buffeted him. Not just growling, but naked snarling; Max couldn't hear his own pounding pulse over the din. He stared in amazement at the fiercely bared teeth of a Great Dane, the pair of Shih Tzus in the kennel next to him equally serious. The tingling turned into heavy pressure on the back of his neck. "Anastasia!"

"Max?" Anastasia's voice came shakily from one of the kennels farther down the row.

Max hastened toward her. Behind him, the Great Dane charged his kennel's door, making the chain link rattle.

"There's something here," Anastasia said, raising her voice over the canine panic. She came out of the kennel, her eyes wide in a pale face.

"I know," Max said. "But I can't see—" Something seized his wrist. He turned back, startled, to look into the terrifyingly blank face of a solid shadow. Its grip was hard and cold. Before Max could react, it flung him against the wall. He thought he heard Anastasia call his name, but his hearing faded and his vision dimmed.

He felt something trying to get in—no, not trying, it was slipping into his core with oily ease. Max frantically bore down with his will to push it away. Though he could no longer feel his lips, he tried to chant as he'd been taught as a child.

"My mind is my own. You will have no vessel in me. You will have no vessel in me. You will—"

And then he was falling, the intruding force retreating like a cat jerking its paw back from something hot, leaving him disoriented and weak. Max blinked furiously at the Great Dane, whose name he dimly remembered was Peter. After a wary look down both ends of the hallway, Peter gave him a slobbery lick up the cheek. Max numbly patted the big dog's neck.

"Are you okay?" Anastasia knelt beside him, quickly feeling his cheeks and forehead.

"Yeah." He licked his lips, finding them very dry. "What the hell was that?"

"I don't know." Her voice broke, and she paused to get control. "God, Max, I don't know. I think if the dogs weren't protecting me it would have got me." She slumped down beside him, shoulder to shoulder. "I've never seen a spirit like that."

"I think I might have," Max said weakly. "Not sure, though. Wait." He turned to frown blearily at her. "Why would it be afraid of dogs?" Peter's tail brushed his arm as the dog snuffled the floor. All around them, the other dogs were watching. Eerily, not one so much as panted.

"I have no idea, but it was. When Peter broke out of his kennel, the spirit took off." Anastasia pointed to the bent door that leaned forlornly away from its kennel.

"Jesus." Max shook his head. "Jesus, what's going on in this town?"

"Max." Anastasia leaned more heavily against him. He found her weight comforting. "Should we talk to Mom about this?"

That cleared his head. Max began to get to his feet, pausing to help her up after him. They exchanged a look.

"She'll worry."

"I know she'll worry. It's just—this might be worth a freak-out, Max. That thing was so strong, and it was clearly willing to forcibly possess."

Max heard panting and the groans and grunts of dogs settling themselves back down for the night. He led Peter back into his kennel and tied the gate closed with a bit of baling twine. Anastasia helped him double-check that all their boarders were where they should be. Neither of them spoke. He knew she was right, but the thought of his mother's hysterical voice brought acid into his stomach.

His first memory, his only memory of being very small, was of his mother screaming. Of the car accident that took his father from this world, leaving him, baby Anastasia, and their mother behind. Being able to speak to his father in the spirit world had softened his grief, but it hadn't hardened Max against his mother's voice when she grew upset. He was still too shaken to want to face such a decision.

"Let's see," he said finally, as they prepared to leave. "We'll see how things are in the morning."

"Okay." Anastasia, thankfully, didn't question him.

Full Moon

Over the past two days Max had made an intimate acquaintance with Theo's voicemail. He was busy enough to put Theo out of his mind during the day. Every night, however, in snuck Theo. Sometimes he wondered about Theo's secrets, but mostly he thought about where he should have taken things after that one kiss.

Max parked his car and peered out his windshield. He could see a faint light inside.

"When you live like a hermit, Theo, it makes it pretty easy to find you." Max took a deep breath and considered things. *I'm not this pathetic.* Suddenly annoyed at himself, he put his keys back in the ignition. Something flickered on a corner pane of the front window when headlights flashed across the house, and he took them out again.

Max got out and walked across the lawn to take a better look. There was a clear crack in the glass, spreading out in weakening patterns of fractures.

Maybe it's nothing. Maybe a kid hit a baseball the wrong way. Yet the damage looked like it was on the inside. A bad feeling came over him as Max looked into the empty living room beyond. *No. Screw manners. Too many bad things have been happening lately.* He climbed the steps to the front door and rang the doorbell. There was no response, so he went in. The unlocked door did nothing for his peace of mind.

"Theo?" Spooked by how cold the house was, he raised his voice. "Theo, are you home? It's me, Max." The more he moved through the quiet house, the more uneasy he grew. He turned on the hall light. "Theo?"

The kitchen was empty; he started down the hall. All the doors were open. He moved to peer around the door frame into a bedroom. His eyes widened and his heart leapt into his throat.

Curled up on the bed was a massive dog, staring at him over the bushy tail resting across the end of its powerful muzzle. Its pale eyes bored into Max.

Dog? Max's brain pointed out the broad skull, the complex gray fur, and the large, upright ears. Dogs didn't come this big. It was half again the size of a Great Dane.

"Hey, buddy," Max whispered. The animal's ears didn't so much as twitch at the sound of his voice. It was far too large and real and alive for this cozy little house.

Max, who regularly worked with aggressive dogs, still couldn't help but tense up as the big animal uncurled. The bedsprings squeaked dryly as it leapt to the floor and trotted past him. He watched it go, eyes stuck wide open.

He knew that Theo didn't have a dog. Even if it weren't so odd that Theo hadn't said anything about it, and even if dogs didn't actively dislike Theo, this was not a house with dogs. There was no fur on the couch, no dog bed or toys in the living room, no food or water dishes in the kitchen, no leashes on the coat hooks by the front door. Max heard the stairs creak and went out to look. Moving slowly, Theo came up, tying shut the belt of a worn housecoat.

"I'm sorry," Max said. "I saw the cracked window and the front door was open and I just, uh—just came in. Are you okay?" Theo's glistening skin looked dull and pale.

"Just the flu," Theo mumbled, leaning his forearm against the wall. The housecoat revealed his collarbone and the top planes of his chest, but Max didn't enjoy this as much as he normally would. He cast about, rudderless.

"Are you sure? You look like death warmed over."

"I'm fine. What're you doing here?"

Gee, he really looks happy to see me. "I just wanted to apologize ... Since when have you had a dog?"

"Dog?"

"Yeah, that big gray one." *That doesn't look like a dog.*

"I don't have a dog." Theo's tone was flat.

"What are you talking about? It was just here. It went down your way. You had to have seen it."

"I'd know if I had a dog. I—I want to go back to bed, and it sounds like you've got a fever or, y'know, or something, too. Maybe you should go home."

At a loss, Max stared at him. Theo glowered at the floor, impatiently wiping at his chin as sweat rolled down it.

"I don't think I should leave you alone," Max said.

"Just go." Theo pushed himself off the wall and returned to the staircase. "There's nothing to apologize for. Just leave me alone."

Those words hit him unexpectedly hard, and Max didn't move right away. Then Theo began to tilt sideways. Max lunged down the stairs. He closed one hand around a wrist alarmingly warm to the touch. With his free hand, Max grabbed the banister before Theo's weight could pull him off his feet. All at once that weight was gone. Max caught the banister in the stomach.

What the—Light flared up from below, obscuring everything. It sucked down to a rough outline, rapidly resolved into a familiar shape, then winked out.

On the floor was the dog. The wolf. It was wrapped up in Theo's robe, one massive, white-tipped paw sticking ludicrously out of a sleeve. Already off-balance, spots on his disbelieving eyes, Max sat down with a thump.

CHAPTER FOUR

Full Moon

Anastasia had spent the last part of her visit insisting to her friend that she was fine, that she didn't regret coming out to her dinner party.

I probably do regret coming out. Anastasia rubbed at her forehead, frowning at the curving rural road. She wasn't at full strength yet. It turned out that drowning took seconds, but recovering from it took weeks. *My head hurts.*

It was a long drive home from her friend's place down on the river flats. Surprisingly, she didn't fear driving; her wrecked memory worked in her favor there. At this time of year the poplars were fancied up with golden leaves, especially nice with the setting sun filtering through them. Occasionally a pickup rattled past, but other than that she was alone on the road. The sedan she drove, bought used for her by her stepfather, had been waiting for her when she got out of the hospital. She'd had no choice but to burst into tears. It didn't quite feel familiar yet, but she enjoyed its solidity.

As she turned the sweeping corner, she saw someone standing in the road. Anastasia gasped loudly and slammed her foot down on the brake pedal. She heard the tires screech. Her heart nearly stopped as the back end of the car skidded to the right. It came to a stop, slightly askew, and she looked around wildly.

She didn't see anyone as she fumbled with her seatbelt. Once free, she threw open the door and ran around to the front of the car. Still no sign of anyone, prone or otherwise. The burst of adrenaline that numbed her lips and quickened her breathing distracted her from the tingling pressure on the back of her neck.

Anastasia turned sharply to her left. Right next to her stood a solid shadow, about her height, in an unfinished humanoid shape. She recoiled in horror, the beginnings of a scream in her throat, as its spiny fingers reached for her. She felt pressure building in her head as she bolted around the car.

"No! I'm not a vessel!" she cried. As she turned the corner of the rear bumper, she felt those peculiar fingers clamp around her shoulder. Its aggression terrified her. "My mind is my own. My mind is my own!"

It felt like successive layers of thin film separated her from her nervous system. Anastasia hurled herself clumsily forward. She hit the car with her side and bounced off to land on her knees. She scrambled up in time for the thing to seize her by the throat.

No! Anastasia glared at it through spots on her vision as its tepid fingertips pressed into her windpipe. It was eerily, blankly strong, but she could feel how clearly it wanted control of her, and that gave her something to fight. She bore down with all her mental power until its grip loosened enough for her to pull free. It immediately came at her again. She wildly dodged one grab. It caught her wrist and she fell hard against the trunk of the car.

"I said no," she spat, tasting blood. "I will not be a place for you. This is my body, my mind. It is not for you. I am not your ..." Inside her skull the pressure grew heavier and heavier. Pain sliced into her body until the parts of her that made actions and words were cut away.

She slid down the car and fell limply to the asphalt.

Yet she was still present when her body got up. It unnerved her that she couldn't feel her feet touch the ground as her body walked across the asphalt and through the dried grasses on the side of the road. It continued down the hill, pushing aside bushes, tangled dead grass, and old fallen branches with rude force.

Who are you? What do you want from me? She got no response; whatever this spirit was, it had no interest in her beyond as a vessel. It frightened her that the shadow was apparently taking her straight to the river, but she didn't ask for mercy. She didn't want it to know how afraid she really was.

As she drew near the edge of the river bank, the spirit left her so suddenly that it felt like her body had been hurled aside. Anastasia fell to the ground, her head reeling. She stared up at the shadow, so impossible, standing there in the dimness of evening. It did nothing.

"What are you waiting for?" she whispered. The answer came immediately.

In the core of her awareness, she felt a new kind of pressure. The stronger the pressure grew, the more she realized it didn't feel the same as connecting to the spirit world. This was an alien energy forcing its way in. Her body jolted and then collapsed, distanced from her; she stared blankly up at the sky, seeing the first hints of stars.

It didn't surprise her that she began to recognize the energy as it filled her to overflowing. It was simply a less coherent form of the shadow itself.

She could do nothing to stop it as it congealed within her, then began to tug its way free. As the new shadow rose next to her, she found the strength to turn her head. The two shadows made no real acknowledgement of each other, instead immediately walking back up the hill toward the road. Anastasia, drained, could only watch them go.

Max sat on the stairs, gazing in shock at the wolf. He didn't dare stand up. The foundations of his world had shifted slightly, and he wasn't sure they'd come to a stop yet.

The wolf lay on its side, ears flattened and eyes squeezed shut. It—he—raised his head and shook it. Theo hunched his back and slid out from under the robe; for a moment he was caught in the sleeve and repeatedly nosed and tugged until he freed himself. Then he made a beeline for the computer desk and tried to fit his massive frame under it. Only partially successful, he gave Max a hunted look around the base of the chair.

Max's next words came in a wild rush.

"Okay, ghosts are one thing. I've been around spirits all my life, and they make sense to me, but—but seriously— what? What the hell? Theo, what the hell?" Theo's head cocked to the side. "Don't look at *me* like that! You're the one who can explain this!"

Theo flattened his ears and gave him a dirty look, then crept out into the open. Max watched in dry-mouthed bemusement as the big animal began nosing around in a pile of cardboard boxes. Backing up, Theo dragged a white poster board over to the bottom of the stairs. It had the alphabet printed on it in capital letters. Theo went to the desk and rose onto his back legs, then returned with a notepad in his mouth. This he carried right to Max, who automatically took it. Theo made the same round trip again, this time depositing a damp pencil.

As Theo started to retreat, Max reached out to push

his fingers into the dense fur of his ruff. It was coarse at the edges and soft near the skin. Theo hesitated, glanced at him, then shook him loose and went to the alphabet poster.

He put his big black nose on a letter. It was "I." He looked expectantly at Max. After about a minute, he made a grumbling noise in his throat. Max belatedly wrote an "I" on the notepad. Apparently satisfied, Theo nosed a series of letters. Seeing him mince around the poster was surreally cute. Max dutifully wrote them all down.

IM A WEREWOLF.

"No shit," he said. Theo's ears pinned to his skull, but he resumed pointing out letters.

FULL MOON. WEAK.

"Huh?" But Theo was at it again.

CANT CHANGE BACK.

"Oh." Max cleared his throat. "Ever?"

TOMMOROW.

"That's not how you spell that." This earned him a growl. "Is there anything I can do?"

DONT TELL.

"Who would I tell? You know you've put a space thing and a period on here, but no apostrophes, right?" Max frowned at the poster. "Or question marks."

Sitting down, Theo gazed at him. One brow was furrowed.

"Look, uh, Theo, my family's got a history with unusual things—not that you're a thing. But that would probably be why I'm not screaming and running away." Max cleared his throat. "Mom, Anastasia, and I can all talk to spirits. Ghosts. I don't tell people about my family's secret, and I'm not going to tell anybody your secret, either. You can trust me."

Licking his nose, Theo looked away. Max just gazed at him for a minute.

"Is this why you avoid people?"

Wrinkles appeared on Theo's wide muzzle.

"I'm not judging, I'm just curious. Seriously, I get it, in my family being a kid was—"

Cold goose bumps rose all over Max's back, and Theo jumped to his feet, growling. Max pulled himself up and looked around warily. He backed down the steps and stood next to Theo, whose hackles were up. Tingles flared up on Max's neck and shoulders. Growing pressure in his head made dark spots dance in front of his eyes.

"Theo, there's something there. Be careful."

Four-legged, Theo was almost overpowered by the inky scent. It sent adrenaline coursing into his body, banishing the aches and fatigue. He couldn't see what was stinking up the basement, only the effects of its actions. Boxes suddenly crumpled and metal shelves rattled. Theo lunged forward to stand before Max, who was wavering on his feet. Then the shadow grew visible just out of reach in front of them. Theo growled. It seemed to understand his warning, hesitating where it stood.

"My mind is my own. I am not a vessel for you." Max was mumbling the same two phrases over and over again. Unnerved, Theo growled louder. He lunged at the shadow, a feint. It dodged him, but didn't fully retreat. Frustrated, Theo made a bolder move, and the thing slipped past him. He whirled, horrified, at Max's strangled cry.

After that inarticulate protest and a grab at his own temples, Max was still. He blinked very slowly as he looked around the room, then down at Theo as if he didn't recognize him. Theo bared his teeth completely and hunched. The scent was still there, although muted. It was blending with Max's scent. That spooked him further. When Max turned as if to move for the stairs, his posture rigid and odd, Theo panicked.

You can't have him! He grabbed Max's pant leg.

Max jumped as if he'd been burned, although he didn't make a sound. Theo tugged and felt fabric tear. One of his canines slid across skin. He didn't smell blood—he hadn't broken skin—but fear he'd hurt Max mingled with the stronger fear of letting go. Theo ground down with his teeth and yanked. Max fell forward onto the stairs.

The shadow peeled itself free. It stood, hands held out warily, and stared at him. Theo stood his ground, all too aware of how still Max was. Finally, his nerve went, and he barked. The shadow flew up the stairs and away.

Max shuddered. He groaned as he turned and sat on a stair.

"God, that sucked," he said, rubbing at his neck and jaw. Theo sat down and gazed at him. It was frustrating not to be able to ask if he was all right. "Spirits don't usually do that," Max went on. "Just jump you like that. It's so weird." He looked Theo in the eye. "Uh, I told you I was a medium, right? I can let ghosts and spirits ride me. I usually keep them out unless they ask nice, though." Max shuddered again, blinking rapidly. "It really sucks when they do that without permission." He rubbed at his own upper arms.

Theo whined. He turned and leapt on the bed, looking at Max. At Max's puzzled look, Theo pawed the blankets. He whined again until Max stood. Scooping up Theo's fallen robe, Max joined him on the bed.

"Okay, I get it." Max tossed the robe over the end rail of the bed, then stretched out, fully dressed, on the blankets. "Yeah, it didn't like you. You're probably better suited for guard duty than I am." Theo curled up near him. Max's hand came to rest on his head, and it was all Theo could do to stop from shaking it off. He could practically hear Grandmother's sharp voice scolding him that one did *not* pet a werewolf in four-legged form.

It's okay, Grandmother. He just doesn't know any better. Adrenaline abandoned him, leaving him without the energy to protest. The familiar ill feeling of moon sickness stole over him again. Everything had happened so fast he was left dizzy.

"Something weird's going on in this town, Theo," Max said.

Theo whined agreement, but despite his best intentions, his eyes sank closed.

His nose was cold. That and the heavy warmth on his thigh were the first things Max noticed when he woke. He was lying on his side on Theo's bed, fully dressed, with the pen and notebook beside him; the poster remained on the floor.

Oh yeah. He peered down at the great head resting on his thigh, then reached out toward it. Just before his fingers made contact, Theo's eyes snapped open and he lifted his head. Max's fingers continued on to delve into the fur of his ruff. Theo shook him off. He got up and climbed off the bed, making it rebound significantly.

Max sat up, then hastily looked away from a blast of golden light. He peered through spots on his vision at Theo standing nude between the bed and the wall. There was a residual glow in Theo's eyes as he leaned over to pick up his robe. This eerie effect should have drawn Max's attention, but he was absorbed in Theo: from the hard angles of his thighs to the tight curves of his buttocks to his ridiculously tiny waist to the intriguing little indents and bulges of his back, Max took it all in. He slid across the bed as if Theo had just turned into a super magnet and he a nail.

"Are you going to—" Theo stopped when Max caught his hand, preventing him from closing his robe. His cheeks colored, but he didn't protest as Max raked his eyes over his body.

"Holy motherf—" Max's left hand swept over his face, cutting his words in half, "—rist."

"Wh-what?" Theo flinched when Max slapped his stomach.

"Where did these come from? How does a guy who lives in his own basement playing video games get abs like *these*?"

"It's kind of our, uh, metabolism or something." Theo cleared his throat. "We just—do."

"Do you know what my weird thing gives me?" Max surged to his feet; startled, Theo fell back against the wall. "Comments on my report card." He yanked the robe down off Theo's shoulders. "Weird dreams. Poltergeists trashing my room. School counselors referring me to shrinks who want to diagnose me as schizophrenic!" He pressed against Theo, catching him by the back of the neck.

"M-Max, uh—mmph!"

Max sealed Theo's mouth with his own, sucking up his next words; jolting, Theo bumped a small computer speaker off the ledge behind him. Max caught it automatically, busy seizing Theo's lips, releasing them, and seizing them again.

"Oh, *god*, you turn me on," he said breathlessly. Wide-eyed, Theo stared at him, his cheeks dark pink.

"Uh—ah—we just—you f-found out—and there were freaking *ghosts* and—"

"Later," Max said, taking Theo's waist in both hands and looking right into his eyes. "I'm done chasing you." He smiled at Theo's quivering mouth and quickened breath. "You're caught, you understand?" Not waiting for an answer, he went at Theo's mouth with serious intent.

There was no resistance. Hands fumbled at his shoulders, feeling more than trying to push away, then began to caress his neck. They were strong, soft-skinned, but a little unsure. Max didn't feel he had time for unsure. He backed onto the bed, drawing Theo after him. Turning to lie on his back, Theo looked into Max's face. His expression was endearingly serious.

"Max," he whispered, "I don't think I can."

"Sure you can." Max slid in next to him and started kissing his neck.

"S-seriously."

"Seriously, you stop me now, I'm going to die," Max said, pressing closer.

Gaze darting this way and that, Theo didn't speak immediately. His cheekbones pulled up into clear view as his mouth quirked. Finally, the smile broke free, just a little.

"What?" Max asked, charmed.

"Just funny," Theo said. "You're usually so cool and together, and right now you're ... really not."

"Well, maybe you're making me lose my cool." Max ran his hand along Theo's side, shaking his head. "I don't understand why you hide yourself away when you're so damn beautiful."

Theo turned a deeper shade of scarlet, but he looked Max in the eye.

"I can't change who I am," he said. "Not for anybody." Running through both his gaze and his words was a thread of rebellion that made Max's body flush with heat. "And it's not—that I don't want—this. You. It's just it's right after a full moon. I'm not sure I physically can yet."

Reluctantly Max made himself slow down and deal with this.

"What do you mean?"

"It's, y'know, not like the mythology says. We don't change with the full moon. We can actually change back and forth all the time." Theo's words gained momentum. "It's just that something about the cycles of the moon affects our energy levels pretty hardcore."

"Not quite getting it yet." Max's hands played across Theo's smooth skin.

"No one's really figured out why, but when the moon's full we feel just dragged out and sick, like, like a bad flu."

"And are you okay now?" Max wanted to get rid of the cloth between them. He could feel the hard shapes of Theo's body but not closely enough.

"Well, I mean, I'm okay, but still pretty weak."

"Then let's just say we see how far we can get." Max quickly unzipped his coat and threw it aside. "Deal?" He pushed Theo's disheveled hair out of his face and tried not to smile at how red he was. Theo closed his eyes and nodded. With great restraint, Max kissed his forehead, then each eyelid, before engaging his mouth again. Now there was no hesitation in Theo's response, and new heat exploded across Max's skin. "God, I'm burning up," he said under his breath as he stripped off his shirt. He watched as Theo, eyes cracked open, unbuttoned his khakis for him; grinning, he caught Theo's hands and brought them to his chest. "Well?"

"Not bad," Theo said, one corner of his mouth lifting and his eyebrows at jaunty angles. The overall effect was quite handsome.

"Gee, thanks," Max said with an artificial pout; they both laughed. He liked that. Laughter was the cherry on the sex sundae: it wasn't strictly necessary, but it just topped everything off nicely. It also, he thought, eased some of the tension in Theo's nervous frame. "What've you got?"

"Hm? Oh. Bedside table."

Max shifted across the bed and reached out to the first drawer; then he considered whose bedroom this was and went for the bottom drawer instead. In it were lubricant, a box of condoms, and a stack of what looked like comic books.

Even though he lives alone, the naughty stuff gets hidden. Half-assed hidden. That's so like him. Right now, this was nothing more than a fleeting thought. His body was telling him just how done it was with this whole thinking and talking nonsense.

When he turned, Theo had straightened himself out on the bed. He watched Max with his lower lip clamped between his teeth. Max didn't take his eyes off of him as he got out of the rest of his clothes. He all but leapt on top of Theo, skating his mouth down his neck. Theo's arms stole around him, then tightened. He tilted his head back, baring his throat for Max to explore as well. His skin smelled smoky-sweet, that scent lingering on Max's tongue when he inhaled. Both of them were breathing faster; Max moaned softly as he shifted against Theo, his hardened cock sliding across that flat belly. He moved downward, mouth playing over Theo's tightly defined chest, until he knelt between his legs. There he got a good look at Theo's half-erect cock and gave it an encouraging stroke. Theo moved his pelvis restlessly.

"I guess you might not be too tired," Max said, hearing huskiness in his own voice. Theo nodded quickly, and relief mingled with Max's throbbing desire. *I want inside him, and I want inside him now.*

Max had been secretly afraid he was dealing with an inexperienced partner, but Theo simply gave a shivering sigh when Max slipped a dampened, exploratory finger inside. While he was more passive than Max was used to, lying spread out and simply watching with a clouded gaze, he didn't seem nervous or afraid. Max groaned, getting a condom on in record time.

"Here we go," he said, putting his hands under Theo's thighs and pushing them up. "You ready?"

"Really ready," Theo whispered.

"Me, too." Max slowly worked his way inside. For a while, it was just their mingled breathing; Max was so excited he had to concentrate to keep himself from going too quickly. Theo accommodated him willingly, relaxing into him. "Theo, you're just so perfect."

"D-don't say that." Theo closed his eyes, exhaling on a moan as Max started to move.

"I'll say what I want, especially when I mean it." His speech grew ragged, thrown off by the sweet pleasure of their connection. It was all incredible: Theo moaning with him, Theo pulling him closer with strong hands, Theo gazing feverishly up at him. Digging in with his feet, he pressed in, curling Theo tighter beneath him; he pounded harder, caught by Theo's lost expression.

"Oh, Max," Theo whispered.

"You're not weird. You're fantastic." Max panted heavily as he thrust urgently. He dimly regretted how quickly this would end, but all he could see, feel, hear, and smell was Theo, with his incredible shapes and textures. Not only was he gorgeous, he was completely present, taking Max in with his eyes as well as his body. Max couldn't remember sex this honest. Powerful ecstasy blotted out any thoughts of impressing Theo, comparing him to other lovers, or anything but the finish he rushed toward.

"Theo!" Climax slammed into him, chasing the name from his lips.

His over-excited hips needed to be reined in before he could free himself and let Theo stretch out his legs. Noticing that Theo's breathing was still tight, Max looked into his face, then down. Theo turned his head, biting his lip.

"It's harder for, uh, us to ... y'know, get off." His eyes narrowed, and he shifted in apparent discomfort. "It takes longer."

For a moment Max just frowned at him. "What are the disadvantages of being a werewolf again?" This earned him an exasperated huff; before Theo could speak, he gave him a kiss on the temple. "Don't worry," he said. "I'll take care of it." Running a finger down Theo's torso, he traced the lines of his abs; then he reached lower and circled the tip of Theo's cock. Shivering, Theo tilted his head back when Max took a proper hold of him.

It was lovely to watch. Theo's eyes were just barely open, his eyebrows jerking. Throaty sounds of approval came from between his parted lips. As he pumped at Theo's hot cock, Max circled the fingertips of his free hand around and around an erect nipple.

He had a long time to look. Long enough that he took a surreptitious glance at the clock.

This is impossible. Nobody has stamina like this.

"Oh, god," Theo breathed. "Max ..."

Max dipped to kiss that rigid nipple, then raised his head as a hand clumsily bumped his cheek. Theo was giving him a plaintive look as he caressed Max's face. Smiling, touched, Max leaned in for a kiss. He shifted up and over to deepen the kiss, feeling the subtle echoes of the effect of his own touch through the uneven pressures of Theo's mouth. Theo's helpless groans hit him hard, making him tighten up. His own recovery was so quick he was surprised at himself.

"I won't stop," he whispered, "but roll over onto your side, okay?" Theo gave a tiny nod and complied. Curving against Theo from behind, he fit himself inside. He watched Theo's face carefully, and saw nothing but bliss there. This spurred on his hips and his hands. He pinched Theo's nipple, stroked his arousal, kissed his neck and back. Theo was hot to the touch everywhere, raising fresh sweat on Max's skin.

"Oh, god, yes," Theo said, one hand clutching the headboard, the other reaching back to flick across Max's side. "Do it, Max, do it."

"You sexy little ..." Max breathed.

"Harder," Theo groaned, pressing back into him. "Don't stop."

"Come on, Theo. Come on."

"Ahhh ... Max!" At last Theo jerked into climax, his body clenching around Max. Hissing through his teeth, Max grabbed Theo's hips. Bearing forward, he pressed him half onto his stomach and pulled nearly all the way out. He slid in deep once, out, in again, out, and on the third full thrust he was done. So quickly Theo was still out of breath, and Max was embarrassed.

"You're a hard man to get finished off," he said as he eased free. *And apparently I'm really not.*

"You're just har—" Theo pressed his face into the pillow.

"What was that? Hm?" Max leaned on his back, speaking into his ear. Theo hunched his shoulders, but Max forced him out of hiding with a pinch on the behind.

"I liked h-how hard you were, that's all," Theo said weakly.

"Would you stop being adorable?" Max gave Theo a noisy kiss on the shoulder, then collapsed onto his back. He gazed at Theo's bright red ear. *There's something about him that draws me in and holds me.* "There's got to be an easier way to get you in the sack than finding out you're a werewolf and getting attacked by nasty spirits together."

"Nope," Theo said, making him laugh. "Are you

going to get that?"

"What?"

"Your cell keeps ringing."

"Crap, it's still on vibrate." Max started digging around for his cell. He found it under the bed, unable to hear it until he'd pulled it out into the open. "You've got pretty sharp hearing."

"Yeah, well," Theo mumbled.

"Fifteen missed calls? It's, what—crap, is that the time?" He pushed the answer button. "Mom? What's going on? It's three in the morning."

"Max! Where have you been?"

Theo didn't intend to eavesdrop, of course, but he suspected anyone would have been able to hear Kaitlyn's voice through the phone. Theo sat up, gazing at Max's back. Sitting on the edge of his bed, Max seemed completely comfortable with his own nudity, though his shoulders hunched a little as he spoke to his mother.

"What do you mean Anastasia's missing?"

"She didn't come home last night either! Max, where are you?"

"I'm just at a friend's, Mom. I'm fine. Are you sure she didn't have any plans?"

He was getting cold without Max, but Theo didn't want to move from where he was. This conversation chilled him in a different way.

"She said she'd be home late, not that she was staying out. Her car's not here, and none of her friends know where she is. Where is she? Where's my daughter?"

"Mom, calm down." Max glanced at Theo over his shoulder, his brows flexed in obvious concern. "I'll be home in a few minutes. Just stay home and wait for me, okay?"

"What if something's happened to her, Max? I want my daughter home, now!"

"Just hold tight, Mom. Please." Max disconnected and jumped up from the bed. "I'm sorry. I've got to get home."

"Where would Anastasia go?" Theo asked, also getting up. Fatigue made his muscles fight him, but the worst of the moon sickness was over.

"I don't know," Max said. "Her boyfriend's on another continent, and her friends are all about as exciting as she is. Late nights for them are having fancy teas and doing hippy, crafty stuff." He sighed as he zipped his pants. Theo handed him his shirt. "Mom freaks out really easily, but I'm ..." He threw on his shirt and rubbed a hand across his face. "I don't like this." Theo picked up a pair of jeans and drew them on. When he came clear of the neck hole of a T-shirt, he saw that Max's eyebrows were raised.

"Can I come?" Theo scooped up Max's jacket and threw it. Max caught it and swung it on.

"What?"

"I might—be able to help." He glanced sidelong at Max as he stuffed his shirt hem into his jeans and then ran both hands through his hair repeatedly. Max hesitated, flipping his cell around and around in his palm. His jaw worked subtly from side to side as he regarded Theo. Trying not to let his exhaustion show, Theo waited for his decision.

"Thanks, Theo," Max said. "You're a good friend." Tucking his cellphone into his jacket pocket, he led the way up the stairs. Theo took a false step, then rubbed briskly at his face with both hands.

Friend? He hurried up the stairs and dipped down the hall to turn the heat back up before catching up with Max at the door. There were more important things to worry about than that. Even so, he fought down the bad taste that word had left with him.

Neither spoke once they were in the car. This left Theo plenty of time to worry. He suspected Max broke the silence to distract them both.

"Do any of your friends know?"

"No." Theo grimaced.

"Then why do you have that poster?"

"Um, it's kind of embarrassing." Theo put a hand to the back of his neck, hesitated, scratched, then dropped it to his lap. "When I was a teenager, for a while I wouldn't stay two-legged. Grandmother tried everything. She even locked up the food so I couldn't get to it without hands." He turned his hands over and looked at his palms, his fingers loosely curled over them; he wondered when he'd become able to talk about this. "Ma was already sick then, but she made the poster. So I couldn't hide from things."

"So you've always been a werewolf?"

"Of course I have," Theo snapped, unable to suppress a surge of irritation at the question. "How else do you think I got this way? It runs in the family."

"Your parents were, too?"

Theo shook his head. An oncoming car's headlights made him wince. "Only on my mom's side. Not everybody inherits. It's just me and Grandmother—" He stopped, biting his lip. "Just me, now, in my immediate family."

"How long ago did your grandmother pass away?" Max glanced at him, tone softening.

"Seventeen months ago, with this moon."

"And the bedroom upstairs was hers."

"Y-yeah. Why?" Theo rubbed at his cheek, feeling stubble. Outside, the streets were half-heartedly busy; it was still early.

"You're still in the basement because you think it's still her house."

"It is." Theo looked uncomfortable. "Territory's—important." Max sighed heavily, sliding his hands back and forth along the curve of the steering wheel.

"Theo, I'm sorry. My dad passed when I was four, so I know how it feels."

"Your dad? But—"

"He's my stepdad. I've known him since I was five, so he's just a dad to me now." Max cleared his throat, then twitched his lips in an almost-smile. "I guess I can actually tell you, can't I? My first dad didn't actually leave my life until I was twelve."

"Huh?"

"He hung around spiritually for years. I heard his voice before I had any clue that talking to dead people wasn't normal." Max smiled weakly. "Being a werewolf runs in your family; being a medium runs in mine."

"So you had a stepdad and a ghost dad." Theo gazed wide-eyed at the dashboard.

"Yup." Max shrugged.

"That wasn't weird?"

"It should've been, but I didn't know any better. It actually helped in a lot of ways. He was talking to Mom, so when she got married again, he knew about it. He'd already seen that Ambrose was a decent guy, open-minded, and it made it easier for him to accept. I don't know, I've got a huge extended family; it was just that much bigger." Bringing the car to a stop at an intersection, he reached out to touch Theo's shoulder. That touch confused Theo; he didn't know if it was meant to comfort him, or to comfort Max himself, or as an expression of affection. And then something struggled through the mist in his brain.

"Anastasia can, too, right?"

"Yes," Max said grimly, removing his hand and driving on as the light changed.

"Then that thing in my basement could, uh, be after her, too?" At last Theo was wide awake, his mouth going dry.

"That's what I was thinking." Max shifted restlessly in his seat, gripping the steering wheel tightly with both hands. "I've got to warn you, Theo. My mom gets hysterical. It's pretty easy for a medium to get overly sensitive because you come in contact with all the baggage spirits are carrying around. But this time, honestly," he gunned the engine, overtaking another car on the highway, "I think she's probably right to be freaking out."

CHAPTER FIVE

They'd lost the entire morning. The sun was high in the sky when they stepped out of the Shevchenko house. Kaitlyn had certainly been upset, but Theo privately didn't see the hysteria Max hinted at. Yet she constantly had popped in and out of the basement, apparently going there to do something in the "spirit world." After convincing Kaitlyn to take a sleeping pill, they'd left her curled up in bed, a twin plastered to either side.

"I think having you there helped," Max told him, leaning on the top of the car. "She couldn't lose her shit with you around. Thanks."

"Uh," Theo said, then cleared his throat. Sometimes Max's kindness blindsided him. "Where do you want to start?"

"I really hate to say this, but I'm thinking of going straight to the police. I mean, I don't think they can do anything this soon after she disappeared, but after her going into the river, maybe they'll keep an eye out for her or something." He looked weary, his eyes at half-mast.

"But the police ..." Theo scratched at his chin, feeling fresh stubble poking through. In his head, warnings from his youth butted up against the sense that Max was making. To his family, authorities were always to be regarded with suspicion.

"I know, I don't like it, either. But do you have any better—" Max abruptly twisted around, staring into the lilac bushes at the corner of the house.

Theo followed his gaze. He couldn't see anything out of the ordinary, but the hair on his nape lifted.

"What? Is there a—I don't smell anything, but—"

"There's somebody there, all right," Max said softly. "It's somebody I haven't seen in a long time. I've never seen him this far out of town."

Cold sweat beaded up on Theo's upper lip. He shoved his hands into his pockets as his back and neck stiffened.

"Okay. Okay, I get it." Max glanced at him. "Can you do me a favor, Theo?"

"What?" Theo demanded, nerves shoving his voice out too hard.

"Stay cool." Max gave Theo a tight, one-sided smile and held his hand out toward the lilac bush. His eyes closed gently, and his face grew quiet for a moment. His eyebrows knitted, and he abruptly scratched at his ear, tilting his head and then giving it a shake. Something about the movement looked wrong; Theo shivered, goose bumps leaping up all over him. When Max opened his eyes, turned to look at him, and twisted up his face in a frown, Theo felt the beginnings of a growl tickle his throat. Embarrassed by acting four-legged when on two, he clapped a hand over his mouth as he stared nervously.

"Max?"

Max's voice took a moment to come to life, low and grumbling. "No. Uh, no. He's just ..." He scratched at his ear again, almost frantically, then gave a jerky shrug. "Just helpin' me talk."

"Wh-who are you?"

"Me, I don't matter. But the girl, y'know."

"The girl?" Theo's over-worked heart leapt. "Who? Anastasia?"

"Don't know the name. But she and him always been real nice to me, so I know 'em. I heard something went down with her by the river.”

“River? Which one?”

Max’s cheek gave a nervous tic.

“The Grand. There’s weird shit in the air lately. I been hiding a fair amount.”

“On the Grand? Where? Down by the cutbanks or—”

“Yeah. Where those farms are. Off the highway there. I’m goin’ now.”

“Sure,” Theo said, coming around the car at speed. Max stumbled back when Theo snatched the car keys from him. Theo had missed the transition, but it was clearly Max blinking back in puzzlement. “In the car.”

“Okay,” Max said. “Sorry, Wallace makes things unclear when he rides you, so I’m not sure what he told you. We got something?”

“M-maybe a place I can find a scent trail. I hope.” Theo jammed the keys into the ignition of Max’s car.

Wallace was an old family favorite. He’d been a young native man, and it was hard to know what he would have been if the alcohol and drugs hadn’t warped his body and mind before ultimately killing him. Max and Anastasia occasionally let him possess them because he was either unwilling or unable to speak without borrowing a body. Max first grew to like him as a teenager because Wallace made his mind a trippy place, but now he admired how helpful Wallace was despite how life had treated him.

Theo drove with his game face on, gazing at the road like he was chasing something down it. The car hurtled along at a speed that matched the urgency in Max’s own mind. Wallace’s mellow aura had calmed him, but now Max’s skin crawled with the need to get there, to find Anastasia, to know if she was all right.

"What did he say?" Max finally shook off the cobwebs enough to speak. Wallace really was like taking something mind-altering.

"The flats," Theo said curtly. "I'm pretty sure I know where."

"Pretty sure?" Max's tone sharpened. "Theo, we can't be wasting any—Jesus!" The car whipped into the opposite lane to overtake a car. Max saw the incoming truck and clutched at his seatbelt. Just as horns started to sound, Theo slid the car around the vehicle they'd passed and opened it up again. Max decided not to look at the speedometer as he clutched his chest. "Do you usually drive like this?"

"No. This is different." Theo's eyes were too busy to give him any attention, scanning the rearview, the highway ahead, and their surroundings. "I've got better, uh, reflexes than you do. Don't worry."

"I know," Max said. "I know."

When Theo ran a red light and cranked the car hard to the left, Max felt the opposite tires leave the road. He closed his eyes. The car lurched back onto all-fours, now heading down the long, low road that followed the river. Theo finally slowed the car. Just to be perverse, Max's adrenaline-fueled state didn't change to relief, but impatience.

"Maybe we should have asked somebody to help us search."

"I trust my nose better than I trust strangers," Theo murmured. He glanced at Max, rolling down the driver's side window. "He said she was around here."

"Okay," Max said, feigning calm, "let's look around." He stared into the bush at the side of the road, squinting when it occasionally thinned to reveal raggedly shorn hayfields and weathered barns and sheds. He became aware of a heavy sniffing sound next to him and looked at Theo, just managing to stop himself from asking what he was doing. Nostrils flared, inhaling deeply, Theo was looking unfocused. Max opened his mouth to suggest he take over the driving, then grabbed Theo's arm. "Hey, stop the car."

"What?"

"That's Anastasia's car!"

Theo pulled over, and they both ran to the sedan parked crookedly on the opposite side of the road. Max peered inside the car, then tried the door and found it unlocked. The keys were still in the ignition.

"Jesus," Max said. Acid tore up his gut, generated by new and real fear. "Oh, Christ." He started when Theo took a vice-grip on his wrist. "What?" Theo was looking around alertly. "Theo, seriously, what? This is Ana's car, let go—"

"I've got her." Theo spoke with tense certainty.

Now Max grabbed back, his fingers digging into Theo's jacket.

"Don't screw with me, Theo. Are you—"

"Shut up." Theo didn't relinquish his wrist as he pushed past. "Don't distract me. It's super weak." He pulled Max along at a sharp pace, straight down the road, his head held high. Max pressed his lips together tightly and just tried to keep up.

She's my sister. I really should be the one making the decisions. He spared a look at Theo's serious expression. *If he was always this guy, he'd never be single long enough for me to get near him.* Max took an emotional hit, for the first time considering that he might not be the better catch in their relationship; it shamed him that he resisted the idea, or that it could even come to mind at a time like this. *I need to find you soon, Ana. Who else is going to smack me back into adulthood?*

Max bumped straight into Theo when he abruptly

stopped. He turned left, then right, sniffing audibly.

"Go back," he mumbled, pushing Max out of the way. "Lost it."

"You lost it?" Max hissed. "How could you lose it? Jesus, find it again. I have to know if she's okay!"

"Just give me a minute!" Theo snarled with sudden intensity, and Max staggered backward, propelled by a rude jerk on his wrist. "I just need to—" Theo threw off his jacket, then his T-shirt. "I need a better nose."

"What are you going to do?" Max hated being so out of balance at such a crucial time.

"Find her." Theo dipped down, shoving off his jeans and boxers. He rose, nude and pale in the night. He briefly touched Max's arm. "Go back to the car and bring it here." Then he handed Max his clothing.

Before Max could say anything, golden light exploded in front of him. He was too slow to throw up a protective hand and had to watch Theo lope away through great splotches on his vision.

"Find her." He shifted closer to the side of the road, numbly compressing the bundle of cloth in his arms. "Yeah. Find my sister for me. Shit." There were no streetlights, so he was left to walk back to the car in darkness, using the gravel on the side of the road as a guide.

Fortunately he wasn't afraid of the dark. With a very few notable exceptions, the things that went bump in the night just wanted to chat. Even as a child, he hadn't seen any need for fear. Still, with no distractions, the walk was unpleasant. The stars and nearly full moon barely peeked through heavy clouds. Their weak light seemed to add to the chill.

Gratefully he got into his car and the civilization of its interior. Then he began to drive, slowly and carefully. Eventually, a great shape galloped into the edge of his headlights' beams and came to a stop. Max braked, but Theo gestured broadly with his head and whirled, trotting back the way he'd come.

"Okay, okay," Max muttered. "Lead the way, then." He inched awkwardly along in the car, keeping Theo in sight. He tried not to think about anything beyond what he was doing. Theo seemed to have found something, but he had no way of knowing what. There was no guarantee that he'd find Anastasia unharmed.

Theo made an abrupt turn into the bush; Max hastily stopped and got out.

"Theo, wait!" He ran to the edge of the greenery. Just into a clump of dried-up berry bushes stood Theo, eyes gleaming. "I'm going to hang on to your tail, all right?" Theo obligingly lifted his bushy tail for Max to grab its tip. When Theo shoved forward into the trees, Max yet again did his best just to keep up. They cleared the bushes and hurried through spindly poplars. Max's breathing was loud in his own ears, the sound of the river competing from nearby. Here the moonlight didn't reach them at all. He wished he'd remembered to grab the flashlight from the glove compartment.

Even so, the figure slumped against the base of a pine tree was clear enough in the darkness. He let go of Theo and ran to it even before he recognized Anastasia's fuzzy brown boots. She was still as he crouched beside her, but he felt her warmth and the movement of her breath as he grabbed her shoulders.

"Ana!"

Her cheeks were cold to the touch, but she wore a jacket and gloves, as well as her boots. Immediately her eyes opened, and she gazed at him.

Max let out a loud exhalation, nearly a laugh.

"Anastasia, it's me. It's Max. Can you stand up? We have to get out of here." Tears of relief prickled behind his eyes as her mouth shaped crackling words.

"Max? Be careful, they forcibly possess."

"They? There's nothing here."

"The shadows," she moaned as he lifted her to her feet and wrapped his arm around her waist. "Like before. Why is there a dog here?"

"It's okay, he's helping. What are you doing out here?"

"I—one possessed me, and—it was dark, I got lost. Oh my god," she whispered, pressing her face into his shoulder. "I was so scared."

"Okay. We'll talk later. It's going to be okay."

"Oh Max," she said, her voice crumbling. "You're so full of it." Smiling in deep relief, he escorted his weeping sister up the hill. *Let's get you home before Mom's head explodes. And think of what to tell her before we get there.*

With a full night's sleep, the worst of the moon sickness had passed. Theo didn't remember much beyond getting back to the car. He'd woken as Max got him out of the back of the car. The next thing he remembered was coming out of a deep darkness on his couch, fully dressed and under a blanket.

Exerting himself so soon after a full moon had left him completely dragged out. Neither his muscles nor his brain worked without protest, and he felt like he could use another full day of sleep, but at least he could drive. Max hadn't answered his cell, but Theo had grown too impatient to stay home and wait for updates. He turned up the music, hoping the dance mix he'd picked would shake off some off the fog.

He set off a different kind of loud when he got out of his car. Nerves worn thin from fatigue, he glared at the kennels.

"Shut up!" he barked, and a shocked silence fell. Before he got any farther, the back door opened and Kaitlyn leaned out to wave.

"Hi, Theo!"

"Hello," he said as he crossed the driveway, looking sheepishly up at her.

"What brings you by?" She beamed at him, wiping her hands on a towel.

"Uh, just wanted to see how Anastasia's doing."

"Hm?" Kaitlyn's expression shifted from puzzled to shocked. "Oh, no, Max didn't tell you? Come in, come in."

Alarm spurred him up the stairs after her, but he caught himself up short at the sight of a stranger in the hallway. A tall, fit, older man, he had neatly styled silver hair and an easy smile on his face.

"Ambrose, this is Theo," Kaitlyn said, as Theo hesitantly removed his shoes and let her take his coat. Ambrose's smile brightened.

"Oh, so this is the famous Theo! Ambrose Shevchenko, Theo. It's a great pleasure to meet you." He padded over sock-footed to shake Theo's hand with a confident grip.

"N-nice to meet you," Theo said.

"Come sit in the living room," Ambrose said. "We were just about to have some tea. Would you like some?"

"Sure." Surrounded by friendly goodwill, Theo didn't have the strength to deny them anything. "Is Max ...?"

"He's taken the two house dogs for their yearly checkup." Ambrose disappeared into the kitchen; Kaitlyn came in with tea for Theo. Once he was in the chair by the window, teacup in hand, she sat down with her own.

"I'm really going to have to get after Max. I'm sure you were just as worried about Anastasia as anybody else."

"Yeah," Theo said, puzzled.

"It turns out one of her coworkers had just gone through a terrible family situation, and Anastasia stayed with her for the night. She thought she'd texted me, but she forgot, and then the battery on her cell died." Kaitlyn shook her head in exasperation. Theo stared into his tea; its creamy surface trembled.

"I'm just so relieved," Kaitlyn went on. "Anastasia's obviously tired, but she felt well enough to go to work today. Unlike her poor mother, who lost about eight years' life."

"They're both adults," Ambrose said, sitting down next to her. "I suppose we don't have to have them checking in all the time, eh, Theo?"

"Yeah," Theo said woodenly. *This isn't right.*

"I don't think I ever asked," Kaitlyn said. "Do you have any brothers or sisters?"

"No," Theo said. "I'm an only child." *The matriarch of the family has to know these things. It's his duty to tell her. How is keeping things from his family going to protect them?*

"Oh, I'm sorry. Is that an uncomfortable subject?" Kaitlyn peered into his face, then blinked in surprise as he drew himself up. The couple sat together in perfect comfort, Ambrose's hand resting lightly on his wife's thigh. To Theo's eyes, they were the image of honesty and kindness. There was only one correct response to that.

"It's not," he said. "I'm—I—" He shook his head in frustration, wrestled with his tongue, and tried again. "I think there's something you should know."

CHAPTER SIX

Theo?" The moment the front door opened, his name shot through it.

Sitting bolt upright in his chair, Theo stared at his monitor with wide eyes. He drew a bracing breath.

"I'm downstairs." He quickly put his hands back on the keyboard and resumed typing an e-mail as he heard Max come down the stairs. He could hear Max's anger in his subtly quickened breathing, even in his stillness.

Keep it together. You expected this. Maybe not the same day, but you expected it.

"What the hell, Theo?"

"Eh?" He had no idea what to say.

He stiffened when Max grabbed the back of his chair and turned it. Mouth in a tight line, Max put a hand on each arm of the chair and looked him in the face. His eyes glittered, looking very hard and more brown than green. Now the faint creases raised by his narrowed eyes seemed more worrying than charming.

"Don't play stupid. Why did you tell my parents about what happened?"

"They needed to know," Theo said.

"That wasn't your decision to make."

"I—I just did what I thought was right." Pushing aside one of Max's arms, he got to his feet and made some space between them.

"And you figure you know how to deal with my family better than I do?"

"Those things are dangerous." Theo folded his arms and glared at Max's knees. "The matriarch has to know about stuff like this."

"Well, I appreciate the concern," Max drawled. "And how much you obviously trust me." Stung, Theo hunched his shoulders. "But then, you didn't have to hear her screaming at you for an hour. I thought she was going to have a fucking aneurism. Why did you want to put her through that? Or me, for that matter? Jesus, Theo, I thought you were my friend."

Friend. The word came as a blow, a direct punch to the gut he was too tired to defend against. He dropped his gaze to the floor, miserably unable to move or speak. Silence reigned for an uncomfortably long time.

Then Max startled him by falling into the chair, making it roll back.

"God, don't look like you're a puppy and I just kicked you," he groaned, tilting his head back and putting his hand over his eyes. "I've got a right to be angry here."

"I'm sorry," Theo whispered.

"Why don't you believe that I sometimes know what I'm doing?" By the word, Max's tone grew less chilled.

"I didn't think about—of it—like that." Theo rallied weakly. "Protecting family's a, a thing with me."

"Believe it or not," and Max came out of hiding, "it is for me, too." He smiled faintly. "Family and friends."

That word, coming again so quickly, hit him like a blow. Theo licked his lips.

"I'm sorry, Max, but could you go?"

"What?" Max asked. Theo shook his head. "What's wrong?"

"Nothing."

"Oh, bull. We need to keep talking to each other, especially with what we have in common."

"In common?" Theo's lip curled. "You think we're the

same?" *You, who can fit in anywhere, who can go home to a big loving family after taking somebody to bed for no other reason than ...*

"You think we aren't? Prove it." Far from looking offended, Max visibly relaxed into the chair. Theo barely dared look at him.

I've had casual relationships. I don't think I can do that with you. It didn't feel casual, being with you. "I really think you should go."

"Not until you talk to me," Max said.

"I said I was sorry, didn't I?" Theo tried, frustrated.

"What, me being around is like a punishment?"

"No!" Theo buried his fingers in his hair.

"This has got nothing to do with me being mad at you, does it?" Max tilted his head.

"Max, c-come on, I don't want to talk."

"Come on, boy, speak."

"So not funny," Theo said, turning away.

"Theo," Max said in a stern voice. There was a new vibration in that easy tenor that hit him in the spine. Woodenly, carefully, Theo turned, his skin seeming to shrink three sizes in an instant. "Come here," Max said, and Theo's fatigue skittered away. "Come. Here." Max's mouth curled sensually around the words. Licking his lips, Theo shifted uncertainly closer.

Why am I doing what he says?

"Down." This was accompanied by a downward-pointed finger. He slowly knelt, unable to look at Max. Stiffening, he closed his eyes as a warm hand trailed down his cheek. His hair was ruffled, his cheekbones traced, and his lips pressed carefully apart.

"Lick." Max's voice was quiet but still firm, so firm it denied the possibility of resistance. Theo felt the word like a jolt of electricity. Goose bumps rose on his flesh. He slowly slid his tongue across Max's knuckles, then between his fingers, tasting nicotine and outside air.

"Good." Max shifted his hips in the chair. He tilted his head, tapping the side of his neck. "Now here." Theo rose up on his knees and stretched until he could taste Max's skin and find the hard curves of the tendons in his neck. With each breath, he inhaled faded aftershave, shampoo, and the spicy scent that was simply Max himself. With the tip of his tongue, he traced the bulge of Max's jaw, resisting the urge to bite. Then he heard the sound of a zipper and slowly leaned back. "And here." Max looked him in the eye.

If we're just friends, then is this just some kind of a game to him? He couldn't pull free of the power of that potent gaze. *Oh, god. I don't care.* Sinking down on his heels, Theo looked at the hardened cock Max cupped in one hand. He wanted it. Leaning forward, he opened his mouth.

"No," Max said. "Just lick."

Frustrated, Theo clenched his teeth for a moment before he put a hand on each of Max's thighs and dipped his head for a taste. The scents here were thick and masculine and made his own cock struggle against the confines of his clothing. He explored Max's full shape with small, lapping motions before moving into long, confident strokes of his tongue. He could hear from Max's soft exhalations that he was doing well.

I'd do it, you know. You think I don't want to take you in my throat? Do you know how good you would taste to someone who can smell what I can smell? Why won't you let me do it? These thoughts battered the inside of his head, trapped by the commands that Max didn't give.

Curving over Theo, Max pulled his T-shirt up; he pushed it into Theo's armpits so he could make swirling caresses of his chest with both hands. His tightly grouped fingers dragged up and over both nipples, then down again. The sensation was too powerful, and Theo drew his torso back. When Max slowly pulled on his nipples, the resulting electric pleasure shot down to his cock, and he groaned in discomfort.

"Off." Max pushed him back onto his heels. He stripped Theo's shirt off and tossed it aside. "Stand up."

Uncertain, Theo got to his feet and looked down. Max was flushed, his eyes glittering. His arousal would have been obvious even if he hadn't been revealing his swollen cock to the world. He put one hand between Theo's legs and slowly squeezed; Theo's eyes widened as he moaned.

"Hush," Max said as he unfastened Theo's pants. "Left leg," he said when he'd brought them down to knee level. Theo pulled his left leg free, and his right leg when so directed. "Fetch." Max pointed past him.

Theo turned to see that he was indicating the bedside table. He walked stiffly to it, his erection making it an uncomfortable trip, so he could grab what they needed to go further. As unnerving as this was, he truly needed to go further.

"Hands and knees." Max took what Theo carried. He'd removed his shirt and let his pants fall. Theo wanted to look at him, but Max's instructions had him turned the other way. He got to his hands and knees on the mat in front of his bed and waited with a loudly pounding heart. He heard the rustle of Max's boxers and the crinkle of a condom wrapper; he closed his eyes, licking his lips, and waited.

Hands ran over his shoulders, his back, explored the shape of his sides. They moved lightly over his hips, buttocks, down his inner thighs, and over his calves in a possessive inventory. Theo gasped as liquid hit him between the shoulder blades. One finger trailed through it, following his spine, and then dipped into him. This process was repeated, each time ending with an exploratory jab of Max's slick finger. It expanded to two fingers, which lingered inside him.

This made Theo's own fingers curl into the mat and his body tense with impatience. When Max started to penetrate him, he had difficulty getting in. Taking a hold of Theo's hips, Max made firm thrusts forward, pinching Theo when he began to breathe too quickly.

"Relax."

Theo gulped and tried to release his tight muscles.

I'm so hard. He's *so hard.* His excitement fought him, and he couldn't relax until Max's deep-seated friction melted him. He shivered in conflicted ecstasy, closing his eyes. *He knows my deepest secret, and he's still here.* Joy rose within his chest at this thought, making him groan again. Max held his hips, fingers spread and gripping, as he slid in and out with lingering thrusts. Every move Max made took possession. Max's thick shaft spoke directly to the pleasure centers in his brain.

"Listen to you," Max said. "I love that noise you make. That I make you make."

"Yes," Theo whispered, hardly comprehending what was spoken to him.

"But what I really love is how good you are inside." Subtle changes to the rhythm sparked new pleasure in Theo. "It's like you were born to have me in you, Theo. No, hold still, I'll do it. That's it, good."

Increasingly breathless, Max held Theo in place and began to really move. Eyes wide, Theo felt Max's urgency, and it added to his own. It was frustrating to be still, and yet it made him feel everything in intimate detail. "Good, Theo. Now tighten up. Come on, now." A slap on his side startled him, and Theo clenched his muscles. "That's it. Good, good—yes!" Grinding in one last time, Max clutched at him with bruising fingers. Max lingered there far too long for Theo's over-excited state. Slowly his grip eased and he caressed Theo's back, then pulled free and away.

Hands trembling, Theo took hold of the rail at the end of his bed, and used it to get to his feet. He leaned heavily on it as he turned around. Max was right there, running his gaze over Theo's body, smiling darkly.

Pressing his face into Max's neck, Theo caressed his chest unsteadily.

"I'm not done," he whispered.

"Hmm?" Max's tone held amusement.

"Would—would you finish me off?" He nuzzled Max's neck and kissed his earlobe.

"What's that?" Max's fingertips very, very lightly traced his side, raising fresh gooseflesh. Theo shivered and clutched at Max's nape.

"Max," he said, his eyes closing tightly. "Please."

"I'm not sure what you want, Theo."

"Max, please," he moaned. "Please."

"Please what? Hm?" Max pressed his mouth to Theo's forehead. That affectionate little touch was not nearly enough, and desperation made the words easier to say.

"Please make me come."

"Oh, is that all?" Despite the teasing, there was a deeper, warmer undercurrent in his tone. Max put his hands on Theo's head and tilted it back to allow him to nip aggressively at his neck. He kissed Theo hard, capturing a shuddering gasp. Then his hands were trailing down Theo's body, his heat gone from his side. Theo's buttocks hit the railing, and he clutched it with both hands, watching through barely open eyes as Max kissed the tip of his painfully hard cock. After that first gentle touch, Max turned ruthless, taking him in deep and firmly. Theo's back arched, and he cried out.

"Max!" The sensation was blinding. Max's attentions were complete and relentless, causing layers of sensation to build upon each other. The tongue that circled the head of his cock, teasing and prodding, gave way to the hot, wet pressure of a skilled throat. Theo was far too caught up in it to notice his own inarticulate cries. Nobody else could make him feel this way, surely; nobody could matter more than Max. Swirling around inside him with his physical desire was a mix of gratitude and sweet affection.

"Please tell me," he whispered fervently, throwing his head back, "that I made you feel this good." Max's hands caressed and clenched his buttocks as he moved his head faster, overwhelming Theo with white-hot pleasure. Theo almost protested, but instead he rocked forward into it. Gooseflesh rose all over his body as Max cupped his balls, then tickled and stroked behind them. Skilled fingertips traced lazy circles down his inner thighs, then leapt back up to seize his hips and push him back against the railing.

Desire for it to go on and on fought with his desperate need to finish; however, Max was in charge, and his punishing rhythm was yet another command. Theo wanted to thrust, but obeyed the hands holding him still. "Max—oh, good god." Theo shook his head wildly, lost. "Max!" He yelled out his climax to the ceiling, feeling his entire body jolt in reaction to the focused and exquisite and unstoppable ecstasy in his cock. It jerked and quivered in Max's mouth, seeming to pull Theo up onto his curled toes. The bed railing squeaked warningly under his weight, and his arms trembled under the burden.

When it all faded, Theo was left with trembling knees. It took effort to remove his hands from the railing, his fingers caught in the imprints he'd made in the metal. Carefully he eased himself away from it as Max released him and stood up. Wiping at his mouth, he gave Theo a tight smile and then pulled him into a full embrace.

"You're so sweet," Max said into his ear. "I want to take you home, put you on my table, and have you three times a day. Fucking you would be like saying grace.”

“Th-that’s …” Theo stared wide-eyed at the ceiling, his hands slack on Max’s hips. *Hot. Scary. I don’t know what.*

“So cute,” Max mumbled. “So sweet, Theo.” He stepped back, patting Theo on the cheek. “Can I borrow your shower?”

“Y-yeah.”

“Thanks.” Max kissed him lightly on the mouth and bounced jauntily up the stairs. Theo moved woodenly to sit on his bed, rubbing at his throat.

Who did I become, just now? Uncomfortable, Theo sat and stared at nothing, listening to the shower running upstairs. His fatigue fell on him at once; numbly, he slid under the covers. His thoughts circled around in his head, chasing their tails.

He was woken from a light doze by Max, smelling of soap and steam, burrowing in next to him. Sighing in contentment, Max wrapped an arm around his waist and snuggled up. Theo kept his eyes closed, because he hadn’t caught anything useful in his head yet.

To Max’s relief, his mother was busy with her show dogs in the exercise pen when he drove up. He slipped into his trailer for a change of clothes before heading the kennels. As he went into the boarding kennel, he met Anastasia coming out.

“Oh, hey. Didn’t get called in to work today?”

“Uh-uh.” She retreated back into the kennel and pulled up a bucket to sit on as Max began shooing dogs into the external runs and closing them outside. “Must be nice having a boyfriend in town. I have to hide in my room.”

“Boyfriend? Who says I have a boyfriend?” Max slid

down the last gate and went back through the kennels, removing bedding and dishes. Normally Anastasia cleaned the kennels on days she didn't work, but family consensus was she should take it easy.

"Oh, come on. Why else would you be out all night?" She picked up a tennis ball and turned it around in her hands. "Was it Theo?"

"What makes you say that?" Max had a hard time keeping his tone neutral.

"Was it?"

Max gave up, and the grin that had been trying to escape broke free.

"I actually went to tell him off. It was supposed to be a *fight*, but ..."

"One, don't need any details. Two, you dog!" She threw the tennis ball at him; he turned so it bounced harmlessly off his arm. In unison they added, "trainer," and chuckled together as he tossed the ball back to her. Then Anastasia's expression stilled, and he grabbed a scoop and garbage bag while he waited for her to speak. The routine was so ingrained in him that he barely noticed what he was doing, instead listening for the first hint she was about to explain her sudden silence.

"He was probably right, wasn't he?"

"I don't care if he was right," Max muttered.

"At least now we can ask Mom about these things. Once she's calmed down. Whatever they are, Max, they're different from anything I've ever heard of."

"I know." Max moved to the next kennel. It said something about how eventful that night had been that Max had been thinking less about the shadow that possessed him and more about Theo's secret. And even more about Theo's body. And most about Theo last night. He hadn't planned anything beyond getting there and expressing his displeasure. He'd only wanted to stop Theo from shutting him out. Then he'd seen the excitement spark in Theo's eyes at being told what to do.

"Max?"

Jesus, we're talking about malevolent spirits and I can't even stay on topic. "Sorry. You're probably right."

"I think I should talk to Louis Wilson."

"Maria's husband? Why?"

"He's the one they found out by the river. I think he might have run into one of those spirits." Anastasia shrugged stiffly.

"And how are you planning to talk to him about that? 'Oh, hey, were you possessed, by the way? And just in case, I should tell you I talk to ghosts.' I don't think that's a good idea, Ana."

"But this isn't just some new ghost yelling in people's ears. I think they're probably why I drove into the river, Max. And they don't just possess; they *use* you. I felt one come through me like I was some kind of portal. I don't think we should ignore these things."

Max hesitated, then went out into the aisle to look at her. She gazed at him steadily, her hands in fists on her knees.

"If you're going to go telling the family secret, you're going to have to be the one breaking that to Mom."

"I will." Anastasia lifted her chin. Max felt his eyebrows lift.

"You're really serious about this."

"I am, Max." She got up and set the tennis ball on the overturned bucket. "I think this might actually be more important than the family secret." She moved for the door, then paused. "And I think you should probably tell Theo, too. He's involved now. We can't be sure he'll be safe."

"Uh, yeah. Good point." Max fought the urge to clear his throat guiltily. Once Anastasia had left, he quickly got on with things. As he swept, scrubbed, and rinsed the concrete kennel floor, his mind was free to wander. To his embarrassment, it didn't manage to stay interested in the shadows for long. He found himself staring at the spray from the hose. It made him think of showers. Theo, water trickling down over his shoulders. Theo, his hair clinging to his cheeks, gazing at him with intent gray eyes. Theo, sliding long-fingered hands over his own chest, one lingering by his nipple while the other travelled straight down over his belly—

Max abruptly released the trigger of the nozzle. A puddle was forming in the corner of the kennel. He'd been so caught up in the image that his heart was beating faster and his cock pushing back against the weight of his jeans.

"I think I have to go over to Theo's again," he whispered.

Theo growled and tossed the controller aside. He couldn't concentrate, which meant work wasn't progressing on his current contract. Max had left at an indecent hour, in an obvious good mood; Theo had buried himself into the blankets and merely grunted as Max whispered goodbye and kissed him on the shoulder.

It's not like you didn't have reason to expect this sooner or later. Theo scrubbed at his hair with both hands. The memory hadn't come back right away, but it now lurked just below his thoughts.

It had been the single most embarrassing conversation he and Ma had ever had. Like all werewolves, he'd been home-schooled until he was eleven, when his control over his changes had solidified. While he'd managed reasonably well in elementary school, high school had been more difficult. Under puberty's full power, he'd entered a shower room full of boys, and the blended scents of steam-heated skin and testosterone had given him a mortifying erection. A bully spotted it and spent the next month hounding Theo. Theo finally lost his temper and hurled the bigger boy through a locker door.

Then he'd had to explain a suspension to Ma and Grandmother. While Grandmother had scolded him for risking the family secret, Ma hadn't been convinced by his vague explanation for the fight. In the end, she'd come to sit on his bed and eyeball him until he told the full truth.

"It's just part of growing up. You know werewolves don't think about 'gay' and 'straight'. Who you're attracted to doesn't matter. The only thing, Theofanis, is you've got to make sure you only get close to the right ones. Just because you won't marry a female doesn't mean the instinct to submit is going to go away." Here he'd desperately tried to shut her down, his cheeks burning hot, but she'd waved him quiet. *"We're werewolves. Females lead, males submit. That's how it works. But whoever you're going to give up that control to had better be strong. Good, kind, and strong."* She'd smiled and pinched his cheek. *"Don't bring home anybody but the best."*

"I never did bring anybody home," Theo muttered. "Especially wasn't going to do that while Grandmother was alive."

He got up from the couch and went to the kitchen. Maybe making lunch would give him enough time to settle down. That was his intention, yet he found himself staring at the instructions to a microwave dinner without being able to read them.

He ordered me around, and I begged for more. Is that really a part of me? He set down the box and leaned on the counter. *As embarrassing as it'd be, I could really use you right now, Ma.* The undeniable truth was he'd loved every moment of it. Another undeniable truth was that Max was strong. Sure of what he wanted. If Max asked for something, either physically or emotionally, that he didn't want, what would he do? Would he be able to resist that sweet urge, or would he just follow along?

"No. Not for just a 'friend.'" Theo clenched his hands into fists, glaring at the unoffending box. He started when the doorbell rang.

When the front door opened, Max found himself looking at a grimly bespectacled Theo. He'd planned to grab Theo and kiss him deeply, but Theo's cool manner caught him up short.

"Hey," Max said. "Are you okay?"

"I'm fine." Theo hadn't fully opened the door.

"Uh, can I come in?"

"I think you should go," Theo said.

"What? Why?" Max was completely taken off guard.

"I just don't want to—see you right now."

"Nuh-uh." Max blocked the door before Theo could close it; he was encouraged by the fact that Theo let him do it. "Let me in, Theo. I think we'd better talk this one over."

Theo turned away, his mouth jerking in frustration. Max slipped inside and shut the door.

"So what's the problem?" he asked Theo's stiff back.

"I'm not an animal," came the sullen response.

"That's funny, because I am."

"You know what I mean."

"I think I do," Max said gently, "but you'd better explain it to me."

"I'm a werewolf," Theo said, almost cutting him off. "Not a dog!"

"I'm glad to hear that, because I'm not attracted to dogs. They're like kids to me. I am attracted to sexy Greek guys who'll play along in the sack, though."

"Yeah, right. What the hell was 'fetch' then?"

"I was trying to be playful." Max heard the defensiveness in his own voice and abruptly firmed his tone. "Why am I hearing about this the day after it happened, Theo? All I heard at the time was you asking me to make you come."

"That's—that's because you sc—"

"Bullshit." Max smacked a hand against the wall, making Theo's shoulders jerk. "I'm calling bullshit on this whole conversation right now." He caught Theo by the shoulders and turned him around; face dark red, Theo stared downward. "Never mind that a simple 'no' would've been enough at any time, you could tear me in *half*. Don't tell me I scared you." He saw the flicker of Theo's eyelashes. "It's just a turn-on, Theo, like silk underwear or handcuffs or whatever. It doesn't hurt anybody when it's between consenting adults, and it doesn't say anything deep about you." He cupped Theo's face in both hands. "So it got you hot to play my pet for an evening." He tried a smile. "It definitely got me hot."

"I think it does say something about you," Theo said quietly. "I know I'm—I'm—lazy, and don't want to make decisions. I'm a follower, so it's easy to see why I'd, uh, be like that in bed. But I have to ask myself why you'd need to make me feel small and weak."

Shocked, Max couldn't reply for a moment. Theo smiled sadly and started to pull his hands away.

"You've got it wrong, Theo."

"You'd better go." Theo turned away.

It took so long for Max to marshal his thoughts that

Theo was nearly to the kitchen when he reacted. He marched after Theo, catching him by the belt; using it to pull him around and close, Max kissed him firmly on the mouth. There was a moment of startled resistance, then Theo's mouth took his in return. It took a couple of minutes for Max to drag himself back on track.

"You've got so much of that wrong," he said, thumbing Theo's lower lip. "One, lots of people with power in their day-to-day lives like to get dominated. Two, what you did for my sister wasn't what a follower would do, it's what a leader would do. Even you telling my parents stuff behind my back was a sign of leadership. And three, if I like dominating you, that's not because I want to make you weak." For a moment he was the one who couldn't make eye contact. "It's because then I have all of your attention and you're ... Truly naked, in this beautiful, amazing way." He tugged Theo yet closer, glancing up at him, then down at his collarbone. "If you don't want to do that again, I'll understand, but I'd like you to stop trying to make *yourself* small and weak."

"To you it's all just that simple, isn't it?" Theo's words came out smoothly, softly.

"I guess it is."

"This is why I can't handle normal people," Theo muttered abruptly. "You all think things are so cut and dried."

"Normal?" Max tried not to get angry. "The gay dog trainer who talks to ghosts? There's a reason I like hanging out with you, you know. It's because we have things in common that we don't have with anybody else except family. Stop playing 'my life sucks worse than yours', Theo. It's stupid."

All at once, Theo's hands were on his waist; Max's breath jumped from him in surprise as he was turned and pushed back into the wall. Theo leaned in close.

"Oh, yeah, you're such a freak you look like you model for Preppy Outdoors Guy Monthly," Theo said. His tone was quiet, but not soft, and the gleam in his eyes reminded Max uncomfortably of just how much stronger he was.

"Is that a bad thing?" Max kept his voice steady. "Would you like me better if I wore a black T-shirt and jeans every day?"

"You think I ... You think the problem is that I don't *like* you enough?" Theo's right hand brushed against his lower lip and then slid over his throat. Max felt one of his eyebrows jerk up. That hand continued down his chest, pressing in to feel through the fabric of his shirt. Theo's gaze followed his hand, then came back up to challenge.

Go ahead. It doesn't hurt my feelings if you want to touch me, dummy. And you don't really scare me. He wanted to speak but pressed his back teeth together and just returned Theo's look. Feeling a tug on his fly, Max fought to keep from smiling. *Go on, take control. Let's see what you come up with.*

As it had last night, anger turned easily to arousal. He swallowed reflexively as he watched Theo's hand pull his pants open. Theo shoved in abruptly, nuzzling aside the collar of Max's shirt to press his face into his shoulder. Teeth grazed across Max's skin, and he shivered, closing his eyes. It was getting crowded in his briefs, and he moaned impatiently. Theo did him a favor and pushed them down, wrapping a hand around him. Max gasped as Theo's teeth pinched his flesh and held it clamped; he twisted, trying to duck out from under the wonderful discomfort of that while at the same time shifting his hips closer to Theo. Just as he was about to break his silence, Theo's mouth released him. To Max's distress, so did Theo's hand.

Theo placed both hands on Max's clavicle, giving him

a defiant glance before starting to unbutton his shirt. As his hands opened the shirt all the way down, his body sank with them. Max watched this with his lower lip caught in his teeth. Theo's long fingers were soft and very warm against his skin as they slowly trailed down it. Caressing his stomach and hips, Theo looked straight ahead; then he leaned forward, dropping one hand to position Max's cock.

Oh, hell yeah. Max's breathing was doing double-time. His fingers curled up into his palms as Theo placed a very light kiss on the tip of his arousal. The kiss made a tender little sound. Then Theo touched his lips to it again, and they parted to take in just the tip. Letting out a sigh, Max lowered his eyelids; his blurred focus beheld Theo's bent head. Every tiny movement of Theo's careful mouth sent burning chills through Max's body. His hardened nipples interpreted air as friction.

Growing more confident, Theo drew his tongue around the head of Max's cock. His head dipped as he took more and more of it into his mouth. Max's hand moved of its own accord to dive joyously into Theo's abundant black curls. As Theo applied pressure, he threw his head back and just barely missed thunking it against the wall. He wouldn't have cared if he had; he now had both hands in Theo's hair, and it took all that was left of his self-control not to yank.

"Oh, god, that's good." Theo's mouth was the perfect mix of aggression and exploratory caution, wet heat and curious tongue; he was letting Max slide in deep. "Where'd you learn—oh, hell, where'd you learn to do that so damn good?" A moan in Theo's throat sent ripples of new fiery pleasure up his cock. Hands massaged his hips, cupped his buttocks, and played down his thighs.

"Theo," Max groaned as Theo sucked harder. "Oh, Theo ..." He could hear that Theo was breathing very quickly through his nose, could feel his big hands clutch at his hipbones. Pleasure built and built until Max could barely feel anything else, could hardly distinguish the different sensations assaulting his senses. "Yes. Yes, Theo—Theo!" His hips jolted, and he bent forward instinctively, curving over Theo as his cock pulsed inside his mouth.

Slowly Theo pulled his head back. Belatedly Max forced his benumbed fingers to let go, regretting the loss of Theo's sweet warmth as his spent cock slipped free. His heart pounded and his knees trembled as though he'd been running a race. Wiping his mouth, Theo got to his feet and looked at him. Max busied himself getting his clothes back in place so he didn't laugh at how red Theo was under the serious expression. When Theo continued to search for something to say, Max hooked his fingers through the belt loops of his jeans and tugged him closer. He wedged one knee between both of Theo's and, pulling slowly, brought Theo's crotch against his thigh.

"Now what?" he asked softly, watching Theo's jaw tighten as he kept up a slow grind against the impressive bulge in his jeans. "What are you going to do with me?"

"Send you home," came the quiet reply.

"What? Are you serious?" Max smiled uncertainly, caressing Theo's lower back. "That's got to be a joke." He leaned in closer, letting his mouth hover pointedly over Theo's. "Go ahead," he said. "Throw me down right here, tear my clothes off with your teeth. Show me you're the big man. I can take it." He was close enough to see Theo's pupils dilate, but then strong hands pressed him into the wall as Theo disentangled himself.

"Not today," he said. "I've got work to do."

"Theo," Max said, uncomfortable, "I don't get it."

"No, you don't get it." Suddenly, Theo's voice sharpened. "You think I'm sometimes a wolf. I'm never a wolf. I'm always a *w-were*wolf."

"Which means what?"

"It means I don't live in a pack. I don't chase caribou across the freaking tundra. And s-submitting might be ... natural to me, but ..." Theo raised his head, his cheeks rosy but his eyes hard. "I'm nobody's b-bitch."

"Theo," Max said again, this time in exasperation, "that was just a game, just a fun screw."

"Yeah. I guess so." Theo held open the door, his expression still unyielding.

At a loss and still rubbery from the wonderful way Theo had pleasured him, Max couldn't find it within himself to fight back any longer.

"Call me," he said on his way out. "Call me for real, okay?" He got a nod in response before Theo closed the door. Then he nearly tripped on his way down the stairs. *What did he just say about submitting?*

Theo hadn't called. Not yesterday, not today.

Max was getting frustrated on multiple levels. Mom was still angry, so he avoided spending much time in the main house. There'd been more news of a local going into a coma, probably because of a shadow spirit attack. Theo wasn't talking to him, which meant he still didn't know what the intriguing statement "submitting might be natural to me" was all about.

He went to Jimmy's. Not much else was open at this time of night, and it gave him an excuse to go for a drive.

Jimmy's was surprisingly lively as he stepped inside. Seeking out the source of all the laughter, he spotted a group of people sitting at a table near the windows. He couldn't miss the tallest figure in the group or his mop of dark curls. Max started to smile in disbelief. He drew a breath.

Theo leaned forward, lowering his head as his shoulders visibly shook and he slapped the table. Then he fell back in his chair, tilting his head back. His laughter was as loud as anyone else's.

Max's smile failed. He stood there uncertainly, watching Theo talk with unfamiliar energy, even give one of his friends a teasing push. The cashier was looking at him quizzically, so he went to order. Once he had coffee and doughnuts in hand, he considered just slipping out. But then the one woman in their group spotted him. She said something to Theo, who turned and spotted him. And all the amusement seemed to drain from him.

That reaction really made him want to leave, but Max walked over to the group. The woman, a freckled redhead, gazed up at him through green-rimmed glasses. Next to her sat a slender, dark-skinned man who wore a friendly smile. Beside Theo was a man with a ragged ponytail. He was much less fit than Theo, but his black T-shirt could have come right from Theo's closet.

"What are you doing at this Jimmy's?" Max asked. "Bit far for you, isn't it?"

"That's my fault," the woman said. "I live out of town. This is the closest place for me. I'm Marnie, by the way. That's Frankie." She indicated the ponytailed man. "And this is Whitney. We're all old friends of Theo's."

"Max." *And your guess is as good as mine what I am to Theo right now.*

Frankie was staring at him, unsmiling. Max supposed this was some sort of protective gesture.

"Everything okay?" Theo mumbled.

"Yeah, fine. Just wanted a doughnut." Max gestured with the bag to a notebook on the table. "What are you guys up to?"

"Planning Halloween," Marnie said.

"Oh, yeah? What do you guys do?"

"Movie marathon." Frankie abruptly spoke. "This year we're doing zombies."

That requires planning weeks in advance? Max nodded.

"Max," Theo said, "Marnie's sister was one of the ones in a coma."

"Oh." Max turned to her. "I'm so sorry to hear that. Is she ...?"

"She woke up, thank goodness." Marnie laced her hands before her on the table. Whitney put his arm around her shoulders. "Doesn't remember a thing, but she's getting stronger all the time."

"That must have been scary." Max put a hand on Theo's shoulder, trying to signal his understanding. Theo was here protecting his friend.

"It was. It was." She smiled bravely. "Are you into zombie movies, Max?"

"Not really." He smiled back. "Sorry." He squeezed Theo's shoulder. "I'd better get going. It was nice meeting you guys. Theo." He leaned down to kiss Theo's cheek, then spoke into his ear. "You need to call me."

Theo dipped his chin. His cheeks were quickly turning pink, and he only made eye contact for a second.

Max escaped the awkward scene, feeling their attention follow him out. He didn't look back, because he didn't want to see how much more relaxed Theo was around his friends. He tore at a defenseless doughnut with his teeth as he drove home.

Either I rock your world or I kill your buzz. Make a decision, Wolf Boy. Ball's in your court.

CHAPTER SEVEN

The highway had gotten slightly less lonely. It was a subtle change, because the highway was still lined with evergreens and birch alternating with relentlessly featureless pastures. The truck shot down the asphalt, sandwiched between semis, to pass a gas station and then a sign welcoming them to the city.

"Almost there, Babe." Adrian glanced at Kelsie in the passenger seat. She was folded casually into it, one booted foot up on the dash, and she rolled her eyes at his assured tone.

"I'm doing fine," she said. "Not as excited as you, though." He chortled.

"I just can't wait to see the look on his face!" He gripped the steering wheel until it squeaked.

"Be nice to him." She toyed with her ponytail.

"What? What bad stuff I ever done to him?"

Snorting, she rested a foot on his thigh. He chuckled as he patted the top of her boot, his hand covering most of it.

"Be nice to him," she repeated as he massaged her calf.

"Don't worry," he said. "It'll just be a nice family visit."

"We're not visiting. We're looking for work, you doof."

"Yeah, but it all starts with family. Grandmother said

it always starts with family." As he said this, he turned onto the street that led into the older part of the city.

Anastasia had felt nervous the entire trip over, yet her urge to do this wouldn't let up. She couldn't manage much of a smile when Louis opened the door.

"Hi," she said. "Sorry to drop by unannounced. I was wondering how you were doing."

"Oh. Well, that's nice of you." Louis blinked in surprise, then stepped back to let Anastasia in.

"How have you been holding up?" Anastasia rubbed her hands together. She peered around the living room, relieved to find it empty. She'd tried to predict when he'd be alone in the house. Friday afternoon seemed a good bet, as she sometimes ran into his wife at the supermarket then.

"I'm actually feeling pretty much back to normal, but the wife doesn't believe me." Louis headed for the kitchen. "Coffee?"

"Love some."

"Have a seat. I'll bring some in."

Anastasia perched on the edge of an armchair, unsettled. She'd been here before for the occasional Christmas gathering, but she couldn't say she knew Louis very well. She certainly didn't know him well to easily broach this subject.

Louis looked a little uncomfortable, too, when he brought her the coffee. He sat on the worn sofa, nudging aside blankets and an open novel.

"Doctor's orders," he said. "It's tough being told to rest when you feel fine. I was a paramedic so long, you'd think I'd be a better patient."

"It's understandable." She smiled tightly. "I tried to do

too much too soon, too. It wasn't a good idea."

For a moment, he looked puzzled. Then the clouds cleared from his brow.

"Yeah." He rubbed his beaky nose. "I forgot about that. You seem like you're doing okay."

"I am. I am." She cleared her throat. "I'm sorry, Louis. I came here to ask you something really strange, and I can't think of any other way to say it than to just say it. When you had your—when it happened to you, what did you see?"

She saw the wariness come into his pale eyes, and it felt familiar. She felt bad for bringing up those feelings that every medium felt at some point.

"Not much," he said. "I blacked out."

"No, I mean before that." She tucked her hair behind her ears and dove in. "I think the same thing happened to the both of us. I think we both became portals to some kind of otherworldly spirits. Awful ones that look like shadows."

Not unexpectedly, Louis didn't immediately respond. He sat with his lips pursed, his gaze flicking around the ceiling. Finally, he started to smile, but the expression wasn't reflected in his eyes.

She didn't feel like hearing the lie.

"It sounds crazy, but you believe me. You believe me because it happened to you, just like it happened to me. That's why I wanted to talk to you about it. Maybe we can figure out something about those things."

Louis's expression fell. He leaned forward and rubbed a big hand over his mostly bare head. For a while, he was silent. She heard a car go by on the road, gravel popping. Finally, she broke that silence.

"I've seen ghosts my whole life. I've let them inside me—been possessed. But it was never like that. I mean, have you ever felt anything like that?"

"No." His voice was a soft grumble. "Not like that." He sighed heavily and sat back. "When I was a boy, my family told me they were hallucinations. Or called me a liar."

Anastasia nodded, feeling a swell of compassion. She knew how lucky she was to have been born into her family, where everyone understood and nobody judged.

"I started to believe it, I guess. But those damn things didn't let the past stay the past. Damn it." He covered his face with his hands for just a moment. "Do you think they'll come back?"

"I don't know, Louis. But I'm going to try to figure out everything I can about them. If there's a way to stop them, I'll tell you about it." She tried to sound sure as she got up. "If you hear anything, or you need any help, give me a call. Okay?"

Louis nodded. They seemed to have run out of words, so Anastasia let herself out.

Max spotted Theo standing, hands in the pockets of his army-green coat, next to a tow truck. Sheepishly Theo walked toward him as Max stopped the car. Max waited for Theo to get in.

"Thanks for coming to get me," Theo said as they buckled up. "My car'll be out of the shop in a couple of days. Just needs a part sent up from down south. Sorry about this. Couldn't get hold of any of my friends."

"It's not a problem, Theo," Max said, exasperated. "You saved my sister's life. I'll drive you anywhere you want to go." *That kind of made it sound like we* aren't *friends. Is he still pissed off at me?*

"Is everything okay? Uh, at home?" Theo cleared his throat.

"It's better," Max said. "Mom's almost talking to me now." He glanced at Theo and saw that his mouth had tightened up. *Yeah, you should feel guilty.* "Mom's really high-strung. She gets herself worked up sometimes, and it's hard to talk her down." Even just thinking about his mother's hysterical voice made his stomach twist. Theo's voice brought him out of his thoughts.

"Do you think she'll know what we can, uh, do about them?"

"We're going to do something about them?" Max asked, bemused. Theo tapped the dashboard with stiff fingers.

"They're causing trouble."

"I'm not used to the idea of doing something about spirits." He rubbed his chin. "It's always been more live—well, exist and let exist."

"They've gone for your sister twice, Max." There was impatience in Theo's tone now. "Plus Louis Wilson, and Marnie's sister. And you, too. They're d-dangerous."

"So are bears, and I usually leave them alone." Theo's insistence was starting to irritate him.

"Max, what—" For a moment, Theo's voice rose, but he immediately stopped speaking, which irritated Max even more. Theo spoke evenly. "Don't you want to protect your family?"

"Of course I do!" Max sat up abruptly, striking the steering wheel with his hand; Theo's eyelashes flickered. "What are you trying to say?"

"I just ..." Theo grimaced. "I just don't get it." He laced his hands together in his lap and looked down at them, his hair falling softly over his forehead.

Max watched the road and didn't say anything.

"I guess protecting people—is just a thing with me." Theo spoke quite softly now. "Maybe it's because of what I am."

They were waiting at a red light. Max reached over to run his knuckles along Theo's jaw. He turned to look into Theo's widened eyes.

"Believe it or not, it is with me, too." He traced the outline of Theo's ear with his thumb. "Are we good, Theo?" The way Theo's eyes widened and his lips quivered was beautiful. Max smiled at Theo's tiny nod. The light changed, and he drove on. *I don't think I want to be done with you yet.* He'd been relieved to get Theo's call, even if it was just asking for a favor.

Someone had parked a big red pickup truck in front of Theo's house, so it took some maneuvering to park.

"Hey, there are lights on in your living room—" Before he could finish the sentence, Theo was on the sidewalk. Max scrambled to get out.

Theo's nostrils flared as he stood on the sidewalk and his eyes narrowed sharply.

"Excuse me," he said curtly, and marched up the stairs to fling open the door and disappear inside.

"Hey, Theo!" Alarmed, Max followed. *What if they have weapons or something?* The irony of his thoughts was not lost on him as he, too, charged into the house. Inside he found Theo standing in the living room, arms folded across his chest and giving the two people on the couch a dirty look. Max stood behind him, uncertain.

The man just getting up from the couch was big— really big. He had long legs and a powerful torso; his jaw and cheekbones were prominent, his mouth broad and confident. Straight black hair swept back from his forehead to his shoulders, and his light brown eyes focused on Theo from under a prominent brow. His eyebrows had the same arch as Theo's, but were thicker and held at a clearly contemptuous height.

"The key wasn't in the same place, but it's not like I couldn't sniff it out," he said to Theo in a quick, brash voice.

"Yeah, Adrian, when the spare key's been moved and you weren't told about it, you should probably take the hint," Theo snapped. Behind the very big man was a much smaller blonde woman. She was slim, her long hair worn simply, her face lean and unremarkable. She gave Max a what-can-you-do smile.

Adrian moved so suddenly Max didn't have time to react. The windows rattled as Adrian pinned Theo face-first to the wall.

"Think you're a tough guy now? Huh?" Adrian pressed bodily against Theo, one hand holding his head in place. He jerked up the hem of Theo's shirt. Theo arched forward into the wall, then yelped and shoved back against Adrian.

"Whoa!" Max started to move before he was sure what he was going to do. The woman caught him by the elbow. She shook her head in response to his startled look.

Theo gave a trembling cry. A laugh.

"Ade, get off!" Theo danced in place as Adrian's fingers scrabbled across the small of his back. He got his hands under him and gave a mighty push, sending Adrian staggering away. The woman put out a hand to stop Adrian from crashing into Max. Face flushed, Theo huffed in exasperation as he straightened his T-shirt. "Jesus, Ade, we aren't kids anymore."

"Says the runt who's still ticklish." Adrian chuckled.

"This is my house now. You can't just come in."

Max's heart beat faster as Adrian drew himself up. He wasn't used to having to tilt his head back to look at someone's face.

I don't think I could do a thing to this big bastard.

"What the hell?" Adrian demanded. "This is Grandmother's house, Theofanis. You can't—"

"Yes, I can." Theo didn't seem nearly as intimidated as Max felt. "She left the house to me."

"Oh, yeah? She tell you to move the key, too?"

"It's my key. I can put it wherever I want." Theo gave Max an apologetic look. "Max, this is my cousin Adrian and his fiancée Kelsie. Ade, Kelsie, this is Max." Theo cleared his throat and rested his hand briefly on Max's shoulder. While Kelsie simply nodded, Adrian turned and gave Max a long look.

Oh, boy. Max forced a smile and held out his hand. Adrian took it readily enough, but then he began to squeeze. Max kept the smile firmly in place, pretending not to notice as his hand started to hurt.

"Next time call first," Theo said.

Adrian abruptly let go.

"Since when?"

"Ade," Kelsie said. Her voice was flat, neutral. "Come on now. We just dropped in. Theofanis, how about I make some Greek food to apologize?"

"That would be great, actually." Theo looked at Max, clearly hopeful. "Kelsie learned how to cook from Grandmother. She's really good."

"Sounds good," Max managed. He felt like he hadn't gotten his bearings yet. *I have to admit I'm curious. I can see if Theo's like other werewolves. What he's like with his family.* He flexed his fingers to get the feeling back in his fingertips. *Except his family seems kind of crazy.*

"Yeah." Theo's little smile rewarded him. "Except I've got nothing in the fridge."

"That's okay. We can go get some." Kelsie scratched at her head. "Except I hate driving that monster in town. Could you drive me to the store?"

"Uh, sure." Theo gave Max a worried look.

"I'll be fine," Max said, trying to laugh it off. He went to Theo and patted his cheek, then whispered into his ear. "I know werewolves don't eat people." He didn't feel as confident as he sounded. *I can take a shower or something.*

Check my e-mail. Try to avoid the conversation I just know is coming.

"Okay. He's a jerk, but at least you'll be, y'know, safe." Theo looked past him, then kissed his cheek. "Be back in a few minutes." He grabbed the keys to his car and led Kelsie from the house. The door closed.

Max turned to find himself still on the receiving end of a penetrating stare. He put on a sunny smile. "I'm just going to wash up. Feel free to get yourself a drink from the kitchen." He enjoyed how Adrian's left eyebrow twitched at this subtle territorial claim.

However, there was only so long that he could usefully stay in the shower. He dawdled long enough to dry his hair, then sighed and went out to face Adrian.

Adrian was, to his surprise, sitting quietly in the kitchen with a pot of tea near him. He glanced up when Max entered.

"Want some?"

Okay, that wasn't quite what I was expecting. "Sure." Max watched as Adrian poured tea into a mug. He doctored it with sugar and milk, looking pointedly at the mug Adrian sipped from—it was Theo's favorite. Adrian didn't seem to notice.

"What you do for a living, Adrian?" *Start with safe, manly, straight guy talk.*

"Drive truck."

"Long haul?"

"Gravel, logging, wherever the jobs are. You?"

"I'm a dog trainer."

Adrian threw his head back and laughed, slapping the table. Teaspoons leapt and the milk spilled a little.

I don't think he even knows what an inside voice is.

"Unbelievable." Adrian shook his head, his thick hair waving. "Ah, shit. A monkey who plays with dogs."

Max grimaced and said nothing. He sipped tea, hardly

tasting it, until Adrian broke the silence.

"So how long you been screwing my baby cousin?"

Max snorted in exasperation. "He's a grown man." His pulse quickened, but he kept his tone level.

"Uh-huh." Adrian abruptly set down his tea and glared right into Max's eyes. "Theofanis, he shouldn't be with somebody like you."

"Somebody like me." Max leaned back in his chair. "Now what would that mean? Gay? Ukrainian? Self-employed?" He tilted his head challengingly. Adrian's expression flattened. His eyes glittered unpleasantly under the shadow of his heavy brows.

"Don't play games with me, monkey."

Max tried not to let the silly insult irritate him.

"You shouldn't know about us, and you shouldn't be anywhere near Theofanis."

"I don't think you get to determine that." Anger warmed Max's face. *Jesus, just how good are werewolf ears?*

"Monkeys aren't good for us. Can't trust you tricky weaklings. You sure as hell aren't good enough for him." Adrian leaned closer. "Trust me. You'll never satisfy him."

"What?" Max snorted again. "I'm not twelve, do you seriously think—"

Adrian leaned closer yet, his wide mouth curving into a dark grin.

"I should know. I popped that cherry. Your weak little dick ain't going to do it for him."

The room did a full turn around Max. He couldn't think of a thing to say. Adrian laughed through his nose, relaxing back into his chair with his tea.

"Don't look like that. We're second cousins and, like, a half or something. Our family's kinda weird. Anyways, he was eighteen, I was probably twenty, twenty-one. I come over one time to hang out. He's alone, and it's real obvious I just caught him in the middle of something. Too fucking funny." Adrian sipped tea. "I couldn't help it, I had to razz him. I've never seen his face so purple." Adrian started to laugh, then sat up a little and hastily swallowed before he choked on his drink. He wiped his lips, his gaze distant. "Just to wind him up, I ask him if he wants any help. If he wants me to kiss him." Some of the amusement left his expression. "Little runt said yes."

"I *really*—" Max's voice broke. His pulse thudded in his ears. "Don't think Theo would want you telling this story."

"I couldn't help it. Seeing him just give it up to me like that was frigging hot. I swear we were at it for hours."

"Really not appropriate," Max said. "Seriously."

"As long as he didn't have to call the shots, he was good with whatever I—" Adrian paused, his gaze sliding to the side. The next moment the front door could be heard opening. Adrian smirked and licked his lips, giving Max a little wink.

"You're an asshole," Max said under his breath. Adrian's upper lip curled.

"*Kane mou pipa, pithikos.*"

Before Max could do more than realize Adrian had spoken Greek, Theo stormed into the kitchen. Plastic bags flying from his hands, Theo hauled Adrian out of the chair and threw him to the floor. Max, startled, got to his feet. Kelsie hurried in, pulling him to the far corner and shoving him behind her. Theo cocked an index finger at Adrian, letting loose a stream of irate-sounding Greek.

"Whoa, Theo, cool it," Max said, left breathless by the sudden violence.

"Stay back. You'll get hurt," Kelsie barked over her shoulder. She was about half a head shorter than Max, but he couldn't deny how easily she'd moved him around. He stiffened as Adrian jumped to his feet and lunged. Theo twisted, dodging Adrian's attack, and then caught Adrian around the waist and drove him against the fridge. The basket on top overturned, raining paperclips, envelopes, and old batteries down on them.

"Jesus! Shouldn't we stop them?" Max hated the sight of Adrian's massive hands clutching Theo, even though Theo seemed to be winning.

"This has been coming for a while," Kelsie said. "We have to let them sort it out."

"But—" Max winced as Adrian hurled Theo aside. Theo spun around, then regained his balance.

"You can't say stuff like that here, in my house. *My* house. Grandmother left it to me. It's mine." Theo's arm shot out, aiming a pointing finger back at Max. "He is also mine." That finger moved to indicate the door. "Get out."

"You're kicking me out?" Adrian's face contorted in disbelief. "Theofanis, you little—"

"Enough." Kelsie's slashing gesture cut off Adrian's words. "Ade, let's go."

"What? Kelsie ..." Adrian gestured in frustration with both hands, his shoulders slumping. To Max's surprise, when Kelsie left the kitchen, Adrian followed wordlessly behind. When the front door closed, Theo underwent a subtle but complete wilting. He slid Max a sidelong look.

"Shit," Max said. His knees were trembling. "I've never seen you get mad like that."

"Ade's—" Theo rubbed his face. "Ade's an asshole. I'm sorry."

"What did he say? Do I want to know?" Max found he still hadn't left the corner. He forced himself to walk toward Theo, to try to regain some sort of normalcy. Theo's nostrils flared.

"Told you to blow him, basically."

Max laughed. "I'm not that fragile."

"That's not the—not the point." Theo licked his lips. "He can't go saying shit like that to you."

"He is also mine." Max felt strange and trapped again at the very thought of those words, spoken without a hint of stammering. "I'll live."

Theo cleared his throat, looking at the plastic bags scattered around the kitchen floor.

"I can't really make dinner. Pizza, maybe?"

"Actually, you know what? I think I'll call it an early night." Leftover nerves killed his appetite. He wasn't finding the rundown little kitchen nearly as comfortable as usual. When Max moved for the doorway, a hand on his shoulder stopped him. He closed his eyes as arms wrapped around his chest and he felt curly hair against his neck.

"Can you stay tonight?" Theo mumbled into his back.

I should go. No matter what I think of that asshole, I love seeing you submit just like he does. Uncomfortable, Max put his hands over Theo's. *I've got a lot to think about.* Not saying any of these things, he turned his head to catch a peck on the cheek. Theo had never asked him to stay, and he wasn't heartless enough to ignore that. "Theo, how do you hurt a werewolf?"

"Huh? Same way you hurt anybody. That silver bullet stuff's just, y'know, a myth. Why?"

"Just wondering." *That big sucker had you up against a wall, and I know if I tried to pull him off, I couldn't do it. If I made him mad, he could probably yank my spine out.* Max picked up one of Theo's hands and kissed it. *I don't think I could ever protect you from anything.* "As long as you're okay with just snuggling, I'll stay."

"Yeah," Theo said in surprise. "I didn't mean we had to—"

"Okay. I'm just somehow not in the mood. Pizza sounds good, though. Maybe we could watch a DVD or something."

"Yeah." Theo brightened. "I'll order. You pick the DVD." He went in search of his phone.

Max dutifully went into the living room and looked at the jumble of plastic cases in the entertainment center. The little house had become so familiar in such a short time that he resented Adrian and Kelsie's intrusion. He'd never felt so at home in someone else's house before. This was all alien to him.

What have I gotten myself into?

Water. He was floating in grasping, dark, slime-thick water. At the same time, he was also walking. His body moved like a wind-up toy, unsteadily marching across the gravel road and through the ditch. He wasn't allowed to come up this way. His feet were taking him up the slope to the highway. And all the while, he felt that heavy, ancient will. At the top of this hill were monsters made of metal; on the other side were trees, so many trees, holding mysteries. If it got him up the hill, he would die. Yet his feet kept moving, his body slowly rising. The light began to change as he drew clear of the tall grasses and spindly berry bushes. He was almost to the top of the hill. A roaring filled his ears. Almost to the top—

Max's body jolted. He stared at the ceiling, his vision swimming as he tried to catch a breath. After a panicked moment of failure, he shook his head sharply, and his equilibrium returned. He rubbed briskly at his face, trying to wipe away sweat and clinging unease.

"It's been a while." His voice came out rusty. Max cleared his throat and, feeling a little ashamed, reached over to turn on the lamp. Sitting up in bed, he massaged his bare chest, which housed a restless heart. "It must be all this stuff with the weird spirits, bringing back memories."

He knew he was talking to himself to put some human noise into his trailer, which felt dark, confining, and yet not enough protection. Being reminded of Deep Murky made the trees visible outside his window into menacing silhouettes. "God, I'm a grown man."

Knowing sleep wouldn't be back for a while, he flipped the covers back. He hesitated, looking at the pillow next to him. It suddenly looked unoccupied.

"I think I've been sleeping at Theo's too often." He reached out and ran his fingers over the pillow, wishing he could touch Theo's ridiculous black curls. Stroke his warm, smooth skin. Slip his fingertips between his lips and feel the wet heat of his mouth, anticipating that heat touching him elsewhere. Max's cock stirred, admittedly a bit half-heartedly. "I can't think of anything that'd make me feel better faster than fucking Theo." He went as far as picking up his cell, then saw the time and sighed. "No, even he's probably asleep at three in the morning."

Max went down the hall to his kitchen, turning on lights as he went. He grabbed orange juice from the fridge and stood there drinking it from the carton. Even in his own house, it was an act of rebellion. He could practically hear Mom's voice as he did it.

The slightly dingy lighting of his kitchen didn't completely dispel his uneasiness, especially with the night peering in through his windows. Max sat down at the desk tucked into the corner of his living room and turned on his laptop, waiting for it to boot up and swirling the remaining orange juice around in the bottom of the carton.

"How boring is this going to be?"

The kitchen table sat almost accusingly empty in the corner of his eye. He pictured Theo filling up some of that space, listening to him talk. He turned his head and tried that image on the couch instead. Theo, back against the cushions and knees bent before him, flipping through a magazine or playing a game on his tablet.

Theo, pointing at him and laying claim.

"Jesus." Max numbly set the juice carton aside. He got to his feet, rubbing his arms. "I didn't even think of anybody else. It wouldn't have to be Theo." The kitchen and the living room together gave him just enough room to pace. "It wouldn't have to be Theo." He paused by the sink, running both hands through his hair and letting them come to a rest on his nape. "Would it?"

Max abandoned his laptop and his pacing both to sit on the couch and stare at his darkened TV screen. He wasn't going to be able to go back to sleep now.

"Max?" Anastasia's voice snuck through the roar of his vacuum cleaner. He didn't stop until he'd finished the circuit of his living room, then turned it off. When he turned and looked at her, she was leaning against the wall, her eyebrows raised. He pretended not to notice as he walked past into the kitchen. He grabbed the dishcloth and started scrubbing the table.

"Something wrong?"

"What's up, Ana?" he asked shortly.

"I went to see Louis Wilson a couple of days ago, and I thought I'd tell you about it. Max, what's going on?"

"What's it look like? I've got some spare time this afternoon, so I'm cleaning up my place."

"You're cleaning up a clean place."

Max stopped and leaned on the table with both hands.

"I'm probably a terrible person," he muttered.

"Probably," Anastasia said brightly.

He made a face and resumed scrubbing.

"I think I've let Theo think things are more than they are."

Anastasia abruptly moved to sit in one of the chairs, setting her elbows on the table.

"Don't tell me your commitment allergy's acting up again."

"Ana ..."

"No, seriously. Theo's wonderful. Why don't you want to keep him?"

"I don't keep *anybody*. I don't get kept, either. We've got secrets in this family, Ana, we can't ..." *He has family secrets, too. He gets it.* Max threw the dishcloth at the sink, irritated. "I don't want a boyfriend."

"Tough, you've got one. Poor you."

"Ana ..." Max settled into a chair himself. "So what happened with Louis?"

"It was just as I thought." Anastasia drooped a little, a crease forming in her forehead. "Which is scary. He was a portal for one of those shadows, just like I was. From what he said, he's sensitive to spirits. They must be using mediums."

"Jesus. Well, that one did come here, where there are three of us." Max drummed his fingers on the table.

"Why do you have the TV on with the sound off?" Anastasia frowned. "I haven't seen you do that in a while."

Before she could go on to guess that his nightmares had returned—he used to use the TV screen to make himself feel less alone—Max got up to turn the TV off.

"Wait, take it off mute," she said, her tone suddenly urgent. "They're talking about Fort Rivers."

"What?"

The noon news break was reporting on a series of people collapsing from unknown causes. Doctors were apparently baffled. Police were starting to investigate the possibility of them being poisoned. They both listened in silence to the entire report; once it was over, Max spun around and they stared at each other.

"Holy shit," Anastasia said. "Do you think Mom saw that?"

"Doubt it. But I think we'd better talk about this one as a family." Max said that through instinctive reluctance. "God, I'd better call Theo."

"What? Why?"

"Uh, nothing. Just reminding myself about something else. Jesus, Ana, we've never seen anything like this before."

"Yeah." She squared her shoulders. "So who gets to tell Mom?"

They looked into each other's eyes. Max solemnly held out a clenched fist. Without hesitation she did the same.

"Rock, paper, scissors ..."

Kelsie unbuckled the shackles around Adrian's thick wrists, then smiled and patted him on the cheek.

"You didn't break them this time."

"It was close, Babe." He chuckled, lifting his head to meet her when she dipped down for a quick kiss. "That was awesome."

"Mm." She climbed off of him and found her housecoat.

He let out a heavy exhalation, tucking his hands behind his head and grinning up at the ceiling. Then his mouth shifted into a grimace.

"This is such a shithole."

"And whose fault is that?" She went to get herself a glass of water, gazing out the gap between the curtains at the drab motel parking lot.

"Theofanis', of course." His tone sharpened defensively.

"No, it's not."

"Hey, whose side are you on?"

"Yours. That doesn't mean I can't tell when you're being a jerk." She sniffed, then took a deeper whiff. "I swear Fort Rivers smells different than it used to."

"Still stinks like pulp mill to me." Adrian sullenly got up. She winced as the bed springs creaked piercingly.

"Not just that. Under it. Something kind of weird."

"How can Theofanis figure he can just kick us out like that?"

She'd clearly lost his attention. Adrian's childishness was at times endearing, at others frustrating. But she gave up anyway, because all she had was a faint uneasiness. She was too pure a werewolf to worry bones that might not even exist.

"You know what you have to do."

"Like hell."

"Ade, just go apologize. That's all Theofanis wants. What do you expect? You disrespected him in his own house."

"I didn't disrespect him, it was the monkey I—"

"Same thing. For crying out loud, Babe, just go over and apologize."

"All right, already." Adrian spread his arms and fell back on the bed, making it shriek. "I'll go tomorrow."

CHAPTER EIGHT

L ast Quarter

Max could generally resist his mother's attempts to over-feed him, but not during Thanksgiving dinner. He escaped before he could get tempted into more pie and whipped cream. It was still only early evening, but his over-stuffed stomach wanted him to lie down, so he went to his trailer to collapse onto his bed.

I should have invited Theo. I know he likes Mom's cooking. He hadn't wanted to, because he still wasn't completely comfortable with how things were going. Having Theo over for a holiday dinner with the family would have felt intimate when he wasn't ready for that. *I wonder what he does for Thanksgiving.* He blinked rapidly for a moment. *He had a life—sort of—before he met me, right?* He rolled onto his side and jammed a pillow into the crook of his arm, irritated. *I still can't make up my mind about you, you nerdy werewolf.* Max let his body's heaviness sink into his mind and take him away from his annoyance.

He woke abruptly, as he often did with naps, with a racing heart and no idea what time of day it was. He reached for his cell, didn't find it by the lamp, and then realized he was still fully dressed. It was a lump against his thigh when he patted his jeans. He froze in the process of reaching into his pocket for it. Cold sweat sprang up on his skin, and pins and needles spread across the back of his neck. Dreading to see what he knew must be there, Max looked at the foot of his bed.

A shadow stood there, staring at him.

"Jesus!" Max lunged clumsily upward, fumbling at the window above his headboard. He shoved it open. Watching the shadow, he put one leg through the window. Its head tilted as if in question. Unnerved, Max awkwardly yanked his other leg through. The windowsill struck him in the ribs as he slithered out backward. Then gravity took hold. His legs wouldn't hold him as he hit the packed dirt under his window. He sat down hard. Ignoring the pain spiking in both ankles, he scrambled to his feet.

The house, got to—no, the kennels are closer!

The shadow flickered into being next to him. Hissing a curse, Max just barely dodged its grasp. Its ill-formed fingertips brushed his neck. He ran into bright light and nearly lost his orientation. The dogs in the kennels began barking, and he tried to follow that sound. Then the light was extinguished and he heard a truck door slam.

Who the hell? Just as Max spotted the tall figure walking his way, his wrist was taken in a vise grip.

"Hey. It's just me, Theofanis' cousin. Adrian. I wanted to—"

"Get out of here!" Max yelled, trying to pry those inhuman fingers free. The shadow grew too close. He could see the strange bumps of its unformed face bare centimeters from his own. "I am not a vessel for you. I am not a vessel for you. Ah, shit!" The shadow pressed its free hand against Max's chest. Its fingertips sank through. He felt them approach his core with unreasonable ease.

"What the hell's that?" Adrian's voice, accompanied by heavy boot steps, came closer.

"No! Adrian, go—get inside!" Max lost traction and

fell onto his back. The shadow went with him, pinning his wrist to the ground. He tried futilely to wrestle its hand away from his chest. Its skin was like polished stone, cold and impenetrable. He couldn't even get a hold of it.

"Hey, get off him!" Adrian seized the shadow by the shoulders. It pulled free of Max long enough to shove Adrian away. The big man flew backward and landed like a sack of potatoes. He pushed himself up and shook his head.

As Max tried to break free, he saw with surreal clarity the sudden fear on Adrian's face. The shadow pressed both hands through Max's flesh and into his mind. Max's jaw tightened, and his thoughts went dim. At the same time, he kept his gaze on Adrian.

"Go," he mumbled. "Or—or change—" Bearing down with his will, he was only able to slow the shadow a little. Max tried to bring the concentration of a chant together and couldn't manage it. His body grew distant from him, barely blinking at the sudden explosion of light nearby. The kennels went abruptly silent.

He heard Adrian before he saw him. His growl was bass and chilling. It preceded the action by only a moment. Then there was a storm of activity above him. Max's breath exploded from him as a massive paw stomped firmly on his stomach. The shadow tore away from him, leaving him winded and nauseous.

"Hello?" It was Anastasia's voice, distant. Then the squeak of the screen door closing. "Hello?"

"Ana, don't." Max didn't have the breath to speak loudly. He could still hear snarling and thrashing, sounding like it was coming from near his trailer. His muscles protested as he dragged himself to his feet. One of his ankles resisted his weight. He limped to Adrian's truck.

"Max? Is that you?"

"Be careful. One of those things is here." Max saw her silhouette, backed by the porch light, come around the front of the pickup.

"No way. Where?" She hurried to his side, looking around nervously. "Whose truck is this?"

"Just a friend's."

"So where's the friend?"

"In my trailer. Ana, we'd better get inside the house."

"But what about your friend?"

"He's, uh, not a medium. I'll call him when we get inside. Come on." He gave her a gentle push. His entire body tingled unpleasantly, one of his ankles throbbed, and he dearly wanted to sit down. He was also afraid dinner was about to abandon him.

"Wait." She resisted his guidance. "Why are there clothes on the ground?"

"You know you shouldn't ask me those kinds of questions," he tried, his heart stuttering. "Ana, in the house. Now."

"Max," she said, inhaling sharply. "You're not—"

"In the house, for fuck's sake! We're not safe out here!" He limped quickly, pushing her ahead of him the short distance to the stairs. When he glanced back, he saw a huge four-legged shadow slip behind the pickup truck. He swallowed hard.

"Max, tell me what's going on." Anastasia turned the moment they were inside the hall. Dad leaned out of the living room and frowned at them.

"I will. I will." Max heard a heavy tread on the stairs. "I just have to talk to my friend first, okay? Then I think we'd ..." He stopped to swallow hard, this time to fight down nausea. "We'd better have a family meeting. Go tell Mom, okay?"

"Okay." Anastasia narrowed her eyes at him. "Are there more kinds of shadows now?"

"Eh? Why?"

"I swear I saw a big animal. Like a bear or something. In the trees by your trailer."

"I don't know. I didn't see that."

"Huh." Anastasia, with obvious reluctance, went to talk to Dad.

Max stepped outside to find Adrian waiting, fully clothed, on the porch. Some of the big man's confidence seemed to have abandoned him; his gaze was unsteady despite the calm way he stood with his hands in his back pockets.

"Not that I don't appreciate the save," Max said under his breath, "but what are you doing here?"

"What the hell was that thing?" Adrian spoke at normal human volume, which possibly was his method of whispering. "What was it doing to you?"

"It was a ghost trying to possess me. How do you even know where I live?"

"You got a webpage for this place. It wasn't hard to figure out. Not so many dog trainers in town. Most of 'em are chicks." Adrian shrugged. "Look, I got a favor to ask."

"You're in a good position to do it," Max said, laughing curtly. "What is it?"

"I want you to tell Theofanis to let me and Kelsie back into his house. He seems to have it pretty bad for you. I bet he'll listen."

Max eyed him for a moment. His blood was still surging, but the bits of him that were trying to remain calm pointed out how unfair it would be to refuse at this point. "Okay. I'll see what I can do."

"Did the, uh, lady—did she see me?" Adrian did lower his voice more, not quite getting it to a discreet level.

"Sort of. Just sort of."

"Shit." Adrian abruptly glared off into the trees.

"I think it'll be okay. It's not exactly going to be her first guess."

Adrian turned a narrow look on him.

"So what's your deal, monkey? With all this ghost shit?"

Max sighed.

"Again, I appreciate the help. But I think you'd better leave. My family and I have some important things to talk about."

"Like really creepy ghosts grabbing you?"

"Exactly. I'll talk to Theo tonight, I promise. Just ..."

"All right." Adrian nodded in a businesslike manner and clomped off to his truck. Max stepped backward into the house, holding the screen door open and leaning out long enough to see the truck drive off. Then he went to the living room to deal with this before it all got to him.

Theo knew who it was by the smell, of course. He opened the door and crossed his arms over his chest, raising an eyebrow. Adrian tilted his head, his mouth working.

"What?" Theo snapped.

"We gotta talk."

"You think?"

Adrian gave him a sour look. Theo relented and stepped away from the door, letting Adrian in. He pointedly didn't pour coffee for Adrian as they sat at the kitchen table.

"What's with the Shevchenko guy?"

"What do you mean?" Theo instinctively bristled.

"I went over to his place."

"You what?" Theo leaned forward. "Why would you—"

"You're dating a monkey. I got to check him out." Adrian leaned back in the chair, raising his eyebrows. His hooded eyes, as usual, showed no remorse. "You're my baby cousin, what do you expect?"

"You to butt out." Theo groaned, putting a hand to his forehead. "What happened?"

"Seriously, what is with that guy? I found him with this, like ... you're never going to believe this, but he was with a *ghost*."

Theo's blood ran cold.

"Is he—?"

"He seemed okay. The ghost thing ran away from me." Adrian shook himself. "Creepy as hell."

"Jesus, Ade."

"What do you see in that guy, anyways?"

"N-none of your business." Theo saw Adrian's lips quirk at the stammer, and he blushed.

"So he knows you're a werewolf, you know he gets beat up by Casper. Holy crap." Adrian shook his head slowly. "What would Grandmother say?"

"Beat up? You're sure he's okay?"

"He'll live." Adrian shrugged. "Except ..."

"Except what?" Theo nearly leapt from his chair, fumbling for his cell.

"I think somebody else at his place might've spotted me." Adrian abruptly found his hands interesting. "Can you cover for me?"

"Adrian, for fuck's sake—" *You're the older one. You're supposed to be the one taking care of me. Not causing me headaches.* "Get out of here."

"You'll make sure, right? That nobody else knows?"

"Fine, whatever. I just don't want to be around you any more tonight." The cell vibrated in Theo's hand; he hastily answered it, pointing to the door. *Go,* he mouthed at Adrian. "Max?"

"Theo. Sorry, I just …" Max's voice tugged at him with its lack of vigor. It was nearly hoarse, barely recognizable. "Could you come over tonight?"

"Of course." Theo glared at Adrian as he left the kitchen too slowly for his taste. "Of course, Max. I'll be right over."

Theo had yet to set foot inside Max's trailer. If he wasn't worried, he would have been curious. So far he'd only seen Max's family's spaces.

When he knocked, Max called him in. Theo stepped into a very tidy white kitchen with blond cupboards and counters. It was a typical trailer, with a hallway leading away from the kitchen on one side and a living room opening up from it on the other. Max sat on a subdued blue couch, a beer in hand, looking at the laptop on the glass coffee table. He closed the laptop and set the beer aside, rubbing his hands on his jeans as he looked up at Theo.

"Hey," Theo said, slipping out of shoes and coat. He put the coat over the back of a chair and hesitated.

"Thanks for coming." Max's voice was subdued.

"Of course." Theo drew closer and saw that one of Max's pant legs was rolled up. His ankle was bound up in fleshy tensor bandaging. "Are you okay?" He quickly sat down next to Max and put a hand on the injured leg.

"Mm." Max, lifting the beer, was caught mid-swig. "I think I just sprained it."

"What happened?"

Max's mouth twitched.

"Did it jumping out the window."

"What?" Theo stared.

Max sighed heavily, leaning back into the couch. He

reached out to rub Theo's lower back, smiling faintly.

"It's been kind of a night. You know, I pretty much hate your cousin, but he saved my butt."

"What was he even doing here?"

"I think it was sort of an attempt at an apology?" Max smiled faintly. "I'm glad you came."

"Any time." Theo gazed at him a little longer, seeing weariness in the faint lines under his eyes. Theo leaned close to kiss Max, caressing his neck gently. Max's lips parted in invitation and Theo shifted closer, deepening the kiss. Yet it remained quiet and slow, without Max placing any demands on him. Theo faltered, withdrew just enough to look into Max's eyes.

"Is it … ch-cheesy to say I missed you?"

Max blinked. Then his face spread into one of those slow smiles.

"I seem to have made an impression on you."

"J-Jesus." Theo looked down, blushing. "You think?" Max's hand continued to stroke the small of his back. Just that gentle point of contact was enough to make his cock twitch. Max chuckled as he turned and leaned back, putting one leg behind Theo and laying the other across his thighs. Theo touched Max's knee, then ran his fingers down to just above the bandages.

"I'm okay." Max was still looking amused, his narrowed eyes gleaming. He nudged Theo's hip with his knee. "Especially now that you're here."

Theo's heart stumbled violently. Emotion made him move decisively, setting a knee between Max's legs for balance as he rose over him. He kissed Max once, twice, then moved his mouth to Max's neck. He tasted his skin, traced the rim of his ear with his lips. But he paused, because it felt right to say what he'd been thinking for some time.

"Friends is … isn't enough, Max." He again looked

into Max's face. Max appeared to be searching his in return.

"Okay." His hazel eyes were hard to read.

"Okay?" *What does that mean?* Before he could speak further, Max took his face in both hands and drew him down again.

"Okay," he repeated, then caught up Theo's lips with his own. His hands slid up under Theo's shirt, exploring his skin. Theo stripped off the shirt. He watched Max's gaze move down his chest. His face grew warm even as he felt himself tighten with excitement. He closed his own eyes when Max's fingertips reached his nipples. Twin pinches shot electric heat straight to his cock and chased an uneven breath from his lips.

Theo's eyes flew open when he heard footsteps outside. He hastily grabbed for his T-shirt and fumbled into it as the front door opened.

"Max? I saw your light was on."

"Ana." Max groaned. "Knock."

"Lock your door if you don't want visitors. Hi, Theo."

"Hi." Theo couldn't immediately look at Anastasia as she came right in and sat in the armchair.

"What's up? You shouldn't be leaving the house right now." Max sat up with a reluctant grunt.

"Mom gave me one of these. It's a charm that should ward off the shadows. She's got one for you, too." She pulled a necklace from her pocket. It was a small leather pouch hanging from a waxed cord. It wafted a stingingly bitter scent at Theo, who had to blink away sudden tears.

"That couldn't have waited until morning?"

"She's worried, Max. So am I. You should stay in the house."

Theo looked at Max, puzzled.

"The house's protected from spirits—they can't get in." Max grimaced. "It's mostly just for privacy reasons."

Theo realized Anastasia was looking rather closely at him.

"You're taking all this awfully well."

"Really? I mean, I guess." Theo quickly looked away.

"Anyways ..." Max intervened, to Theo's relief. "I'll be fine. Theo's here."

"We don't know for sure that they care if you're alone or not. No offense, Theo, but just having a random person around isn't any kind of a guarantee."

"I'm not offended," Theo said quickly. "But I think it'll be okay."

She frowned at him, tilting her head slightly.

"Why?"

"I—"

"Ana, don't be rude."

"Don't you try to tell me what's rude."

Theo could see the deep worry in the crease between her brows, hear it in the uncharacteristic edge in her voice.

"Don't worry," he mumbled.

"But I *am* worried. Max, this isn't the right time for one of your independence things. It came really close to getting you. Who knows where it would have taken you? And you're not telling me everything about what happened. I can tell."

"Ana," Max snapped.

"What, Max? There's the thing with your mysterious 'friend' and his clothes on the ground, and why you even got away from the shadow. Now isn't the time to be hiding secrets."

Anastasia's sharp tone reminded Theo of how angry Ma got (and even more so how angry Grandmother got) when he did something that made them worry. The tension in her voice put tension in his own muscles, made him rub the palm of one hand with the thumb of another as if he could press away the thud of blood in his veins.

"There's not much to tell; that's why I'm not telling you." Max's tone was heated, and it bothered Theo in a different way. This was a different kind of anger than he'd brought to Theo's house. It seemed to lack self-awareness. "I'm fine, and now that Theo's here, I don't have to worry about the shadows. He's—" Max gave Theo a speculative look before continuing in a calmer tone. The back of Theo's neck burned as he stared at his hands. His thumb came to a stop in his palm. "The truth is that Theo's run into spirits before. He's not a medium, but he's—"

"A werewolf." The words came out with surreal normality. Even with his head lowered, Theo saw Max's abrupt turn in his direction. He glanced up through his hair to see that Anastasia was paused with her mouth open, her eyes tracking the movements of her thoughts. She ended with a blink and a frown, one of those expressions that increased her resemblance to Max.

"What did you say?"

"Theo, what the hell are you doing?" Max said it in his throat, his lips barely moving.

Generations of ancestors seemed to yell at him in Greek as Theo drew a deep breath. But it was out; he'd said it. The thing he must never say, he said again.

"I'm a werewolf."

After staring a few moments more, Anastasia fell back in the armchair. Her hands flew up, then came down on the arms.

"Is that why you have that vibe?"

"What?" Max demanded. "You believe him, just like that?"

"He's got that distinctive aura. Strong. Protective, almost. You never noticed that about him?" After Max's almost edged silence, Anastasia gave a little shrug. "Well, you never were very sensitive."

Theo sat there, ears full of his pulse, and struggled

with misery. He could feel Max, prickly with anger.

"Uh, I can walk you back to the house." Theo started to get up.

"Wait, I have so many questions to ask you. I mean, can you do something to the shadows? Are they really scared of you?"

"I don't know. They seem to be."

"They were scared of the dogs, too." Anastasia seemed to be reanimating as she went, her eyes taking on a gleam. "I'm pretty sure in some cultures they used to use wolf teeth as charms to ward off evil. Maybe they were right."

"I'm not a d-dog or a wolf." Theo instinctively pressed his lips together to hide his own teeth.

Max abruptly stood.

"I need some fresh air."

"But you shouldn't—" Theo shifted, alarmed.

"I'll yell for help if I have to," Max snapped. "I'm just going to be outside."

Theo felt the slam of the door like a slap. Anastasia gave him an apologetic smile.

Leaning his hips against the concrete foundation of the trailer, Max clenched a cigarette between his teeth and glared at the moon. He heard occasional barks from the kennels and snorting from the paddock; he heard Anastasia's excited voice inside the house. He took the cigarette from his mouth and forcefully expelled smoke into the night.

"I don't even know where to start getting mad from," he said to nobody. He heard the door open as he inhaled, then held in his breath as Anastasia thumped lightly down the stairs. Once her shoes had crunched out of earshot and he heard the house door, Max coughed out the smoke. He wandered away from the trailer a few steps as next he heard Theo's greater weight on the stairs.

Theo came up next to him and put his hands in his pockets as he looked through the trees.

"I'm sorry."

"What the hell, Theo?" Max snapped. "I mean, seriously. I thought this was your deepest, darkest secret."

Theo shook his head, digging with the toe of his shoe into the gravel.

"Something I had to find out by chasing you around your house," Max ignored how much he was exaggerating, "you just spew out to my sister."

"I'm sorry," Theo repeated.

"So now what? Huh? You going to tell my whole family? Or just call up the newspaper next?"

Still looking at the ground, Theo lifted the cigarette from Max's hand and threw it aside. He stepped on it as he shifted closer. Cupping Max's face in both hands, he kissed him. When Theo drew back, he rested his forehead against Max's and closed his eyes.

"I just did what I was taught never, ever to do. I don't know how to be sorrier than I already am," he whispered.

"Jesus, Theo," Max said, sighing heavily. Theo's hand caressed his neck. Max could feel Theo's body radiating warmth. "Why is it easier for you to talk to other people than to me?" His anger had faded enough for him to hear exactly how childish that sounded. Theo's heavy eyelashes parted to reveal startled eyes.

"Th-that's not true." He stood back and buried his hands back into his pockets.

"I mean, we've seen each other in some pretty embarrassing and some really fucking scary moments. I just want ..." Max gestured in frustration. *I don't even know.* "One sentence from you, saying something important, with no hesitation or stuttering." He crossed his arms over his chest and glared at the dark. He heard Theo draw a breath and make a false start.

"That's—not fair."

"Is it? Do you try to hide every smile and laugh and bit of emotion you've got from your friends?"

"Max, I don't even get what you're mad about now."

"It's just so much goddamned *work* with you, Theo." Max sighed again, rubbing at his lower lip. When he looked up, Theo's eyes were wide open and he was completely still. "How much more do I have to do to even get you to just talk to me? Why do you have to go out of your way to make it harder for me to get to know you?"

"I'm trying." Theo's voice was barely audible.

"So am I, but how far's it actually getting me?" Max demanded. Theo said nothing for a while, and Max let him stew, wishing for his cigarette back. Finally, the silence irritated him too much. "Seriously, Theo, I ask questions so I can get answers."

Theo drew a breath, hesitated. Then he shook his head.

"Screw you." Shoulders hunched, Theo turned away.

"Theo, I need you to—"

"I'll sleep on the couch. That's—d-don't talk to me." Theo's footsteps punctuated the end of the argument as he hurried back into the trailer.

Max stayed where he was, angry with Theo, angry with Theo's jerk cousin, angry with his own sister, but most of all angry with himself. Branches near him started to shift without wind, and his skin prickled, warning him that his anger was drawing unwelcome interest from the spirit world. Poltergeists in particular found anger intriguing.

Max gave up and went inside. To do that, he had to avoid looking at Theo stretched out fully dressed on the couch.

"Blankets are in the cupboard by the bathroom," he said, and went into his bedroom before Theo could respond.

CHAPTER NINE

Theo hadn't been sleeping very deeply when something drew him back to awareness. He didn't sleep well in unfamiliar places to begin with, and the couch didn't offer much room. When his eyes opened, he felt no disorientation—it was as though he hadn't slept at all. He waited, senses on edge, to see what had woken him.

A voice, although he couldn't make out what it was saying. Max's voice, sounding distressed. Theo leapt to his feet and ran for the bedroom.

Max was alone in the bedroom. He lay on his side, his hand curled by his head. His fingers twitched frenetically as his eyebrows flexed and jerked. Again, he made tight noises that weren't quite words, full of strain and urgency.

"Max." Theo couldn't sense anything unusual in the room. *A nightmare?* It made him nervous that Max's breathing grew quicker and his body shifted restlessly under the blankets. "Max, wake up. It's okay. It's just a dream. Max—"

Max gasped loudly and flung himself back against the headboard. He stared at Theo, panting raggedly, his wide eyes gleaming in the dark. The terror in his expression held Theo in place. Max moved first, stretching out an arm and clicking on his lamp. Yellow light splashed across Max's face, turning his hair and eyes dark gold, picking up the droplets of sweat tracing lines down his neck.

"Shit." Max wiped at his face with a visibly trembling

hand. That single word broke Theo loose and he went to sit gingerly on the bed.

"You okay?"

"Yeah." Max cleared his throat. "Yeah. It was just a dream." He glanced sidelong at Theo. "Did I wake you up?"

"D-don't worry about it." In spite of himself, Theo reached out to sweep away the sweat with his fingertips. Max closed his eyes briefly.

"Comes with the territory." He shifted his hips, sitting up. He looked at Theo, then away, and for a while it was awkwardly quiet in the room. Then Max turned to him, leaning an elbow on the top of the headboard. "I've known you for over a month already, Theo, but there's still a few things I don't know about you."

"What do ..." Theo saw that the smile on Max's face wasn't as relaxed as it pretended; there were tight lines around the corners of his mouth. Even so, it was such a pretty mouth. Just a hint wide for Max's face, it was gracefully shaped, lips just full enough to suggest lushness without excess. "You already know ... a lot."

"Do I?" Max's eyebrows quirked mischievously. "I've been wondering." He ran his fingers along a fold of Theo's rumpled T-shirt. "Are you versatile?"

Theo watched that finger caress fabric, not getting anywhere near his skin.

"Wh-why?"

"I'm curious." Max looked at him through chestnut eyelashes, that lovely mouth curving up higher on one side than the other. "I'm not a very versatile top, but how can I not think about it when you can go forever?"

Theo pressed his lips tightly together. He could smell Max's skin all too clearly, his masculinity coming through in his sweat.

I'm still pissed off at him. He needs a distraction, but

that doesn't mean I have to play along.

"I was actually thinking about it. I mean," Max's tone turned wry, "it'd have to be some time I wouldn't have to move around much the next day, obviously. But still."

"I d-don't usually. I have, but I don't—I don't usually." Language grew more difficult for him as he tried desperately not to imagine what Max was suggesting.

"Would you for me?" Max shifted closer. Theo looked at the far wall, swallowing hard. "I don't mean tonight, but let me run the idea past you." He leaned closer, lowering his voice. "I'd start by opening your fly, of course."

That half-whisper scratched across Theo's skin. His cock twitched in reaction.

"Push down those goofy boxers you wear." Max's hair lightly brushed Theo's temple. Gooseflesh sprang up on Theo's skin. "Just start touching you, nice and slow. Nice and slow."

"Max—" Theo felt imagined fingers on his cock, and it stirred for real.

"Shhh. I'm going to be letting this big cock fuck me, I should be allowed to get to know it." Max made an amused noise in his throat. "Wait, I already do, don't I? I've had you in my mouth. In my throat." His voice deepened. "I want to do that again."

"Oh, god." Theo's heart rate tripled.

"I'm too impatient, though, to go slow. I take you in for a suck, no games. As deep as I can, as quick as I can."

"S-slow down," Theo whispered. Every word was hardening him.

"Nuh-uh. You taste too good. But I'm getting too excited. I'd better get the show on the road. I have to let that hard cock slide out of my mouth."

The word drew Theo's gaze back to Max's mouth. The world narrowed down to it. Before he could touch it with his own lips, Max casually moved his head.

"I'm not very used to being on the bottom. You're going to have to be gentle with me."

"Of course." Theo breathed the words out.

"I take some of my clothes off. Or maybe all of them? Hm?"

"All." Theo's own clothes caged him painfully. He didn't dare move, afraid of just how much he'd feel every fiber of his boxers.

"You, too, then. We're both naked, on the bed. I lie down on my stomach and wait. You're going to have to use your fingers first. You'd do that, right?"

"Mm." Even speaking seemed too dangerous. Theo was sure even his hair was starting to stand up on his head.

"Get some lube on those bony, manly fingers, and work it all the way in. Until you find the gland, and I just about come right there." Still Max's whisper was ruthlessly calm.

"Before, you said I made you lose it." Theo put a desperate hand on the blankets, finding Max's knee beneath.

"That was the first time, Theo. I lost control." The tips of Max's teeth showed between his lips. "I got it back." As Theo felt his way along Max's thigh, Max reached out in return to cup his crotch. Even that gentle pressure made Theo groan. "You're too turned on to wait."

"Yes," Theo said fervently.

"In the fantasy, Theo." Max's voice went throaty with amusement. He quickly unbuttoned Theo's jeans, then held up his hand. It took a moment for Theo to understand. He caught Max's wrist and touched his tongue to his palm, tasting salt. Glancing between Max's fingers, he saw Max's lips purse around his lightly clenched teeth. The arousal hidden in that expression increased

Theo's need to please. He took a firmer hold of Max's hand and started licking his fingers from base to tip. But when he tried to take one of those fingers between his teeth, Max pulled his hand away. He then shoved down the waistband of Theo's boxers and took hold of him. That damp, warm touch caught all of Theo's attention. Unlike in his description, Max didn't take it slow at all. Each stroke was quick and aggressive.

"I can tell you're trying to be gentle, but you're not." Max abruptly continued, his voice adding a fresh shock to the overwhelming pleasure of his insistent stroking. "You're too big. Too hard. But I want it, so I'm pushing back."

"I'd never want to hurt you." Theo's words came out mostly air. "Never."

"I know, but you just can't help yourself. I'm too sexy."

"You are," Theo groaned.

Max, who had been about to keep talking, snorted, then put his free hand to his face. "God, Theo."

"Don't stop talking." Theo saw his chance and yanked the blankets aside. He saw the bulge in Max's pajama bottoms and reached for it. Max quickly caught his forearm and shoved down.

"Not yet."

"Max, I want you to feel good."

"I am feeling good." Max's tone grew sultry again. "You're inside me, just pounding away, and I'm loving it. You start speaking Greek to me, but I don't understand it. For all I know, you're calling me your bitch."

"I wouldn't," Theo breathed.

"Or a slut." Max's hand abruptly moved faster, making Theo groan.

"I wouldn't, Max."

"Hm. You probably wouldn't. I wouldn't care." Max chuckled. "I am a slut."

"No—"

"Shhh." Max licked his lips, watching his own hand work. "I don't care, because I love hearing you speak Greek. It's sexy. And I love that you're so into me you can't even keep straight what language you should be speaking. I think I'm going to come soon."

"No." Theo shifted restlessly closer. "I want to finish with you on your back. So I can see you. Your face." He drew closer still, holding his mouth over Max's. "So I can kiss you."

Max grinned as he tightened his grip and pumped vigorously; Theo shivered, thrown off the kiss.

"You're fucking me so hard now. You must be close. Are you just about there, Theo?"

"Yes—"

"Okay, then." Max finally released his arm.

Theo reached desperately for Max, running hungry fingers over his cock. When he took hold, Max's composure slipped; they leaned into each other, hands pumping with equal urgency, until their mouths came together. It was a hungry kiss, lips parted and tongues darting at each other. Theo could barely tell his own moans apart from Max's. The heated friction of Max's grip created shocking pleasure. He had a hard time believing the elaborate fantasy itself could feel better than this.

"Theo, I'm going to come. Slow down."

"I want you to come," Theo said fervently. Fierce desire spurred him on, made him work harder and harder at Max's erection.

"Oh, yeah? You going to make me? You think you can—oh, you can." Max's brows knitted, and he hissed through his teeth. "Jesus, Theo. That feels so good. So good." He shook his head sharply, then pressed his forehead against Theo's shoulder as he cried out. The sensation was almost lost on Theo because he was so close himself.

Max abruptly shifted onto his knees, looking fiercely into Theo's eyes as he stroked him with long, thorough movements. That commanding gaze startled Theo, but also sent a thrill through him that his overworked nerves couldn't take. He couldn't look away from Max's eyes, gone green and dark. Beyond words, all he could do was drown in every firm sweep of skin against skin. Then Max resumed a quick, punishing rhythm, and the shock of that shoved Theo over the edge. The ecstasy that surged through his cock forced a yell from his throat.

That embarrassing cry faded, leaving them in too much quiet. The game was over, leaving them back where they'd started. Theo took a box of tissues off the bedside table so they could both tidy up. That intent glow in Max's eyes was completely gone now, as was any hint of a smile. Theo felt empty, uncomfortable. Max tossed crumpled tissues past him into a garbage can, his mouth pulled into a thin line. He glanced at Theo.

"You don't have to sleep on the couch." With that, he slid over to the side of the bed and turned away.

Theo stared at his back, blinking. After a moment, he got woodenly to his feet and stripped out of his clothes. He got under the covers and turned his back to Max. Urges argued within him, one to punch Max in the face, another to hold him and tell him it was all going to be all right.

I said I wanted to be more than a friend, not to be a stress reliever. He remembered the genuine fear in Max's eyes upon waking from the nightmare, and sighed. *Maybe I'll tell him some other night.*

Max had woken up refreshed yesterday morning and done his chores in a good mood, but had gone back in to discover Theo had left without so much as a note or a text. Add to that another night of poor sleep in a bed he'd begun thinking of as empty, and Max's mood went straight downhill again. He tried to push his irritation out of his mind as he went into the house.

"Oh, good. You're home."

When Max passed by the kitchen, Mom straightened up from in front of the oven.

"Technically I'm not," he muttered. She gave him a raised eyebrow, but didn't respond. He went into the living room to find Anastasia waiting. She was setting out teacups and gave him a tight smile. Mom came through with a teapot on a tray.

"So glad you actually want to talk to your mother about the evil spirits coming into our town."

Instead of the bait, Max took a cookie from the plate on the coffee table.

"So do you know what we're dealing with, Mom?" Anastasia asked, taking the tray and pressing her mother down by the shoulders. Max poured tea and kept his mouth shut.

"Clearly they're malevolent spirits," Mom said. "Shadow ghosts. Or shadow spirits."

"Seriously? I thought those were hallucinations caused by sleep paralysis dreams." Max belatedly sat down.

"I thought they were a hoax, too. I'm not sure I have any real information on them." She bit her lip. "They're always described as malevolent, though."

"They sure felt that way," Anastasia said.

"Mm." Max shook his head. "Theo wanted to know if we can do anything about these things."

"I'll make some calls," Kaitlyn said. "See what my friends know. Until then, I think we should stay in contact as much as we can. Don't be alone. I'll call your Uncle Yuu in the morning, when the time zones work. In the meantime, you two …" Her voice sharpened abruptly. "Don't you dare keep any more secrets from me."

"Yes, Mom," they chorused. Max slurped tea rather desperately.

Shadow spirits in Fort Rivers. A werewolf for a boyfriend. A sister who knows too much about my life. Man, I need a smoke.

The past four days had not passed easily. Theo had tried to bury himself in work and was only partially successful. He welcomed Anastasia's text inviting him out to coffee at a nearby café as a chance to get out of the house, although it puzzled him.

Anastasia was already seated at a table when he got there. She raised a hand in a casual wave to draw his attention.

"Uh, hi," he said as he sat down opposite her. He made eye contact with a waiter as he turned over the coffee cup in his place setting.

"Hey, Theo. Thanks for coming to meet me."

"Of—of course. What's up?"

Anastasia waited for the waiter to fill Theo's cup and leave. Then she put both hands on the table and leaned forward.

"We haven't had a chance to talk since."

Theo's neck went hot. He turned the coffee cup in slow quarter turns with his fingertips, watching the surface of the coffee tilt in reaction.

"And, more to the point, it doesn't sound like you and Max have either." At his startled glance, she smiled grimly. "I know my brother. When he started talking vague about you, I figured something was up." She leaned on her elbow, idly stirring her coffee. "But with those things out there, we need to stay in contact. I read in the paper that another person's been hospitalized. It's only a matter of time before somebody gets killed."

Theo nodded, his stomach sinking. At the same time, he felt vindicated by the determination hidden in her words. He clearly wasn't the only one who felt that they had to keep looking for a solution.

"Do you know anything new?"

"Mom thinks she knows what they are." Anastasia swallowed a mouthful of coffee and sat back in her chair. She was subtly more restless than her brother in her movements.

Theo wished he wouldn't keep comparing her to Max. He didn't want to think about him right now.

"Shadow spirits," she went on, oblivious to his distraction. "I always thought they were just an urban legend, but I guess not. I'd never have thought they were this dangerous."

"So what—what do they do?" Theo carefully looked over his shoulder. They weren't completely alone in the café, but the tables nearest them were empty.

"They're spirits from another dimension. Well, the spirit world's sort of another dimension, but these ones are from one farther away. That must be why it's so hard on the mediums they use as portals. Most reports aren't clear about them, but it sounds like they drain people of energy, doesn't it? With all these people collapsing." Anastasia coughed a little, then rubbed at her throat. "We really don't know much—not even if Mom's charms will work on them. They aren't really normal spirits."

"*Normal spirits.*" *Jesus.* Theo grimaced. "What do you think we should be doing?"

"I'm not sure. Just keep your ear to the ground. Or nose." Her eyes met his for a moment. "There can't be that many other people with the spiritual capacity to become portals in Fort Rivers, so hopefully there haven't been more and more getting through."

"How many do we think are around?"

"Two that I know of," she said. "Mine and Louis'." She cleared her throat, then raised her shoulders and dropped them. Her tone changed as she gazed at a random point on the tablecloth. "So what did my brother do now?"

"Wh-what?" Theo blushed, blindsided.

She smiled tightly, glancing at him sidelong.

"Like I said, I know my brother. It was his fault, wasn't it?"

"I don't know." Despite his fierce blush, Theo fought to keep talking. He hadn't been able to talk about it with Marnie or any of his other friends because his secrets were too bound up in what had happened. "He's mad I told you."

"God." She shook her head in exasperation. "I swear he just makes up things to be mad about sometimes. So why are you mad at him?"

"Because ..." Theo smiled in spite of himself, rubbing at the back of his neck as he leaned back in his chair. "Because he's mad at me, maybe."

Anastasia's expression remained serious. When she didn't reply, he felt compelled to fill the silence.

"He—I don't know, accused me of making it harder for him to get to know me, or something like that."

"Because you told me?" Her brows knitted.

"Mm." Theo gulped coffee.

"He's what, jealous?" Her eyes widened, and she stared at Theo. "How does that make sense?"

He shrugged stiffly, watching Anastasia deflate. Her mobile face took on a pained expression next.

"I'm sorry, Theo. Max really can be a jerk sometimes." Her gaze went a little distant. "But you have to remember something. I mean, I'm not saying you have to forgive him for anything. Selfishly I want you guys to be happy together, but ... The thing is, Max likes to pretend that things haven't affected him as much as they have."

"Things?"

"Our dad passing away when we were little, growing up different, things like that. What happened when he was a kid with Deep Murky."

"The, uh ..."

"He was forcibly possessed. Trust me, that leaves scars." She gave a shiver. "You have to remember, Theo, that he's really ..." She suddenly looked down. "He's scared. A lot of the time, he's scared."

Theo's heart twisted in sudden, intense sympathy. He stared out the window at the street outside as he tried to get his emotions under control.

"But," and her voice regained brightness, "the other thing to remember is that he gets really mad sometimes, but he doesn't stay mad very long." She reached out to give his hand a pat. "Don't worry too much."

"I do," Theo said, not very loudly.

"What, worry?"

"Stay mad." He licked his lips.

"Well, fair enough. It'll serve him right to get a little reminder that people aren't there just to suit his needs." She smiled at the waiter who came to refill her coffee cup, then began doctoring the coffee with sugar and milk. "So how's work going, anyways?"

Theo was grateful for the change in topic. They chatted about unimportant things for about an hour before he went home to get back to work.

He sat at his desk and looked at his computer screen. It seemed to reflect back the image of Max, staring at him in naked terror. Theo shook his head, as if he could shake it away, and started typing.

If I don't forgive him, I can't protect him. But if I

forgive him, he'll probably start treating me like crap again. Theo sighed heavily, his fingers coming to a stop. *But if he needs me, I'll go.*

CHAPTER TEN

Yet again, Theo's voicemail message. They'd last spoken on the ninth. It was now the fourteenth, and Max was down to his last scrap of patience. "What the hell, Theo?" Max frowned at his cellphone as he hit the disconnect button. "Are you seriously just going to keep ignoring me?" He grunted with effort as he peeled himself off his couch and picked up the crumb-detailed plate and empty coffee cup from the table. "I'm going over there." He put the dishes in the sink and paused, staring at them. "And still I'm chasing after you, Theo. Do I ever get to stop doing that?"

But the drive to town gave him plenty of time to reflect on how he'd acted. While he didn't think he'd been completely out of line, he knew he'd lashed out, and Theo had obviously taken his words too hard. Playing around after had made Max feel a little better, but he had to admit that things had still felt awkward. The worst part was that when he replayed the night in his head, he realized Theo had some reason to be upset.

"So do I," he muttered to himself, drumming his fingers on the wheel. "But I guess it's a day for being the bigger man."

Max pulled in to a gas station to refill. As he stood by his car, watching the numbers roll by on the pump, a truck pulled in to the diesel pump behind him. He glanced at the big red pickup, then did a double-take.

You've got to be kidding me.

Adrian was grinning as he got the pump going. He put a hand on the side of his truck, looking Max up and down.

"Hey."

"Hey." Max cleared his throat. "Thanks for, uh, before."

"No problem." Adrian's grin weakened for a moment. "That was pretty wild."

"Yeah," Max said. "So you're still in town."

"Yup. I'm lookin' for somebody to haul logs for. Somebody who don't know me yet." Adrian chuckled.

"Well, good luck." Slamming his fuel tank hatch shut, Max turned away. Normally he disliked that all the gas stations had gone to pre-pay, but now he was grateful that he could just go.

"Hang on." Max turned, then raised his eyebrows at Adrian's outstretched hand. "Who Theofanis wants to be with ain't any business of mine. Sorry I was gettin' on your case before."

Max took that rawboned hand in a businesslike shake. "I appreciate that." He tried to sound like he meant it.

"Yup." Adrian squeezed, not letting Max pull away. His grin turned naughty. "You're gonna be real glad you just ran into me."

"Adrian, what are you doing?" Max lowered his voice. There was a truck parked at another pump; although he couldn't see the driver, he could hear the pump ticking and churning. He didn't want to be witnessed like this.

"The thing is, Kelsie's outta town." Adrian's eyebrows quirked. "She was just keeping me company on the phone. I had to pull over to take care of it or go right off the road."

Skin crawling, Max jerked his hand free.

"Not cool," he breathed.

"Trust me," Adrian said, leaning in close to lightly

slap Max on the cheek. "You're gonna thank me later."

"What the hell are you talking about?" Max recoiled from Adrian's touch.

"We can smell 'em." Adrian lowered his tone dramatically as he tapped the side of his nose. "Pheromones. You're in for a fun afternoon."

"You're disgusting," Max snapped, backing away. Adrian's laughter chased him into his car. As Max drove, he dug a bottle of hand sanitizer out of the glove compartment and applied a generous amount. "No wonder Theo lives alone! I wouldn't live with that family either if they're all like that!"

It took him the rest of the drive to calm himself. The whole point of meeting Theo today was to smooth things over, which he wasn't likely to do if he was biting his head off.

"God damn, what a jerk," he said, and did one more round of hand sanitizer before getting out of his car. He was still rubbing his hands together when he reached Theo's door. He found himself hesitating before it, uncertain of whether to knock or just go in as usual. Before he could decide, the door opened and he was face-to-face with Theo. "Hey."

"Hey." Theo's expression was almost aggressively neutral. He was reasonably dressed and groomed, and he didn't look exhausted; Max was annoyed that he looked so good.

"Look, last time, at my place ..." It abruptly got harder to talk. He wondered if this was how it felt to Theo all the time, like his jaw didn't want to unlock. "Things were said. Things that we should probably talk about." He looked into Theo's increasingly puzzled eyes. "Are you in the middle of something? Do you want to go have lunch?"

"Sure." Theo's easy agreement relaxed Max's jaw.

"Let me grab my coat."

"Okay. I'll be in the car." Max jogged back down the steps, amazed at how much lighter he already felt. He was even able to smile a little when Theo got into the passenger seat. "You up for Greek?"

"Honestly? Always." Theo bobbed his head sheepishly.

"All right. That place near the highway has a decent lunch special." Max put the car into drive.

God, I'm pathetic. Theo didn't feel pathetic when he looked at Max. He felt amazing, like a jolt of caffeine but to something more important than his bloodstream. He glanced sidelong at Max in the driver's seat. The sunlight coming in through the windshield turned his eyes very pale gold and warmed up the color of his lips. *I swear I've never seen anybody so gorgeous in my life.* It didn't change the fact that sometimes Max turned difficult to handle—as well as difficult to resist.

"How's your ankle?"

"Fine. I must have just twisted it. It was good after a couple of days."

Theo nodded. Neither spoke for a stretch.

"So did your grandmother make good Greek food?"

"Really good," Theo said, grateful that Max had broken the silence. "She was always complaining about ingredients she couldn't get here, though."

"So she came from Greece originally?"

"When she was a kid, so Ma sometimes called her out on acting like, like she was so authentic." Theo found himself losing focus on his own words. "Ma was an awesome cook, too. So's your mom."

"Yeah," Max said, smiling. "She really is. A real feeder, though."

"Uh ... Eh?" His entire body flushed with heat and the world went too bright. Theo closed his eyes.

"Just can't stop feeding people. There's six of us, you'd think that'd be enough, but she's always baking and making extra stuff to put in my fridge. If I didn't go running every morning, I'd be in serious trouble."

"Mm." Max's words were flowing over him, almost tickling his skin. He had no real interest in their meaning. It was hard to think of anything at all as his cock pushed vigorously against the confines of his underwear. His hand crept over to Max's side of the car.

"Wait, what does that mean?" Max turned his head, frowning.

Theo leaned across and put his hand on Max's shoulder. He drew close to Max's neck and inhaled slowly. Max's skin smelled so warm, so deeply masculine and at the same time just slightly sweet, that Theo moaned deep in his throat. He watched Max's lips curve.

"What's gotten into you?" Max murmured.

"I'm sorry." Theo's skin tingled, a delicate counterpoint to the intense pressure in his cock. "Could you pull over?"

"Right here? Why?" Max had to look away, taking his gaze back to the road. Theo nuzzled his shoulder, squeezing.

"I just really need you right now."

"And you want me to do you in my car in the middle of the afternoon?" Max laughed. "You naughty, naughty—" All at once Max went quiet and stiff. "You've got to be kidding me."

"What?" Theo fought the urge to bite, to sink his fingertips in deeper. "What's wrong?"

"Your fucking cousin," Max snapped. "But all right, let's do this at my place."

"Hurry," Theo groaned.

As soon as they were through the door, Theo caught his jaw in both hands and pressed up against him, gaze locked on his mouth. Max tossed his keys blindly at the basket, pulling back before Theo could kiss him.

"I just need to get some stuff," he said. "Be on my couch with your clothes off when I get back."

"Okay," Theo mumbled. Max jogged down the hall to his bedroom and dove into a box at the bottom of his closet.

That complete bastard. He was shaking his head as he stomped back to the living room. *Theo coming on to me in my car should have been so much fun. Now I've got to deal with him being so horny he can't see straight because of his asshole cousin. Not because of me.*

He paused, hands full, as he came into the kitchen. Theo was sitting uncertainly on the couch; nude, his hands fisted on his knees, he looked sidelong at Max. That was incredibly endearing, enough to begin melting away Max's anger. Kicking off his shoes, Max moved to stand in front of Theo, and his eyebrows lifted. He crouched down and set aside his collection of items.

"You really are good to go."

"You're telling me?" Theo replied faintly. He blinked when Max stretched up to fasten the collar around his neck, but didn't protest.

"This isn't a dog collar," Max said, giving the leash a tug. "So don't worry about it. I got it from an adult place online long before I ever met you."

"O-okay." Theo licked his lips, his face tight with discomfort, as he watched Max strip off his own clothes and throw them aside. "You seem kind of mad."

"I'm not mad," Max snapped. He paused, lube in hand, and sighed. "I'm not mad at you."

"Then who are you mad at? Ngh..." Theo's back arched as Max reached between his legs.

Max looked up into Theo's face as he worked lubricant into his body. He should have taken it more slowly, but Theo's quickened breathing urged him not to.

"We're going to use a safe word, okay? I don't think we'll need it, but just in case."

"Yeah," Theo said breathlessly, a hand going to his own mouth.

"The safe word will be, uh..." Max glanced around. "Grapefruit." There was a bag of them on his kitchen counter. He hadn't put them there, so obviously his mother had been at it again.

"I hate grapefruit," Theo whispered, and Max laughed.

"Then that's perfect." Finally, anticipation overtook the last of his anger. He had Theo collared and naked on his couch, and no matter how it had come to be this way, that was a wonderful thing.

"Max, hurry up."

"Hey, now," Max said, getting to his feet. He put his thumb on Theo's lower lip. "I'm the one in charge here." Picking up the loop at the end of the leash, he held it up in front of Theo's mouth. "Kiss it." Theo leaned forward to touch his lips to the leather, and Max flushed with darkly sweet excitement. He drew the loop down Theo's chest, tracing the lines of his muscles, then slid it under each nipple. Groaning, Theo clutched at the back of the couch with both hands. "You naughty boy, now you're getting me all turned on."

"I want you to be. I want you."

"Shhh." He pressed the leash to Theo's mouth. "No talking." Simply getting the condom on was enough to get him fully erect. Licking his lips, Max gradually took up the slack in the leash. "Come on over here." Of course he didn't need the leash; Theo eagerly followed him off the couch. Pausing in a clear space on the carpet, Max took a moment to just look at Theo in his entirety, tall, strong, and beautiful. Then he kissed Theo very lightly. "Down you go. On your back." Sinking down, Max followed Theo most of the way down so he didn't catch him up short with the leash. Then, putting the end of it between his teeth, he caught Theo's hips in both hands and raised them. Theo willingly pushed up to meet him as Max began to penetrate him. Each thrust going downward, Max felt like he was diving right into Theo. Right into the intense pleasure that Theo gave him every time.

Every time. How is it always good with him? Max looked into Theo's face, seeking answers.

Theo gazed back up at him through half-closed eyes, his breath quivering from him with every beat of their quick rhythm. His calves pressed against Max's shoulders as if trying to fuse to him. His moans grew so blissful Max felt almost ashamed of himself for making him wait this long.

"Max, ah—" Theo pressed his lips together tightly. He turned his head to the side, his brows knitting fiercely.

"Good boy," Max breathed. He clenched his teeth into the leather, which made it too awkward to talk. Already this felt so good he wanted to talk, but it wouldn't fit with the collar to start telling Theo how wonderful he was. Instead, he hissed out each breath around the strap in his mouth, his hips moving in short, quick thrusts into the supportive spring of Theo's curled body. One of Theo's hands lifted unsteadily into the air. He brought it down on the leash, running the undersides of his fingers very carefully down along the thin leather. Max watched that exquisite little caress, his blood throbbing harder at the sight. When Theo whimpered, the sound excited Max further. He spat out the end of the leash.

"Who's making you feel good, Theo?"

"You are," came the instant reply. "Only you could."

"Don't lie to me. I know this isn't because of me."

"What?"

"Look at me," Max commanded. Theo did so narrowly, his gaze unfocussed. "I know that this is a werewolf thing. I didn't do this to you."

"Max, I—" Theo gasped, bracing himself as Max drove himself home with extra vigor. "All I can see is you. All I can feel is you. All I want—"

"Stop talking," Max said, the words lacking authority because his own body was tightening up. Theo was an overheated mass of muscle; inside, he was tight and hot. He pushed back into each of Max's thrusts, working his muscles around Max's cock. Max couldn't keep up the game; his body arched and he nearly staggered as a yell tore from him. Breathless, he looked down at Theo's cock, which was clearly nowhere near done. Max withdrew and let Theo drop his legs and pelvis back onto the floor.

"I planned for this, you dirty little nerd." He plucked a toy from the pile on the table and then retrieved the leash, giving it a jaunty tug. Theo curved up from the floor, his gaze still too bright with arousal. Guiding Theo around the coffee table, Max shoved him back onto the couch. Theo bit his lip, burying one hand into his own hair. Max slung one of Theo's legs over the back of the couch and pulled the other onto his own lap. Then he held up the dildo, seeing Theo's eyes widen. Despite that first startled reaction, Theo rolled his shoulders back into the couch, and lifted his hips in encouragement. Max eased the dildo in, watching Theo's face intently. Theo's gaze was distant. His cheekbones lifted, and he tilted his head back as Max begin the work the dildo in and out.

"It's cold."

"Haven't you used one of these before?"

Theo gave a quick shake of his head, his attention plainly elsewhere.

Max took a moment to strip off the used condom. He

pulled out a fresh one, but the sight of Theo distracted him. Gazing up at the ceiling, Theo looked beautifully lost. Max felt a wicked smile shape his lips. He leaned over Theo to pinch his nipple between the folds of the loop at the end of the leash, allowing the rough inner surface to slide across that hardened nub. Theo's chest jerked toward him; Max shoved his shoulders flat again.

"I'm doing this. I don't need your help." He got a plaintive moan in reply and gave the other nipple the same treatment. Theo's powerful thigh trembled restlessly against Max's hip. "That not enough for you? Hm?"

"Max," Theo whispered, barely audible.

"You better not tell me what to do. I'm calling the shots here."

"Mm." Theo's chin dipped in a nod.

"I don't need your permission." Max slid the loop of the leash over the head of Theo's arousal. Theo's pelvis bucked as the raw side of the leather brushed his skin. His hands went to his own chest, caressing blindly. Max twisted the leather tight, and he cried out.

"Bad boy! I should have handcuffed you to something. One day I'm going to do that to you, Theo."

"Anything," Theo groaned. "I love you. Do anything you want to me."

For Max, everything went still. Unaware, Theo was writhing, his hands clutching at his hair. Max could hear his own pulse, his own breathing, very clearly, while all other sounds came from a distance. When he reached out to lay his palm on Theo's knee, it was like a new, unfamiliar skin he touched. He plucked out the dildo, slung Theo's legs over his shoulders, and worked himself inside. He'd jumped from half-recovered to full attention so quickly it dizzied him, and his need rivaled Theo's.

"How does this feel, Theo? Talk to me."

"So good I think I might die." Theo closed his eyes.

"Have you ever felt like this before?"

"No, never. Never, Max, only you—"

"Shut up." Max pounded into Theo wildly. "There's a reason for that. There's a reason." He shifted, trying to get closer when he already had Theo's body flexed and himself as deeply in as he could go; he had to catch his balance on one hand on the couch. "It's because you're mine, Theo. Mine!"

"Yes," Theo groaned. "Oh, yes."

"I'm going to make you come harder than you've ever come before, because you belong to me!" He was completely out of control, in a place physically and emotionally new to him. Feeling how close he was to completion, he ran the palm of his free hand up the full length of Theo's arousal. Encircling that sturdy cock with his hand, he stroked down every time he brought his hips forward; this rapid pace had both of them beyond words. There was no breath, no coherent thought left to him, and to judge by Theo's inarticulate cries he was in the same state. Max couldn't even tell if this white-hot world wrapping around him felt good, because it was too intense for judgment.

When the break came, he dug his feet into the couch and threw himself into the last thrust; he felt Theo's body stiffening and shoving back; he heard both of their voices but was only distantly aware of his own yell. While the echoes in his ears revealed that Theo had called his name, the word that had left his mouth was, "Mine!"

And then, after all the urgency, they were both still. Unfortunately, the incandescent desire and the blind ecstasy slipped away moment by moment, letting coherent thought back in. They looked at each other, both out of breath. Theo's cheeks were dark pink, and Max felt his own face burn.

Don't panic. Everybody says stupid things during sex.

We both did just now, just because it was incredibly hot. Unbelievably hot. It did not hurt Max's ego in the slightest that Theo seemed convinced he had a special ability to make him feel good, but it unnerved him that Theo had already come to represent some of his own best sexual experiences. That Theo could make him feel fantastically good, and that there was a big, obvious reason for that. *I've never claimed ownership of anyone. Oh, god.* Slipping away from Theo, he sat up on the couch and put a hand to his forehead.

After a pause, Theo got up and sat next to Max. He slid in close and kissed him on the mouth, then the temple.

"Thank you," he said. "That was incredible."

"Yeah," Max mumbled. "Any time."

"I really liked that we, uh, finished at the same time."

"Did I hurt you?" Max didn't make eye contact.

"No." Pressing his forehead against Max's cheek, Theo tickled him with his breath as he chuckled. "In some ways I'm tough."

"Sure you are," Max said, softening. Then his eye fell on the unopened condom packet. "Oh, crap!"

"Don't worry about it," Theo said quietly. "I don't think we get the same diseases. And I trust you."

"Jesus. I appreciate your trust, but I don't forget stuff like that. I just don't. I'm careful." Max rubbed his face. "I never lose it that bad."

"Do you want to tell me what had you so ... so ticked off?"

"You didn't figure it out?" He shook his head just a little, hindered by Theo's proximity. "That dickwad cousin of yours put his pheromones on me. That's what got you so hot for me."

"Ade? Why would he do that?" Sitting back, Theo frowned at him. Max threw up his hands.

"Because he wanted to prove that I could never turn

you on as much as he—" Too late he stopped, internally cursing himself.

Theo abruptly withdrew. He sat with his hands pressing down into the couch as he gazed at the floor. His eyelashes fluttered and his Adam's apple bobbed.

"S-so he did tell you."

"Yeah, he told me. Bragged about being your first and how I'd never satisfy you."

"That's not true," Theo whispered.

"Which part?"

"Th-the last one. He really did, y'know, my virginity. I know it's really lame for that to be your cousin, but I wanted to lose it so bad that ... Max, could you look at me?"

"It's hard to look at you right now," Max said flatly. *That was either the best fuck I've ever had or a complete train wreck. Or both. I go bareback without asking first, he throws out the l-word, and now we're talking about his first time with his goddamn, redneck, werewolf cousin.*

"It was only the one time, I swear. Everybody after him was, was just normal, and there weren't exactly a lot of those—"

Relenting, Max turned and took hold of one of Theo's hands. The desperation growing in Theo's voice got to him.

"That's not why, you dork."

"Then what?" Theo gazed at their joined hands.

"Don't you remember what you said?"

"Not really. I was kind of out of it. I remember something you said, though." Lips curving just a little, Theo looked at him through a screen of messy curls.

"And how do you feel about that?" It was Max's turn for his voice to falter. In response, Theo cupped his cheek and leaned in to kiss him.

"First thing, Ade's a moron. They're just plain old

hormones, not pheromones, we just smell them better. Second, they can get us, y'know, going, but ..." Shifting, he whispered into Max's ear. "But we still have to want you first." He sat back and stroked Max's shoulder. "They couldn't make me do something I didn't want to do."

"Could I?" Max gazed into his eyes.

"You wanting me to do it would make me want to do it."

"Remember you said that," Max said, laughing quietly. Shaking his head, Theo buried his face in his shoulder. Max pulled him close and tried not to over-think things. "Oh, crap."

"What?" Theo's voice turned alert.

"I completely forgot. I actually wanted to talk to you." He looked into Theo's surprised expression. "I thought of a way to test those charms out. Want to help?"

CHAPTER ELEVEN

New Moon

Max exhaled a visible breath into the night air as he looked around. The mall had closed three hours ago, and there wasn't a car in the parking lot besides Max's. They'd chosen the mall because two different people had collapsed there for unexplained reasons; Max was betting that meant a shadow spirit was lurking in the area.

"Okay," Max said. "The coast is clear."

"Are you sure?" Theo asked from inside the car; leaning on the door, Max peered inside.

"I don't see anybody," he said in exasperation. Grimacing, Theo nodded and slipped out next to Max. Then he slapped a hand down on the front of his robe, sucking in a shocked breath as a cool wind struck.

"Oh, *shit.*"

"You sure you're not going to freeze to death?" Max said, wrapping his arms around Theo's shoulders. Theo pressed close with a shiver.

"It's all I've g-g-got that I c-c-can get out of f-fast." This time it wasn't nerves that made Theo stutter, but his chattering teeth. He wore nothing under his robe.

"You sure you don't want to change now?"

"D-do you th-think they'll, y'know ..."

"No," Max sighed. "Sorry. I don't think they'll show if there's a werewolf here. Come on, let's get out of the light just in case somebody does drive by." He closed the car door and drew Theo over to the wall. They leaned their backs against it and looked around. Theo toyed with the belt of his robe; the attached charm dangled against his hip, too cute for his ragged robe.

"I'm so buying you a new one of those," Max said.

"Why? It still works," Theo said stonily, making Max chuckle.

"Trust me," he said. "You'd look a lot better in something without holes in it." That got him a longer silence than he'd expected. Not sure what was up, Max suppressed impatience and waited. Eventually, Theo audibly drew a breath.

"How can you?"

"How can I what?"

"T-trust."

Such a fundamental question put him on the back foot, but Max understood immediately. He thought carefully about how to respond.

We managed to skip over the making up right to the make-up sex. I doubt I'll ever be that lucky again in my life. But it wasn't only a wish to keep things calm between them that made him hesitate. He'd started feeling an unwelcome old ache in his chest.

"I mean—for both of us, other people are ... They could even be a threat."

"That how you see your friends, Theo? Hm?" Max rubbed at his throat, looking up at the dark blue sky. There were too many lights around for the stars to show through.

"No, but they ..." He licked his lips. "They know what it's like to be different." He sank in on himself. "And even then ..."

"You can't tell them," Max said. "I get it, Theo. I do."

"But I can mostly forget and feel like I'm with my

own, with them. Do you? I mean, when you're with your friends."

"Yeah," Max said lightly, but that felt too dishonest. "For a few hours, anyway."

Theo reached over to curl a hand around the back of Max's neck. He leaned in to lightly brush his lips against Max's.

"Theo," Max said, laughing softly, "I'm fine."

"I know," Theo said.

"You're so shocked I don't really fit in either? Hm?" Max hooked his thumbs into Theo's belt and tugged him closer. "What?"

Theo was looking over his shoulder, his eyes narrowed. As much as he knew Theo would hate his thinking this way, Max was reminded of how a cat or dog would gaze fixedly at something unfamiliar. Prickles turned to cascades of tingles down his back. Max jerked around, searching for the presence he felt.

Near his car, as bold as anything, stood a shadow spirit. Max broke out in a cold sweat, but bared his teeth in a grin.

"Well, that didn't take long. This one must just hang out around here."

"E-everybody comes here sooner or later," Theo said softly. "Pretty smart."

"We'll see about that," Max said, pushing off the wall. The shadow spirit turned to watch him as he walked across the parking lot. With every step, he felt a little more pressure in his skull. Max ground his back teeth together as he pressed forward. He could hear Theo's bare feet brushing against the asphalt behind him. It was easier to fight his apprehension with a werewolf at his back. He held out the charm when, as if reaching a decision, the shadow spirit made a sharp move in their direction.

The shadow spirit jerked back as if it had touched

something hot. It stretched sideways, torso slipping too much to one side of its lower half to remain humanoid, and made another tentative reach. Jerking again, it retreated a step.

"Hot damn," Max breathed, legs trembling with built-up adrenaline. "I think it works." He swung the charm in the shadow spirit's direction, and it turned to run. After a few steps, it flickered out of sight, but Max still sensed its presence. Sharp movement in his peripheral vision made him turn in time to see Theo jerk the belt open and let his robe fall. Max gasped, raising a hand to block the worst of the light.

"No, Theo, don't chase—" By the time he'd spoken that much, Theo was well across the parking lot. Numbly he bent to pick up the robe. "Holy crap, but he's fast."

Lights flashed behind him, making his heart leap. He looked over his shoulder to see a car driving slowly toward him. It was a white car bearing a security company logo. As casually as he could, Max sauntered back toward his own vehicle. He sighed inwardly as the security guard stopped his car and got out, flashlight in hand.

"Something I can help you with, sir?" The young guard was about Max's height but not very fit; he carried himself with a slight swagger he probably thought gave him more authority. Max decided not to tell him it wasn't working.

"Uh, just looking for my dog," Max said. The guard looked at the robe in his hand, frowning. "Oh, this is just his favorite thing to sleep on."

"Uh-huh. What's the dog look like?"

"Big gray one. Really big, like a malamute." *Except anyone who knows malamutes would know he isn't one.* Putting two fingers in his mouth, Max did his best whistle, wondering how ticked off Theo was going to be. "Theo! Come on, boy!" Feeling the guard's gaze burning into the side of his head, Max stared across the parking lot. He sagged in relief when he saw the great wolf bounding back their way. Ears popping up at the sight of the security vehicle, Theo made a half-circle and came in behind Max.

"That a boy." Max patted Theo's head, making his ears flatten against his head. "You had me worried."

"Wow, he is a big guy, isn't he?" The guard's manner had noticeably softened. "Hey, wait just a sec." He jogged back to his car; Max and Theo exchanged a look. Dropping his haunches to the ground, Theo opened his mouth to pant. He abruptly closed it again as the guard came back, tossing something around in his hand.

"I've got a shepherd-lab cross," he said to Max. "Sometimes he comes along for the ride, so I usually have some cookies in the car. Can I give him one?"

"Sure," Max said. *Oh, I have got to see this.*

"Here you go, buddy." The guard leaned forward and held out a dog biscuit. Theo swiveled one ear toward Max, then turned his head to the side and casually took the treat. He crunched it up, pretending great interest in something way off across the parking lot as the guard petted his ruff with both hands.

The longer this went on, the harder it was not to laugh. Max coughed to disguise a plaintive sound that escaped his throat.

"Come on, boy," he said. "Let's go home. Thanks, eh." He nodded to the guard.

"Hey, I'm glad you found him. Too many pets go missing around Halloween." With a wave, the guard went back to his car.

Max watched the other car leave as he opened the back door so Theo could slink inside.

"Okay," he said, tossing the robe in after and closing the door. Getting into the driver's seat and starting the car, he closed his eyes too late as light bounced off of the rearview. "Oh, man. Don't ever do that when I'm driving."

Theo said nothing as he stepped out, then got into the passenger seat. He sullenly buckled his seatbelt and rested his elbow on the door, glaring out the window. Max blinked until the worst of the spots were gone, then drove on. He didn't dare watch how Theo's mouth jerked at the corners. He still didn't trust himself not to laugh.

"They taste good, all right?" This came out in a low rush. Max snorted, then choked down the rest of the laughter trying to fight its way free. "Look, what tastes good when, when, when you're four-legged—and—What, you think my body ch-changes but my, my freaking taste buds—"

"Nobody's saying anything," Max said. Theo lapsed into bristling silence. "Just I'll know what to bring over next time." An unmanly giggle escaped him; Theo gave him a sour look, which only spurred him on.

"What, you think—" Theo's voice broke; he pressed his knuckles to his lips, then slid Max a little grin. "You think I can't buy my own dog cookies?" The tension gave way and they filled the car with laughter together.

This late in October, every day it grew a little colder. Max found the first part of his run uncomfortably cool, but his body warmed up as he went. His feet struck the familiar dirt road in an automatic rhythm. He let the trees slip by without much attention, his eyes on the slowly disintegrating barn on the Wang property. Since the Wangs had bought the place a couple of years ago, they'd been building up a vegetable farm, but they hadn't cleaned up the entire property yet. The barn was blackening and caving in, not an unusual sight around Fort Rivers.

He personally used the barn as an impromptu timer. He'd run this route so long that he knew approximately how quickly the barn should appear to approach him. Today it only reluctantly grew closer, a sign that he was frustratingly off-pace.

I've got to start sleeping better. The dreams hadn't laid off yet. He was reluctant, like most mediums, to take sleeping pills, because the dream world could be too close to the spirit world and he wanted the option of waking up. He didn't want to sleep through a shadow sneaking into his bedroom again. He shivered, and not just because of the cold which was starting to sear his throat. He drew up his fleece neck warmer.

A glitter caught his eye, and he looked up. Very fine snowflakes fell from the pale sky. They disappeared before they reached the ground.

Looks like it might be a white Halloween this year. His childhood had been full of trick-or-treating with his costume under a winter coat and snowball fights with Anastasia. Those memories reminded him of another type of Halloween. *Oh, I am so dragging Theo to the association dance this year. I want to see him—*Max's toe caught on the opposite heel. He stumbled badly, flailing, until he regained his balance. He put his hands on his waist, made aware of his quickened breathing now that he'd stopped. *Glad nobody was around to see that—*

As his lungs tried to catch up, they pulled in strong gulps of air. That air felt warmer, damper. The sweat droplet trickling down the back of his neck was abruptly chased by icier cousins.

The scent came again, swampy and rich. It set his heart racing and opened up all his senses.

Oh, shit. He twisted and turned, scanning his surroundings with wide eyes. *Shit, shit, shit.* This wasn't the pressure of the shadow spirits. The road narrowed down and stretched in both directions. His fingers suddenly didn't work as he tried to get his jacket open. The charm probably wouldn't work on Deep Murky anyway, but he wanted to feel the rough little pouch and know it was there. Then something snapped inside, and he was running unrestrained, barely feeling the half-frozen road underfoot.

At that punishing pace, he soon ran out of lung power, yet somehow kept going. The sight of the yellow house pulled at him like a hook and line. His legs couldn't find more speed, and his knees felt like they could give way at any moment, but still he ran. He dove down through the ditch and up again, then tripped up the front stairs and burst into the house. Max collapsed in the front hall, nearly hyperventilating.

"Max?"

He felt the vibrations on the floor as Anastasia approached, but he didn't have the strength left to lift his head.

"Max! Are you okay?" She turned into rustling and a hand on his back.

"Maybe," he croaked.

"Jesus, Max, breathe. Calm down. You're safe in here." Her hand rubbed briskly across his shoulder. "Was it a shadow spirit?"

He managed to shake his head.

"Then what ... oh."

"I'm going to be sick."

"Oh, crap. Hang on, I'll get a bowl!" She thumped away as he dragged himself up to all-fours, and was back just in time with the beaten-up plastic bowl from the hall closet. He emptied his stomach into it, pushed it as far away from himself as he could before the smell could get to him, and collapsed onto his side.

"Are you sure?"

"No," he said, finally able to take a real breath. "Not sure. But I can't remember feeling him this strongly in a long time."

"Maybe he is around." Anastasia sat on the floor beside him. "Well, why isn't he?"

Max rolled over to glare at her. She crossed her legs under her skirt and spread both hands.

"Think about it. You said Wallace was nervous. Why wouldn't the local spirits be upset about these shadow spirits moving in?"

"Actually, that old lady, too." Max blinked at the sudden memory.

"What old lady?"

"She showed up in my car, talking about ... something about how 'they' got through. Jesus. I thought she was just some crazy old lady's ghost." Max put a hand to his forehead. His fingers no longer trembled, making them feel more like his own fingers. "It's not real fun being a medium right now, Ana."

"Yeah." Her voice went unsteady. "I don't want to have to stay in the house all the time. And these things stink." She picked up the charm and grimaced at it. "So does that." She nodded at the bowl. "I'd clean it out if I were you."

"Seriously? The guy who just got sick has to clean it up?"

"Makes sense to me." She got up and headed up the stairs.

"Some little sister you are." Now that he'd been reminded of the bowl, the thought of it made his skin crawl. He got up to deal with it. Deep Murky—or his own paranoia—would just have to wait.

Hearing the horn outside, Theo stuffed his cellphone in his jeans pocket and caught up his house keys on his way out. He hit the passenger seat, immediately leaning over to kiss Max. Max had turned, probably in anticipation of a light peck, but Theo went for more than that, and he felt Max chuckle. He chased the vibrations of that chuckle with his tongue until Max pulled away.

"That's a big friendly greeting," Max said, putting the car in gear.

"I just missed you," Theo said, his blush feeling guilty. "I'm used to, y'know, having you around now."

"Well, we're not going to get anything too exciting done for a while," Max said.

"Where are we going?" Theo asked, putting on his seatbelt.

"My friend Paul invited us to lunch at the golf club," Max said. Theo looked up at him, startled.

"Who's Paul?" He felt his chest tighten and tried to pry his ribcage loose with a deep breath. It didn't work.

"He's a sales rep at the radio station. I met him when we bought a couple of radio ads for the boarding kennel. Oh, and my friend Josh, and my racquetball buddy, Willis. Everybody's straight, but they're all decent guys." He cast an easy smile in Theo's direction. "They want to meet you."

You couldn't have told me that? Theo pulled at the hem of his T-shirt. *Would I have said no?*

"Have you ever been to the golf course restaurant?"

"No," Theo said, staring out the window. Outside, snow wafted down in dry, sporadic flakes.

"It's really good," Max said. "I mean, it kind of has to be, or else nobody'd bother being a member of the club. The day fees aren't that bad there."

"I've never played golf."

"Do you want to? In the spring, I mean, when the

greens open up again."

"Not really interested," Theo said.

"You should give it a try before you write it off. It's pretty interesting stuff once you get into it."

"Video game golf's good enough for me," Theo said.

"A little fresh air now and again would probably do you good, Theo."

"There's a million other ways I could get fresh air." This continued assault on his lifestyle, no matter how mild the tone delivering it, made his skin crawl. Theo fought to keep his voice from sharpening too much.

"Well, your loss."

The golf course was out to the east of town, heavily treed and surrounded by tall fences; the low buildings were sided with mock cedar panels and not particularly remarkable. Nevertheless, Theo felt under-dressed as he stepped out of the car.

"Hang on a sec," Max said. He stood in front of Theo and reached up. Uncomfortable, Theo felt those sure fingertips rearranging his hair, then straightening his collar. Max smiled, nodded in satisfaction, and gestured toward the clubhouse.

Once inside, Max signed him in, and they went into the restaurant. The interior was decorated with stuffed moose heads and fish, as well as award plaques and wildlife artwork. The sturdy furniture was probably antique; the tables were covered with heavy, white tablecloths and vases of flowers. For Fort Rivers, this trite styling passed for up-scale.

One of the tables had three men already seated at it, and they rose at Max and Theo's approach. Despite basic physical differences, Theo found them quite uniform, especially standing as they were in a semi-circle: dress shirts, ties, dark trousers, short hair, clean-shaven.

He got through the handshakes and introductions fine.

For a blessed few minutes the conversation was more to do with weather and ordering their meals, topics he didn't need to contribute much to. Then, in the time in between ordering and the arrival of their food, the awkwardness settled onto him like a damp film.

"So, Theo," Willis said, leaning back and picking up his beer. "What went through your head?"

"Eh?" Theo glanced up from playing with his fork.

"When you picked this guy," Josh interjected, slapping Max on the chest. The others burst into laughter, Max included. It was the unfettered laughter of men in their element and made Theo feel weird—less normal than he normally felt, which wasn't very normal at all.

"No." Willis chuckled. "When you went in after Ana." Theo's internal hackles rose. He didn't like this man, a stranger to him, using Anastasia's nickname. At the same time, it was a small kick in the gut as well. Anastasia was a comfortable person for him to be around, open-minded, accepting, with a hint of social awkwardness of her own. Apparently she was able to move in the circles that Max did.

"I didn't think," he said, realizing by their looks that he'd paused too long. "I just w-went on automatic. Just saw the car and jumped." He saw, in his periphery, the glow of pride in Max's eyes.

"That's something." Paul let out a heavy exhalation and shook his head.

"Right?" Josh said. "I mean, we all want to think we'd do that, but until you're in that situation, you just can't tell, right?"

They pushed him for details, finally letting him be once the food arrived. Hoping this would be a good excuse to not have to talk, Theo dug in to his meal.

"I never asked what you do, Theo," Josh said.

"Josh and I work in management at the North Central

mill," Willis said. "And Paul works in sales at the radio station, while Max, of course, plays with puppy dogs all day."

"He has his own business," Theo said. The words shot out of him, and he heard their sharpness too late. Max reached under the table to squeeze his knee. "And so do I," he went on stiffly. "Or, well, I'm an independent contractor."

"Theo's a consultant," Max said. "For media companies. He tests their products for them and tells them how much they suck." He gave Theo an indulgent look that did much to soothe his confused feelings. "We're self-employed, which means we get to decide how and when we work and what we'll charge to do it. Yeah, Paul, loosen that tie some more. We don't even know how to wear a tie, do we, Theo?" Theo smiled weakly as Max nudged his side, and the others chuckled. He was grateful that these men had regular jobs, because that meant they had to go back to work soon. This lunch could only last so long.

Once the others had left, Max took Theo outside the restaurant. The golf course stretched out before them, blanketed with snow that had yet to amount to much but did make everything look clean and fresh. As Max lit up a cigarette, Theo put his hands in his coat pockets, raised his shoulders, and then deflated with a long sigh. Max spewed smoke on a laugh.

"What? What was so bad about that?"

"I'm not good with people."

"You were fine," Max said. "It really bugs you that much to meet new people?"

"Yeah." *That's why I stick to people I've got things in common with—other geeks. I don't want to go to all that trouble when it's just some mainstream person.*

"Well, we'll get you out more," Max said. "Get you

used to it." Theo looked sharply at him. Not appearing to notice, Max gazed out over the course and puffed away. "Well, how about this? Come home with me, and after I've got my chores done, I'll cook you dinner. And see what else I might be able to do to make you feel better." His hazel eyes slid in Theo's direction, and as usual, they made his heart stumble around in his chest.

"Can we stop to get my PSP?"

"Oh, for—" Max suddenly dipped down, scooping up a handful of snow. Theo half-heartedly raised a hand to block the snowball; powder exploded against his palm, spattering his face. Snickering, Max ran down the path that led onto the course.

It wasn't a decision. His body had him off after Max before any sort of thought process had taken place. Max ran with speed and assurance, but Theo went straight into high gear. His focus narrowed down to nothing more than Max's athletic figure making autumn colors in a winter background. His thigh muscles flexed, turned his run into a lunge. When he caught Max around the waist, his momentum carried them both into the snow piled up next to the path.

The snow wasn't deep enough to soften the landing, and Theo winced at the explosion of Max's breath into a wheezing grunt. Nose-to-nose with Max, he had nowhere to hide. He felt his neck and ears go very hot as he realized what he'd just done.

"What the hell was that?" Max's wide eyes blinked quickly.

"Th-there's a reason were—we don't ... Sports and stuff," Theo stuttered, deeply embarrassed and ashamed. "When we chase, we ... We really kind of—mean it. Get carried away."

Max threw back his head and laughed. Theo pushed himself up into a kneeling position, then sat back on his heels. He rubbed at his burning cheeks, then gasped in surprise as Max threw a handful of snow at him, hitting him in the throat. Theo grabbed two handfuls of the cold stuff and showered them down on Max, making him twist around underneath him and laugh harder. Each of them made new snowballs and used their free hands to try to fend each other off.

"Excuse me!" A flustered employee hurried up to inform them that the greens were closed, looking at them with veiled disapproval as Theo got up and helped Max to his feet. They sheepishly brushed themselves off, and Max casually apologized. As they made their escape, breathless and rosy-cheeked, Max chortled all the way back to his car.

"Ah, Theo," he sighed, finally back under control. "You turn me into such a dork."

"Gee, uh, thanks," Theo said, making Max chuckle, but his answering smile didn't want to stay on his face.

So what are you turning me into, then?

CHAPTER TWELVE

Theo sighed audibly in relief and pushed back the woolly hood as they stepped out into the chill night air.

"Hey," Max said. "Stay in costume."

"It's really hot," Theo complained.

"You're hot. You're my hot Greek—"

"—wolf in sheep's clothing."

"—wolf in sheep's clothing!" They spoke in unison, Max's voice pitched high with barely contained amusement, Theo's low and distinctly not laughing.

"That wasn't funny the first ten times you said it." Theo waved a cloven-hoof glove at him.

"Wrong," Max said, claiming Theo's elbow. "It's hilarious. I have no idea who would make a sheep costume in your size, but when I saw it at the thrift store, I just had to get it. You look," he dragged his voice back to its native range, "adorable." They made their way down the rickety back stairs, and he added, "Well?"

"Well what?"

"Glad we came?" He tugged and was amused by Theo's exaggerated loss of balance.

"Y-yeah." Theo smiled at the gravel underfoot.

"Good. Me, too." Max chuckled. "You think we're going to get a cab looking like a slutty shepherd and his hot sheep?"

"I don't know." Theo gave the street ahead a concerned look. "It's not even Halloween tonight."

"Halloween's on Monday. They couldn't have done it any other night. Besides, you've already got Halloween plans."

"It's a tradition," Theo said, as they moved slowly through the alley. "You're welcome to come."

"I'm not sure I want to watch a bunch of horror movies in a row with your friends," Max said. "Are you going to dress up?"

"Yeah, of course. It's Halloween." There was a pause, then, "But no non-fandom stuff."

"I don't have my geek-to-English dictionary on me, Theo."

"We cosplay—uh, dress up—like specific characters. Not like, y'know, just witches and stuff. Depends on what you're into." The words were coming out quickly.

"So what are you going to go as this year?"

"You wouldn't have heard of him."

"Hm." Max looked into Theo's rosy-cheeked face. "Do you want me to come?"

"Kind of."

"Does that mean you don't want me there?"

"It's not your scene, obviously. But it'd be nice if you knew my friends, and I could—" He paused.

"You could what?" Max let the last word linger.

"Sh-show you off," came the mumbled reply. Max stepped in front of Theo to stop him.

"Don't make me mess up your lipstick," he said. Theo smiled, then kissed him lightly on the mouth.

"I hope we can get a cab," he said softly. "I don't want Ana to come get you."

"Oh, I like drunk Theo," Max replied in a matching tone, wrapping both arms around the floss-covered body before him. With his black lashes augmented by mascara, Theo's eyes were incredibly beautiful, and they focused on him alone. Then Theo's brows drew down.

"Wait."

"Okay, that's not fair." Max gave up on his complaint when he felt sickeningly familiar tingles on his neck. "Oh, shit. Theo?" Theo was hastily getting out of his costume. Max watched despondently. "Theo, you're not—"

"It's close," Theo said, shoving his clothes into Max's arms as he looked up and down the alley. Max closed his eyes defensively, light battering at his eyelids. When he opened them again, all he saw was the tip of a tail disappearing around the side of the building. Max slipped between two buildings and waited, shivering. His half-pants left his calves at the mercy of the night air. The buzz of alcohol had been replaced by adrenaline, irritation, and an unpleasant sense of uselessness.

When others left the dance and passed by his place in the shadows, Max held his breath. He didn't want to attempt explaining anything. He did worry about them, but suspected that leaping out of the dark warning about evil spirits wasn't going to get him anywhere.

They're going off with other people. At least they're not alone.

Theo had been clearly intimidated by the press of people but danced readily and with a decent sense of rhythm. It had been tremendous fun to watch him, to press against him, to laugh and smile with him. On the other hand, Max's head reeled from all the drinks he'd downed to try to keep from noticing the attention Theo had been getting.

This monogamy stuff's a pain.

After a small eternity, a big shadow trotted up to him. Panting, Theo sat down. Steam rose from his mouth, and his ears were at half-mast. Finally, he stood, shook, and flashed into light.

"Lost it," he said in disgust as he dressed. "Those things, I don't know where they go, but they just—go."

"Well, spirits move through worlds we can't," Max said, ambivalent. "If they're afraid of you, why do they keep coming near you?"

"I—I don't know. Is it me?" Theo was buttoning up the sheep suit.

"It's a possibility."

"Either way, I ... We shouldn't be alone tonight."

"We weren't planning to be, remember?" Max gave him a playful pat on the side, but when they went out into the street, he could see the fatigue in Theo's expression.

Goddamn things. First they mess with my sister, now they steal a night with the sexiest sheep in Fort Rivers.

To his relief, the taxi driver who took them home barely blinked at the sight of them; apparently it was close enough to Halloween to forgo explanations. Once at Theo's, they stood side-by-side in the tiny bathroom to wash the makeup off, which revived Max's mood. Wearing makeup was funny, but not as priceless as having it smudged down their faces while trying to figure out how to get it off.

When he climbed into bed next to Theo, he got a wan smile.

"What's wrong?" Max asked.

"I don't think I can tonight. I ran full-out, and I'm just really ..."

"Yeah, the mood's kind of gone, isn't it?" Max patted Theo's hip under the blankets. Theo wasn't looking reassured. "What?"

"You're—not mad?"

"Mad? Why would I be?" Max pushed himself up on one elbow. "Are you kidding me? Theo, what do you take me for?"

"No, I'm sorry. Th-that was stupid." Theo looked at Max's chest, biting his lip. His eyelids drooped in a new kind of Theo-cute, so Max kissed his forehead and left things at that. He rearranged himself under the blankets as Theo fumbled at the lamp, dropping them into darkness. Max lay awake for some time after, thinking about shadows and werewolves. As things stood, he wasn't sure he had a good handle on either.

He picked up his cellphone to check the time. It was close to four in the morning. He sighed heavily, wishing that he could sleep. Then he glanced at his cellphone's display again. In the bottom corner was a little image of a moon—he'd found an app that kept track of the phases of the moon. The tiny glowing moon was nearly full.

Full Moon

Coming out of sleep this close to the full moon was like pulling himself out of tar. Startled awake, Theo blearily raised his head to see Max stroll into the bedroom holding paper bags and smelling richly of fried chicken.

"Max, I said ..."

"I know, you want to be alone tonight. But I just thought of you sitting here feeling like crap and figured that probably meant you weren't exactly cooking for yourself." Max sat down on the bed next to him. "I don't know what passes for chicken soup with Greek werewolves, so you'll have to make do with fried chicken."

Theo sighed and turned his head, surreptitiously wiping the corner of his mouth. It was true that he couldn't risk cooking when he was this weak, and his mouth had instantly flooded with saliva at the scent of meat.

"Plus this for dessert." Max grinned and held up a box with a picture of a dog on it. Theo sat up, a hand to his aching head.

"Are you serious?"

"Open it," Max said gently, holding it out. As he took

the box, the scents revealed the trick. He opened the lid and peered in at a bag of chocolate chip cookies. "Ana baked them when I told her this would be a rough night for you."

Staring helplessly at the box, Theo sank under guilt and gratitude. He bit his lip.

"Tell her thanks for me."

"Of course." Max bumped his elbow with a fist. "Want me to get some plates?"

"Sure." He continued to stare at the box while Max was gone. *It's been so long since I spent a full moon with someone—on purpose. It used to be we all got through it together.* It had always meant frayed tempers; it had often ended with them curled up together in winter or sleeping under the back stairs in the yard on warm summer nights. Theo put a hand to his mouth, horrified, as tears suddenly filled his eyes.

"Theo?" Max gave him a look at he came back in with plates and napkins. "You okay? Oh, hey." Quickly sliding in next to Theo, he put a hand on his shoulder.

"Mm. I ..." Theo wiped futilely at his eyes. "I just remembered."

"What did you remember?" Max stroked his neck with his thumb. "You know you can talk to me."

That's right, I can. He hated the feeling of wetness sliding down his cheeks; he hated the lack of control he had over it. He'd last cried after Grandmother's funeral, and that only when he'd finally had time to himself. But this was exactly the kind of thing he could tell Max about.

"When I was little, Ma'd—she'd kind of curl up around me, and I'd fall asleep with my nose under her neck. Just when I was little. But on her last moon, even though I thought it was stupid and I was bigger than her by then, she came up and did that. And she was sick, so I—I mean, I was a teenager, so it embarrassed me, but she was sick, so I snuggled up like we used to. And three days later she was ..." His throat closed up and he could no longer talk. As warm arms came around him, he buried his face into Max's shoulder.

"Shhh," Max whispered. "I know how those memories can hurt."

"Yeah," Theo said raggedly. He choked on a sob, then clenched his teeth and bore down on the lump in his throat. He pushed free, hitching up his shirt to use its hem to dry his face.

"Theo."

"I'm okay," he whispered.

"Don't fake it, okay? I really don't think there's anything wrong with guys crying, especially when it's stuff clearly worth crying about."

I do. I hate crying.

Max stroked Theo's cheek with the heel of his hand, his gaze very gentle; Theo quickly looked down.

"I'm really okay."

"Yeah." Max slid his hand around to the back of his neck and gave a squeeze. "Seriously, I want you to get this. You don't have to hide what you're feeling from me. Just remember that." He shifted away, retrieving the greasy paper bag and the plates. "Let's eat." Theo watched him serve out chicken, fries, and salad. His chest was full of intense warmth, as well as an incongruous ache.

Am I still too much work, then? He numbly took the plate Max offered.

Once they'd finished eating, Max took the remains away. Theo struggled to keep his eyes open. Max laughed when he came back into the room.

"Don't hold back just because I'm here."

"But ..."

"I can keep myself busy." Max held up a novel.

"So you're staying?" Theo hoped his ambivalence

didn't come through in his tone.

"Yeah." Max walked around to the other side of the bed and bounced onto it, finding his place in the novel. Theo pulled off his shirt, pausing as dizziness rolled over him. His joints burned, and he felt a million years old. Finally, he got to his feet and got out of his pajama bottoms. Then he straightened, looking blearily at the pale floral wallpaper.

I should change that out. Grandmother would think it's ridiculous I left it on when there aren't any women left in the house.

"Max?"

"Hm?"

He imagined Max's gaze on his back, and it pleased him even as it made his skin twitch.

"Thanks." With that he changed, avoiding any further conversation. When he leapt onto the bed and curled up, Max's hand came to rest on his head. He closed his eyes quickly and resisted a powerful urge to move away. It was absolutely not done among werewolves to pet someone in his four-legged form, but it would have been uncharitable to protest.

Last Quarter

"Hey, guys." Theo slid in next to Whitney in the usual booth. "Sorry I'm late."

"No problem," Whitney said. "Frankie just got here, too."

"Ordered you a chocolate milkshake," Frankie said, giving him a little salute.

"Thanks." Theo ran his fingers over his hair, carefully exploring its unfamiliar shape. Quite a bit of it had been cut off, especially on the back and sides.

"What's with the new do?" Frankie asked, pushing around his knife.

"Max recommended a guy," Theo said, blushing.

"It looks good," Whitney said. "Professional."

"Theo shouldn't look professional. He's a working geek, like me."

"Does it look—like, too preppy?" Theo looked from one to the other, a hand on the back of his bared neck.

"Never mind him," Whitney said, exasperated. "Are you guys ready to order?"

Once they'd ordered, Theo leaned his elbows on the table to prop himself up. All the time he was spending with Max, on top of work and hunting for shadow spirits, was starting to wear him out. In this position, he could see white, button-down cuffs peeking out from under the sleeves of his sweater. His arms looked like they belonged to someone else.

"You look tired," Whitney said.

"Busy night," Theo replied, swallowing a yawn.

"I bet it was." Frankie grinned.

"*That's* not why." All he'd done with Max yesterday was text. He turned to Whitney. "How's Marnie?"

"Good," Whitney said evenly, his eyes sparkling. "She misses you."

"Misses me? Halloween was six days ago."

"But usually she's at your place twice a week or more," Frankie pointed out.

"You guys can still come over whenever," Theo said guiltily.

"We know," Whitney said.

"Relax, Theo. We know you need more space now. That's what happens when you're in a relationship." Frankie leaned back as the waitress arrived with their plates.

"Says the single guy," Whitney said.

"Hey, I'm pretty okay with that." Frankie wrapped both hands around his cheeseburger.

"We'll find you somebody. Marnie's working on it."

"Oh, great." Frankie rolled his eyes. "Look, I'm not cutting my hair or letting anybody change how I dress or anything like that. I've still got my games and my comics and my webpage, stuff like that. I get a girlfriend, she's got to understand that that's what I do."

"Get a geek girlfriend," Whitney said, gesturing with a French fry. "Then it all works out."

"Why *are* you dressed like that?" Frankie asked.

"It was kind of a fancy place," Theo said. "The hairdresser's. Look, I was going to get my hair cut anyway."

"Yeah," Frankie said, reaching for the ketchup bottle.

"You're making too big a deal about that, Frank."

"Aw, I'm just bugging you," Frankie said. "You know that."

Theo stared at the plate of pasta in front of him, his fingers hesitating by the fork. He knew that Frankie was only partially teasing. Whitney was munching on his sandwich, giving Theo worried glances, but not saying anything. Grateful for that courtesy, Theo nevertheless wished one of them would change the subject and distract him.

"How do you know?" he found himself asking.

"Know what?" Whitney asked.

"If—you're being asked to change too much."

All three of them went quiet; he didn't miss the look they exchanged. Sighing, Frankie leaned forward.

"Come on. Out with it."

"It's probably nothing, but ..." Theo fingered his hair again, then slumped against the back of the booth. "It's all just little things."

"Theo, you can just tell us. We're not going to judge

you. We're your friends." Whitney's reassurances made Theo wonder whether this was worth bringing up. And they were small things: comments on how he dressed, recommendations on where to go for clothes or his hair, trying to "fix" his shyness, affectionate but patronizing remarks about his games, his anime, his figures. He'd walked out of the hair salon excited at the thought of showing Max his new look, but now doubt set in.

"No way, dude," Frankie said. "Tell him to back that bus up."

"Well," Whitney said, his expression pained, "he probably has no idea how he's coming across."

"He has to be into you for who you are, not who he wants you to be."

"Talk to him first. I'm sure he just doesn't know that stuff bothers you. And I'm sure you haven't told him." Whitney held up a hand. "Hey, I get it. It took me months to just ask Marnie out. But it's probably the fairest thing to do. Give him a chance, you know?"

"You're just saying that because you're in a couple and think everybody else should be," Frankie said, his tone losing some of its edge.

"No, I'm saying that because when they're together Theo looks happier than I've ever seen him before," Whitney said primly. Theo rubbed at his burning neck and picked up his fork.

"All right, all right," he said. "I'll talk to him. Now can we talk about something else?"

"Okay," Frankie said after a pause. "Question: should I subscribe to Showvo just to watch *Stake to the Heart*, yea or nay?"

Theo was very grateful for the distraction as they got back to familiar territory. Yet he left the restaurant with a sense of relief. Talking it out with his friends had only defined the problem, not solved it.

CHAPTER THIRTEEN

I'm so going to do it," Charli said, nudging Kuh-Cake with her heels to bring him in line with Ay-Muff. Chrissi laughed, her voice clattering about in the trees. The sound of hooves scritching over packed snow was overpowered by their voices. They also took over the empty road as the horses moved away from each other like magnets with the wrong polarities matched. Unlike their riders, the horses had strong opinions about personal space. "Tomorrow's November nineteenth. His birthday. I'm asking him out."

"I dare you," Chrissi said. "I'll, like, video you do it."

"Don't frigging video me. That'll be too embarrassing."

"You're going to ask out a total freakjob. What do you care about getting embarrassed?"

"How is Joe Tamura a total freakjob? You're such a jerk, Chrissi."

"He sits there and plays cards with his loser friends all the time. Who does that?"

"I don't know, somebody who likes cards. Jeez, what is your—whoa!" Kuh-Cake swerved away from the trees. Charli went with the motion. Ay-Muff nearly crashed into her and her mount. When she looked, startled, she saw his saddle was empty. "Chrissi!" Instinctively grabbing at Ay-Muff's flopping reins, she tried to see around his head. "Chrissi, are you okay?"

"Ow. What the hell?" Chrissi's voice sounded weak, but normal enough to ease Charli's growing panic. She had her hands full. Kuh-Cake wouldn't stay still beneath her; his head was raised, his neck rigid. Ay-Muff was equally tense, snorting loudly in challenge. When he pulled sharply away, she lost hold of his reins. He bolted, and before she could react, Kuh-Cake went with him. Kuh-Cake became a powerhouse beneath her. Nothing she did with the reins seemed to matter. Then he stumbled, and she flew out of the saddle.

The fall went in slow motion. She had time to anticipate belly-flopping on the ground, but not enough to prevent it. The impact knocked the wind out of her, but she felt compelled to get up. Clutching at her aching stomach, Charli got to her feet. She could see Chrissi in the distance, still on the ground. Charli gritted her teeth and started jogging.

As she grew nearer, her vision seemed to come over in black spots—or there was just one spot, and it was growing larger, clearer. It wasn't a spot at all, but a person-shaped hole in the air. It was leaning over Chrissi, holding her arm.

That's one of those shadow ghosts Mom was talking about. Her first reaction was calm. She'd grown up around talk about such things. But Chrissi wasn't moving, not even screaming. Charli started to run for real, pain forgotten.

"You get away from her! Go on! Don't touch her!" Her shrieks didn't seem to make an impact. She caught up stones as she went. "Get away from my sister!" The first stone she hurled bounced off the thing; the second went through it. It turned, as if to look at her, but didn't move away. Belatedly Charli remembered the charms that Mom had given them. She'd left hers in her jacket, which was currently tied to the back of her saddle. Chrissi hadn't brought hers at all because she hated the way they smelled. "Shit!" Charli stared helplessly at her sister, who weakly moved one of her legs. Charli picked up more stones and drew a deep breath to keep screaming. In return, the shadow dropped Chrissi's arm and moved her way.

Max had just put his last training client in the kennel when he saw Theo's car drive in. He went to await Theo outside his car door. He smiled when Theo stood and immediately kissed him, hands diving into the hair at his nape.

"Well, hello to you, too."

"We've both been so busy," Theo mumbled. "I've only seen you five times in the past couple of weeks."

"You don't have to make excuses." Max chuckled, kissing the tip of Theo's nose. "It's not like I hate it when you kiss me."

"Yeah." Theo put his hands on the car door between them and grinned sheepishly.

"You don't even care if anybody sees anymore, do you?"

"I guess not." Theo glanced at the house, his brows suddenly knitting. "Did anybody?"

"I doubt it. Mom was in the basement last I saw, and nobody else is home." Max bumped Theo's shoulder. "So what do you want to do tonight?"

"I'm not—" Theo turned sharply.

Max heard the sound of galloping hooves. He felt his expression harden.

"How many times have I told those girls not to run those horses on that goddamned road? It's too hard, and at this time of year there's ice—"

The horses barreled into the yard, snorting like steam engines. Max, alarmed by the sight of their empty saddles, ran toward them making soothing noises. They were both skittish, their necks dark with sweat. Max had never seen either horse this worked up before.

"Easy, guys. Easy. Where'd the twins, go, huh?" The flash of light startled him and made Ay-Muff leap away from him. Max turned in time to see Theo's dark form burst through the front hedge and onto the road. "Shit!" He waved his arms at the horses, shooing them into their paddock and closing the gate. Then he ran for Theo's car, threw aside the pile of clothes in the driver's seat, and drove off in belated pursuit.

It only took about ten minutes, but it felt like an hour before he came upon the twins. They were both on the ground, Charli over top of her sister. Time slowed further as he leapt from the car. When he touched Charli's hunched back, she made a terrified whimper.

"Charli, it's okay. Let me see your sister."

"Are the monsters gone?"

"Yeah, I don't see anything." Max peered into the trees. "Come on, are you two okay? What happened?"

Slowly Charli rolled off of Chrissi. Max fought for calm as he saw the blue tinge to Charli's lips. Chrissi looked pale, though she looked at him and seemed to recognize him.

"I think there were two," Charli said, putting a hand to her temple. "The shadow one and then something—it was growling, like a bear or something." She gave him a gloomy look. "I was too scared to see what it was." Her attention immediately went to her sister. "Chrissi, you okay?"

"You squished me." Chrissi's voice came out very hoarsely. "And I feel like I got the flu, but, like, a bunch of 'em at the same time."

"Oh, thank god," Max breathed. *Maybe it drew on them both. Maybe that's why neither one's in a coma.*

"For me getting the flu?" Chrissi croaked.

"No, not for that."

"God, I feel so cold." She was rubbery weight in his arms as Max lifted her to her feet. He supported her to the passenger seat, Charli a half-step behind him. Once he had both of them in the car, he took one last look around. He was finally able to pick out the pair of eyes peeking through a low-hanging branch. Max nodded curtly and got in the car.

Theo knocked on the back door, then stepped inside. He heard Max and Kaitlyn talking in the living room.

"Hello?"

"Hey, Theo. Just a sec." Max's voice was overly casual. Theo lurked by the back door until Max came to him with a grim expression and a lowered voice. "They're both resting upstairs."

"Are they okay?"

"As far as we can tell. Both of them are talking normally, but they've got no energy. Chrissi can barely move." Max cleared his throat. His gaze was slightly evasive. "What did you see?"

"There was a shadow spirit there." Theo's lip curled of its own accord. "Charli was, uh, throwing stuff at it. Then she threw herself on top of Chrissi, to protect her maybe. I think m-maybe she distracted it before it could totally, y'know."

"So that's why Chrissi isn't completely drained." Max shook his head. "Crazy kid."

"Your sister." Theo tried a smile, but Max simply glanced at him and then down the hall.

"I want to stay close tonight."

"Of course. Do you want me to—I could go get some

food or something. For everybody."

"That's nice of you, Theo." Max leaned in to kiss him on the cheek. "But I think this'll just be a quiet family night, okay?"

"Oh, okay. Sure." He tried another smile, this one feeling less successful. "Keep me updated, okay?"

"You bet. See you tomorrow maybe?" Max patted Theo's arm, then slipped away to talk to Kaitlyn.

Theo opened the back door, trying not to feel hurt. *When stuff happened in our family, Grandmother didn't want strangers around either.* Theo went out into the cold. *I guess I just didn't think I was a stranger anymore.*

"I still don't think this is a very good idea," Max said as Mom bustled by with one of the twins' suitcases. "Shouldn't we stick close to home?"

"We have to go outside sometimes. And obviously the girls can't be trusted to keep themselves safe."

"I'll talk to them."

"It's already settled, Max. Your aunt's expecting us." Mom paused, setting down the suitcase. "Hopefully we'll have a better idea of what to do in a week or so."

"Mom—"

"Max, you can't be there to protect them all the time. They'll be safer this way."

Apparently I can't be there to protect them any of the time. Max clenched his jaw, keeping his words contained. Mom didn't appear to notice, looking distractedly around the front hall as she patted at her pockets. Then she pulled out her keys.

"I really hate these things. I've never been chased out of my own home before." She gave him a keen look. "I'll talk to that side of the family, call your Uncle Yuu. You stay close to this house and watch over Anastasia. All right?" She slapped him lightly on the stomach.

"All right, Mom."

"And get Theo to stay here. He needs to be safe, too."

He's about the only one who doesn't have anything to fear from them. But Max just nodded and started carrying suitcases out to Mom's car while she yelled for the twins to hurry. *Yet again he's doing the protecting, and I'm good for nothing more than carrying stuff.*

CHAPTER FOURTEEN

First Quarter

Theo stood uncertainly in the hall, duffel bag dangling down his back, laptop bag resting against his thigh. Considering how little he liked sleeping away from home, he'd surprised himself by quickly agreeing to stay over for a week. Perhaps it was because he could be useful or because it would apparently make both Kaitlyn and Anastasia more comfortable.

Or it was just because Max had asked.

"Hey, Theo." Anastasia came to rescue him. "Come on in. I'll show you which room you can use." She frowned at him. "Is that all you brought? Even for a guy, that's not much."

Max came out of the living room, a crooked smile on his face.

"Don't worry, Ana. Theo only has about two outfits anyway." He leaned over Anastasia to kiss Theo lightly on the mouth. "Smile, Theo. That was a joke."

"Come on, Theo." Anastasia slid out from in between them and led Theo upstairs. "We'll put you in Mom and Dad's room, because then you can use Dad's study to work." She paused in front of the door at the end of the upstairs hall and pointed back. "That's my room, and Max'll be in his old room right next to it."

Theo nodded confirmation, hoping his disappointment

didn't show on his face. Anastasia opened up the door to a dark room dominated by a large bed; it was backed by an elaborate headboard filled with knickknacks and hardcover books. The duvet, upon closer inspection, was covered in delicate flowers and vines. The room itself smelled distinctly of dried lavender, a scent he'd noticed on Kaitlyn herself. He felt very much the intruder as he set down his bags.

"Do you want to get right to work? Or would you like a coffee first?" Anastasia lingered in the doorway, watching him.

"Coffee," Theo said. "Uh, would be great."

"I know this is all kind of weird, but I'm hoping it'll be fun." Anastasia was dressed more casually than he was used to, in jeans and a sweatshirt; her energetic stride showed through more clearly than when buried in long skirts. "Kind of like going on a trip with friends or something. Man, I've got low standards for trips, don't I?" She gave him a wide-eyed look.

"Trips are overrated," he said.

"Maybe." She smiled and bustled down the stairs. Max was waiting at the foot of the stairs. He caught Theo by the waist and kissed him. Theo wrapped his arms around Max in return as the kiss shifted, deepened. Max made a sound of approval in his throat when their tongues found each other. Then, slowly enough to demonstrate his reluctance, Max withdrew and looked into Theo's face, brushing aside his hair.

"Not that I'm not happy to see you," he said, "but it's going to suck having to behave myself around you all week."

"Maybe, if we—" Theo sagged against the circle of Max's arms. "We're never going to be alone, are we?"

"Doubt it." Then Max's eyes started to glitter. "So we just save it all up for the end of the week. I'll think of something really special for us to do." He put his thumb on Theo's lower lip and lightly caressed it. "I bought handcuffs." That soft murmur hit Theo in the spine. He swallowed hard as his entire body turned warm. Max chuckled and slipped away, leaving Theo reeling.

Am I going to last a week?

Various scents had been sneaking through the lavender—oregano, vinegar, olives—and now they grew strong enough to distract him completely. Theo gave up on the report he was typing and escaped the study through the bedroom.

He could hear Max and Anastasia talking in the kitchen, could hear sizzling and the clatter of plates. The smells of hot oil and steam and meat drew a grumble from his stomach. He peered into the kitchen.

Anastasia was chopping up cucumbers near the sink while Max stood at the stove. As he watched, Max flicked the cap off of a bottle of balsamic vinegar and splashed some into the frying pan before him on the stove with a hint of a flourish.

Okay, that's sexy. Theo cleared his throat.

"Hey, Theo." Max didn't look up from his cooking.

"Can I help with something?"

"Don't worry about it. You're our guest." Max deftly flipped mushrooms in the pan.

"The kitchen's too small for more than two people to do much in at the same time," Anastasia said more apologetically. "Have a seat at the table."

"Sure. I'll just wash my hands." Theo went to the bathroom on the other side of the staircase to do so. The door to the basement was closed, but through it he smelled the only really odd part of the house. Whatever they kept down there, it smelled of soil, herbs, and things he couldn't actually identify. Instinct told him to go down and investigate, but manners helped him resist. *Spirits seem to have a weird relationship with smells.*

When Theo returned to the kitchen, Max and Anastasia were chatting about tomorrow's chores. He sat down at the table and listened, taking in their normalcy for a while. Before it could start making him feel too bad about himself, dinner was ready and their bustling moved in his direction.

"Oh, my god, but that smells good," Theo said as he looked down at the plate Max set before him. A golden chicken breast lurked under a luxurious tumble of mushrooms bedded on pasta; nestled next to it was a simplified Greek salad, lettuce with feta and olives. Theo swallowed as his mouth filled with saliva. Max grinned as he took his own place. Theo tried a bite and nearly moaned in pleasure.

"You really need to learn how to cook," Max said. "You're too easily impressed by normal food."

"Where did you learn?" Theo mumbled around a mouthful.

"Watching Mom, checking out recipes." Max shrugged. "It's not rocket science." He frowned sidelong at Theo. "You not shave today?"

"Eh?" Theo self-consciously rubbed his jaw.

Anastasia gave Max a look.

"He's got black hair. His whiskers are bound to show."

"Actually, I did kind of forget," Theo mumbled, blushing.

"He's not actually a hairy guy," Max said. "Not like you'd expect him to be."

"I'm not the W-Wolfman. My two bodies are different." Theo's face went hot.

"Two bodies?" Anastasia frowned up at the ceiling.

"Is that how it works? So do you feel that other body around right now? Like a spirit, hovering nearby?"

"No." Theo was taken aback by the idea. "It's ... I don't know where it is. It's where I am. I can just—switch. Why?"

"I don't know. I'm just trying to put my finger on something. Why they're scared of you ... Why you can track them down when they don't really exist physically."

"Ana, it's dinner-time," Max said. "Theorize some other time. Maybe not right in front of the person you're theorizing about."

Theo stuffed his mouth with olives and feta, seeking comfort from the familiar flavors.

"So you hear from Lawrence lately?" Max distracted Anastasia by bringing up her boyfriend. Theo didn't know much about him, especially considering he seemed to be traveling around the world at the moment. He was curious about what kind of a boyfriend Anastasia might have. She launched into a detailed description of the work he was doing with NGOs in Cambodia, which wasn't a particularly personal way to talk about him. Theo was grateful to be left to listen, eat, and wonder.

Once dinner was over, Anastasia went outside to feed and water animals. Theo rose to help Max clear the table and was cut off by a sharp gesture.

"No, I can take care of it."

"I c-can help."

"I think I can manage to load the dishwasher by myself, Theo. Believe it or not, I can usually take care of my family and my own place."

Theo sank back down into his seat.

"Max ..."

"I know. I know how shitty that was to say." Max leaned one hand on the counter and threw the dishcloth over his shoulder. "My only excuse is that I'm not used to it—this. Somebody else running to the rescue when my little sisters need it. You can do things I can't."

"Well—" Theo scratched at his neck. "Everybody can do things other people can't, y'know?" *Max is seriously jealous of me?* That made him feel rather guiltily pleased, and he was emboldened to continue. "You can do stuff I can't."

"Like what?"

"Like cook, deal with dogs ... Talk to people." He got up and went to stand next to Max, who still had a wary expression on his face. Theo smiled and kissed his temple. "I'll protect you from the shadow spirits, and you protect me from everything else. Okay?"

"Maybe not *everything*." Max's lips twitched.

"Maybe not." Theo didn't feel sure Max's irritability had really faded. "I'd better go get some work done. Thanks for dinner."

"Hey." Max caught him before he could move away. He put a hand on Theo's cheek and ran his fingertips along the budding stubble there; then he dipped in to kiss Theo, putting the taste of chicken and mushrooms into his mouth. "You don't have to thank me for everything. I asked you to come here. The least I can do is feed you."

"Uh-huh. You taste good." Theo, a little lightheaded, spoke freely. Max laughed out loud.

"I can't feed you that way, unfortunately."

"Yeah." Theo grinned hesitantly. Humor made Max seem more himself.

"Now get back to work." Max swatted him on the backside, and Theo dragged himself away.

Theo managed to squeeze out enough work to fill in the evening hours. He went to the kitchen for a glass of juice, drank it feeling a little odd in the now-quiet main floor, and then went back upstairs. Max, smelling of steam and soap, came out of the bathroom just as he got to the top. Theo gave him a tight smile, awkwardly out of things to say.

"Off to bed?" Max asked, opening the door to his bedroom.

"Yeah."

"Want me to wake you up in the morning?"

"Uh, maybe not. I'll probably want to sleep in."

"Okay. Let me know if you need anything. Good night." Max gave him a half-hearted salute and went through the door.

"Night." Theo turned to go into the master bedroom. He paused, startled, when Max abruptly reappeared, housecoat slung over his shoulder.

"Screw this. Come on."

Theo grinned a little uncertainly as Max followed him in. They climbed into the bed together, Max with a firm bounce, and met in a rather chaste kiss. Max sighed and sagged, patting Theo's shoulder.

"I'm just not kinky enough to do anything in Mom and Dad's bed."

"It's okay," Theo said. He eased himself down onto his back, shifting to accommodate Max, who slid in close to press against his side. Max rested his head on Theo's chest, slipping an arm around his waist.

"You've gotten me into snuggling, Theo."

"Nothing wrong with that, is there?" Theo gazed up at the ceiling. Max's hair felt dry, almost crisp against his skin.

"Mm. I used to like to keep things casual." Max's heat and weight seemed to soften against him. Theo put his hand over Max's. "I wonder when I decided this wasn't what I wanted?"

"What?"

"Never mind." Max kissed his shoulder and slipped away. "Lots of stuff to do in the morning. Get some sleep."

Max put away a training client and decided that was it for the morning. He did a quick check through both kennels to make sure the water dishes were all full before returning to the house. He slipped off his charm at the door, then frowned at the sounds of music and Anastasia's raised voice.

"No, no, no! Ah, let me at least—Theo!"

Theo's voice joined in, laughing freely. Max moved toward the living room, bemused by that rare sound. He smiled dubiously at the sight before him: Anastasia kneeling on the couch, leaning over the arm as she flailed with a video game controller; Theo sitting on the stool, moving with considerably more finesse. Cartoon creatures fought with swords on the TV screen.

"Ah, man," Anastasia complained as music announced the demise of her character. She slumped back and shook her head. "I thought you were going to go easy on me."

Theo turned his head and gave Anastasia a sly smile. It, like the easy laugh, was rare enough to take Max aback.

"I was," Theo said. Then he turned further to smile a welcome at Max.

"What *are* you guys doing?" Max asked. He raised an eyebrow at Anastasia. "I thought you were going to work the show dogs while Mom's gone."

"I will. We're just breaking for lunch." Anastasia pointed to a pair of plates, hers holding a half-eaten sandwich.

"Oh, sure. Don't make me one." Max leaned on the

doorframe, his irritation eased by the pink rim of Theo's ear visible amongst his thick hair.

"Sorry." Despite the blush, Theo looked Max in the eye. "I didn't want to poison you."

"Anybody can make a sandwich, Theo." Max rolled his eyes. Anastasia resumed eating her sandwich, obviously watching them both.

"Fine. Don't, y'know, complain." Theo quickly rose and disappeared into the kitchen.

"Is he seriously—?" Max blinked a few times, then grinned. Anastasia munched with overdone innocence as he sat down beside her. She swallowed and wiped a crumb off her chin.

"Nice having him around, isn't it?"

"Never mind." He pushed at her knee.

Theo came back in with a sandwich for Max. It was clumsily cut on a rough diagonal. Max took half and lifted the top slice of bread. He tried not to laugh at the messy tangle of lettuce and ham.

"I said don't complain." Theo resumed his place on the couch. "Another round?"

"Yeah," Anastasia said. "I haven't taken enough abuse yet." She wiped her fingers on her skirt and picked up the controller. Max sat eating a sandwich that, despite its slabs of cheese and chunk of lettuce, went down easily. He'd slept well last night with Theo next to him. He watched his sister and his boyfriend laugh over a silly game and felt strangely content. The noon sunlight warmed the room both in temperature and in light quality. It made it feel like there were no shadows anywhere.

Things were quiet, so Anastasia took advantage of the solitude. She went down into the basement. The creaking stairs, the rich herbal scents, and slightly damp air should have given her the creeps, but she'd rarely been frightened here. As she lit the candles that formed a circle on the floor, the light became friendly and familiar.

The cement walls, cracked and stained, were old friends. Bare old friends, faintly etched here and there with the symbols Mom had added years ago. Those symbols allowed access to the house in a limited way for spirits, which meant that someone within the circle could also search outside. Even with the protections, the spirit world wasn't entirely kept out of the house; individual spirits couldn't come in, but the other worlds remained where they were, on the other side of the air.

The house really was quiet. Normally, when she didn't have work, she would at least hear Mom rattling around upstairs, and once the twins got home quiet was banished. That might have been what sent her down here.

It wasn't just quiet in the house. There hadn't been any signs of shadow spirit activity, either here or on the news. Anastasia sat down in the middle of the circle on the worn cushion meant for that purpose. She sat cross-legged and closed her eyes to let her senses relax.

At times, the spirit world was just a dark film and silence beyond it. Now it was like a waiting audience, murmuring with voices she couldn't quite make out. She didn't try to call out to anyone. That didn't always work well. Spirits liked to talk, but on their own terms. Even the ones who had once been people didn't always remember what it had been like to be human. It was better to eavesdrop.

She forced herself to be patient, hoping something would come clear. It came only in snatches, some of it hardly verbal. Spirits were nervous, staying away, but not so far they lost their connection to the world. Something had them shaken. Yet none came close enough to become distinct or open to her. It wasn't urgent panic she was sensing.

Anastasia opened her eyes and rubbed at the back of her neck. Four days had passed since the shadows spirits had attacked her sisters right down the road from the house. She wished she could find that reassuring. She blew out the candles and made her way back upstairs.

CHAPTER FIFTEEN

*I*t was more convenient when he was staying with us.* Max snorted in amusement. He was in good spirits as he made his way to Theo's. Understandably, when Dad had come home unexpectedly for an overnight stay, Theo had taken the opportunity to spend some time in his own house. Now Dad had gone back down to see Mom and the girls. *Maybe I can talk him into a quickie before I drag him back to the farm.*

Theo was washing dishes when Max hurried into the kitchen. He turned his head so the peck Theo aimed for his cheek hit his grinning mouth instead.

"Hey, you."

"You're in a good mood." Theo smiled quizzically.

"Take your shirt off."

"What?" Theo laughed.

"Come on, come on." Max started pushing at the hem of his T-shirt until Theo dried his hands and stripped it off. From one of the plastic bags Max pulled out a white dress shirt with thin, blue stripes; this he threw around Theo's shoulders. Still looking puzzled, Theo slipped his arms into the sleeves, chuckling as Max buttoned it up.

"This seems backwards."

"Mm," Max agreed.

"What's going on?"

"You'll see." From the other bag, Max pulled a dark gray cashmere sweater. "I saw this on sale and figured you just had to have it."

"It's, uh, really nice," Theo said. "But why?"

"I don't know, because you're my boyfriend and I saw something I thought would really suit you. Is that weird? And that blue one you had on the other day is looking its age. Try it on." Max didn't let his enthusiasm be dimmed by Theo's unwavering uncertainty.

Theo put the sweater on, and Max helpfully pulled the shirt's collar out from under the v-neck. Then he ran both hands through Theo's hair, arranging it so it sat properly in its new cut, sides shortened and top waving gently down over his forehead. Leaning back to take a look, Max nodded in satisfaction. As expected, Theo's eyes turned the same color as the sweater, and the olive tones in his skin sprang to life.

"Yup, I got that right. You look really good in that."

"Really?" Theo frowned.

"The sweater's comfortable, isn't it?"

"Yeah." Theo bit his lip.

"I want you to come with me to a party next week, wearing that."

"Party?"

"Yeah, just a thing with some guys I know. Lunch with Paul and the guys wasn't so bad, was it?" Shamelessly Max threw a plaintive note into his voice. *I'm going to get you over this hermit thing you've got going on, Theo. The world's got a lot to offer a guy like you, and you're missing out.*

"Uh ... Sure."

"Great. We'll have you BS-ing with the local business community in no time." Max smoothed down the sweater with both hands. Its softness contrasted delightfully with the hard torso beneath it.

"Why would I—want to do that?"

"Huh?" Max was genuinely taken aback. "Theo, you're basically an independent businessman. It only makes sense to network."

"Those kinds of, uh, business guys can't really help me."

"You don't know that," Max said in exasperation. "You never know where the next client or person who'll pull your ass out of the fire is going to come from."

"I do. Game companies that aren't here, and my friends," Theo said.

Max took a moment to phrase his response to that.

"This is just a different kind of making friends—a practical type of friend. You don't have to marry them, just get them to like you enough to remember you when you could help them out."

"Why does it, y'know, matter to you?" Theo's expression was growing stony.

"Theo, I'm just giving you advice. What's gotten into you?" Max fought down irritation.

"Like the hairdresser, and how my clothes fit, and ..."

"Well, yeah."

"Max, stop trying to change me," Theo said, without hesitation or any hint of a stammer. Max's hands grew cold as his face went hot.

"What's that supposed to mean? Since when is just wanting to see your boyfriend dress in more flattering clothes changing him?" He heard his voice jump in volume and quickly shut his mouth.

"That's just the symbol of it." Theo rubbed at his forehead, sending his hair pinwheeling away from his fingers. "I know that you're dating down, but ..."

"How am I dating down?" Max couldn't help the edge in his voice, sharpened by guilt.

"The stuff you think is stupid—the games, the costumes, the figures, the, uh, black t-shirts." Theo looked up, his expression troubled but unafraid. "That stuff is me. It's who I am."

"What you do for fun and who you are, they're different things."

"Not to me. They're really important to me."

"Come on, Theo, you've got more going on than that."

"No, I don't." He shook his head. "And I don't want to. That's the stuff I choose, and it makes me happy."

"Seriously, what are you talking about?" Max tried to rein in his voice.

"It—" Theo clutched at his own shirt with both hands. "It's awesome that you ... That my body turns you on. That makes me really happy, because I could, could never have dreamed I'd get a guy like you. But my body isn't me."

"Theo, I'm not only into you for your body." More anger slipped loose. "I'm not spending all this time with you just to get into your pants. I like being with you."

Theo closed his eyes for a moment, swallowing hard in a way that looked painful, and went on as if Max hadn't spoken.

"And the fact that you accept my heritage, all of it, that's—But every time we're together, it's just little things. I can feel you trying to change what I do. My heritage, you know, either one, or my sexuality, I didn't choose them. You can't change them, and you wouldn't. But the rest of me ..." He shook his head, and when he spoke again his words were throaty. "I'm weak, I know I am. It'd be so easy to just let you do it. You could just swallow me whole."

"Whoa. Hang on here." Max felt his fingertips trembling. He lost interest in holding back. "I know you like to play the victim, but you've got to stop deluding yourself." He didn't realize he'd made a fist until he thumped the table with it. "Everything in this relationship is on your terms. Anything you don't like, you start playing weak whether you could handle it or not, and me and everybody else around you feels bad. Adjusts. Takes care of you." The disorientation of true anger was always sweet, irresistibly so. Max dragged in one deep, rough breath. Theo's face had stiffened, and he watched Max with narrowed eyes. "The one with all the choices and all the options is you. You've got no family in your back pocket to worry about, barely any responsibility, nothing but supportive friends." The hairs on the nape of his neck rose; he clamped them down with a forceful hand as tingles shot across his shoulders and arms. "You're selfish, Theo. You don't try to understand anybody but yourself, but you won't even take responsibility for that—won't even tell people what you want or don't want, because it's easier to get mad at them when they don't deliver than be honest! You are the one who could say no at any time, and you choose not to say it!"

Finally, the words stopped shooting from his mouth like silk from a cannon. The prickling of his skin grew louder. His strong emotions were attracting the wrong kind of attention.

And being who I am, I'm not even allowed to get mad.

Theo was looking at him, arms crossed protectively over his stomach. His saddened eyes were steady as he cleared his throat.

"Then I'm saying no now."

Max's head jerked up, and he glared into Theo's face. His back teeth ground together.

"I think we both need some time to figure things out." Theo spoke gently, as if he was trying to be kind.

Infuriated, Max buried both hands into his hair, fingernails digging into his scalp. He wanted very badly to hit something. His hands slid down his neck, then down his chest, to hang in fists at his sides. When he spoke, the hoarse near-growl that came out seemed to belong to somebody else.

"You just keep running and running. Don't think I'm going to keep chasing you forever."

Theo's eyes flashed, and he looked away, his mouth jerking. In profile his face was particularly handsome, making nothing easier.

The chill breeze ruffling his hair told Max he had to leave, and he heard something smash behind him as he stomped out of the kitchen. Once he'd slammed the front door shut, he leaned against it, lightheaded. The neglected shrub next to the stairs began to rock back and forth, brushing against his shoulder. He hadn't made it out alone.

"I'm sorry," he said. "I didn't mean to call you." The collar of his jacket flapped against his cheek hard enough to sting. "No. You can't stay here." His entire jacket rippled around him, and he was pushed against the door. "You can't stay here. Go!" He glared into the distorted air hovering in front of him. Shapeless, the poltergeist still managed to give him a dirty look before it slunk off.

Heart pounding, jaw tense enough to give him a headache, Max ran down the stairs and slammed his way into his car.

Like hell. Like hell!

Max wanted to sit alone in the dark of his trailer and smoke. Yet he knew that he wouldn't be allowed to have that; even if he did go to his trailer, Anastasia would come looking. Instead, he marched into the house. It at least meant that the last clinging poltergeist fled, scared off by the protections on the house.

"Hi, Max." Anastasia's voice came, muffled, from the living room. Max cursed under his breath and went into the kitchen to pretend to be interested in things in the fridge. As expected, Anastasia came into the kitchen. She was wearing rubber gloves and carried a dust rag. "Hey, where's Theo?"

"He's not coming over."

"What? Why not? That was the plan, wasn't it?"

"Plans change." He slammed the fridge door.

"What's going on?" Anastasia started stripping off her gloves.

"Leave it."

"Max—"

"I said leave it!" Anger chased him out of the kitchen before he could take more of it out on her. Unfortunately, she followed, catching him by the back of his shirt. He whirled on her, glaring, but she just glared back. He couldn't remember the last time he'd actually been able to intimidate her. Max spoke through clenched teeth. "He's not coming over because he just ended it with me."

"What?" Anastasia's eyes widened, and her hand released his shirt. "Why? What did you do?"

"What did *I* do? Christ, Ana." He waved her away. "Don't you put this on me. I did my best with that cowardly prick."

"Max, we need him. How are we going to deal with the shadow spirits without him?"

"Fuck the shadow spirits. Why are they my responsibility, too? Huh?"

"It's not about responsibility, Max. They're hurting people. One of these days somebody's going to die if we don't do something."

"So why do we have to do something? We can scare the fucking things off, but that's it. And we can do that with or without—" His voice broke and he hastily looked away.

"No, we can't. This family needs Theo. Whatever happened between you, we can't be cut off from him.

Max, do you understand what I'm saying to you? Max!"

"Leave me alone!" Max fled to the only place he could: his old bedroom. He leaned his back against the door and dug into his pocket. The only thing in it was his cellphone; he'd left his cigarettes in his trailer. "God damn it!" He hurled the cellphone at the wall. Splinters of plastic went one way, the battery another. "Ah, fuck me." He went to pick up the pieces. The cellphone was obviously a lost cause. He sat on the floor with his back against the end of the bed and turned the pieces of plastic around in his hands. "Fuck him." Max threw them aside, put his hand over his eyes, and leaned his head back. "Fuck everybody."

She had the charm bouncing off her chest, but Anastasia still felt a little nervous as she walked up the sidewalk toward Theo's house. She knew Max would be furious with her.

That's fine. I'm not too happy with him. She walked up the steps to ring the doorbell. Anastasia found herself a little excited, too; she'd never been in Theo's house. It wasn't charitable of her, of course. He was bound to be quite upset after yesterday's breakup. She took a deep breath and toyed with her purse while she waited.

"Anastasia?" Theo's tone matched his wide eyes as he rather quickly opened the door. "Are you okay?"

"Um, that's what I came to ask you." She put a hand to her mouth, trying not to smile. So much of what Theo did was so endearing. "Can I come in?"

"Yeah, of course." He opened the screen door to let her in.

"Oh, you've got company." She was startled to hear voices coming from within.

"Uh, yeah. M-my cousin and his fiancée. It's okay. Got tea on."

"You?" Anastasia peered around curiously as Theo led her down a short hall and through a doorway into the kitchen. *What a cute little house. Somehow it doesn't seem like a place he'd come up with, though.*

"Ade likes tea," Theo muttered. "Adrian, Kelsie, this is Anastasia Shevchenko. Max's sister."

"Max's sister, huh." Adrian lounged in a chair he was clearly too big for, while Kelsie sat more circumspectly with both hands wrapped around a mug. Kelsie nodded mildly while Adrian looked Anastasia over more thoroughly than she liked. "Nice to meet you."

"And you." Anastasia chose to stay standing, seeing there weren't enough chairs. Theo looked unhappy about this, but she quelled him with a smile. She stood near him by the sink with a cup in hand. "I don't know how to ask this, Theo, but can we talk? I mean, really talk?"

"Yeah." Theo cleared his throat. "She's in on the family secret."

"What? Did you tell everybody in the whole freaking town?" Adrian demanded.

"Says the idiot who got himself seen on their farm," Theo snapped.

"Wait." Anastasia frowned at Adrian. "Do you drive a red truck?"

Adrian shrugged stiffly.

"I think I've seen your underwear, then." She tilted her head challengingly. Adrian's eyebrows shot up. A moment later, Kelsie made a sniggering sound into her tea.

"Like what you saw?" Adrian asked, smirking.

"Naw. Tighty-whiteys are kind of boring, don't you think?" She looked at Theo, who was watching her sidelong. "Just because Max—just because of what happened, it doesn't mean we should lose track of each other. The shadow spirits are still out there. There was another collapse at the mall last night."

Theo's shoulders crept up toward his shoulders. "We have to do something."

"I know. I just don't know what. Mom found out that they can move between dimensions pretty much at will. That's why they shift back and forth from being solid. Only getting through all the layers between where they come from and here seems to require a place of boundary and a medium to be a portal. After that they can kind of jump around in the spirit world."

"A place of boundary?" Theo asked.

"Usually a place where two elements meet. Water and land is a big one—that's why Fort Rivers draws so much spirit activity, with the rivers meeting and the land in between." She gazed down at the dingy linoleum. "The spirits are scared of them, too."

"So they can t-touch spirits?"

Anastasia felt like she was almost, but not quite, picking up on the idea buried in that question. "I don't know."

"Because maybe spirits could touch them ... Y'know, could touch them back."

"I don't know." Anastasia bit her lip. "That's a really interesting question. I think maybe tonight I'll see if I can't summon somebody to ask." She bumped Theo's elbow. "Good idea."

"This is some crazy bullshit you two are talking." Adrian's upper lip was slightly curled.

"Seriously, are all werewolves skeptics?" Anastasia demanded.

"Pretty much," Kelsie said, the first time she'd spoken. Unlike her fiancé's booming baritone, she had a slightly flat, terribly normal voice. "Are all ghost hunters—"

"Mediums," Theo said quickly.

"Mediums, then. Are you guys all not scared of werewolves?" Kelsie looked directly at Anastasia in a way that was uncomfortably steady.

"I'd be dead if it weren't for Theo," Anastasia said, irritated. "Why would I be afraid of someone who jumped into a river to save me?"

Kelsie and Adrian exchanged a look. Kelsie straightened up.

"What's this all about?"

Theo's face turned dark pink. Adrian crossed his arms over his chest and gave Theo a narrow look.

"Who was getting after me for almost getting seen saving that Max guy?"

"Just how obvious were you?" Kelsie demanded. "You know what your grandmother would say."

"Nobody saw," Theo mumbled, then repeated it vehemently. "Nobody saw!"

"But you sure as hell told people after. You stupid runt—"

"Let's talk in the living room," Theo said hastily. Anastasia nodded eagerly.

"We'll still talk about this later, Theofanis." Kelsie's tone didn't change much, but it was clearly not willing to accept denial.

"What did I just do?" Anastasia whispered as they sat down on the couch.

"Uh, old family argument." Theo removed his glasses to pinch the bridge of his nose.

"Are you okay, Theo? Be honest."

"Don't worry about me, Ana." Theo spoke too quickly. "And if you need my help, just call. Just—not tomorrow night." He pointed upward. "You know."

"Oh. Gotcha." She tried again. "But I really do want to know if you're okay."

"I—" Theo smiled tightly, and the strain visible in the

corners of his mouth made a lump rise in her throat. "I'll be okay. I've got family here."

"Yeah, you do." Anastasia finished her tea in a series of hasty sips. They sat in silence, and Anastasia could swear she heard Theo's thoughts in it. She answered the unspoken question. "He's not happy, Theo, but he'll live." She patted Theo's forearm. "And you'll always be welcome at our house, no matter what."

"Thanks," Theo said hoarsely.

"I'd better go. I'll keep you updated, though." She hurried away before he could offer to show her out.

"Anastasia?"

"Hm?"

"Be careful." Theo gazed at her with calm concern. He looked haggard, but at the same time trustworthy and steady.

"Thanks, Theo. You, too." She smiled and let herself out. Outside, she shook her head ruefully.

My brother is such an idiot.

Full Moon

Max hadn't yet taken the app off his laptop that told him what phase of the moon it was. He kept glancing at it as he typed an e-mail to Dad. The tiny full moon seemed to be trying to get his attention, leaping into his peripheral vision when he looked away. It wasn't doing anything, of course; it was a static picture of a moon. Max finally gave up and closed his laptop.

Unfortunately, everything he had to do involved his laptop. He looked for something to procrastinate with; none of the books on the shelf interested him, being mostly the historical novels his parents liked. If he went downstairs, Anastasia was likely to start in on him again.

If he went out to his trailer, she'd be pounding on the door in no time.

It was so quiet in the house. No dogs, no twins, no parents, no ... Max abruptly went to the door. He'd put on a charm and go check the kennels. He'd top up water bowls and brush coats. That would pass some time.

The TV was on downstairs as he went by, but so was the light in the bathroom, so he managed to dodge his sister. He went out into the dark, feeling the cold hit. It numbed his sense of smell so the charm's fragrance wasn't immediately obvious. A dog barked, almost conversationally, as he came down the stairs. Max paused and looked left and right; the driveway was so empty, with only his car and Anastasia's present. Not even Theo's car was there to fill space. It wasn't just the emptiness that bothered him; it was his own need to check his surroundings.

Can't I feel safe at home anymore? Have those goddamn shadows taken that away from me? Max yanked the cigarette pack out of his pocket. He put a cigarette into his mouth, lighting it. He was in full sight of the house, if Anastasia happened to look out the kitchen window. Somehow he didn't care if he got caught right now. He forcefully expelled smoke and flicked ash away. One of the Weimaraners stood in her kennel, giving him a tentative wag when he glanced in her direction.

"Go back inside, Betty. It's too cold for you out here." He wandered over to hold his knuckles against the fence so she could sniff them. Her tail cut through the air as she wagged harder; some of his simmering anger cooled. "Seriously, I can tell you're cold." He turned his head to take another drag. As he inhaled, he felt the cigarette shudder between his lips. Just as he realized his fingers had begun to tremble, he tasted more than smoke. He tasted swamp, moisture, and moldering fear.

Max whirled around, his heart thudding. He heard the scrape of nails on cement and the squeak of a dog door as Betty fled. Yet it was his other senses he turned to now, casting about for any indication of a spirit nearby. There was a little tickle from what was probably a poltergeist out in the trees somewhere, but that was all. He no longer felt that he was about to drown in brackish water.

Shit. The last thing I want to do is go crazy. He'd heard of mediums who did, although it was all second or third-hand information. Mom had always been high-strung, meaning at times she'd withdrawn into emotional or even physical isolation. He still wouldn't call that crazy—who hadn't gone through the occasional dark patch? But once he started to doubt his own senses, his own ability to tell what was actually there and what wasn't ...

"I refuse to let my life turn into that." He aggressively dragged on the cigarette, welcoming the searing in his throat. His fingers had steadied, but he still had the urge to get inside, where light and safety beckoned. Max stubbornly held out where he was. "It's not that dark anyway." Between the yard light and the full moon, there were thick shadows, but also blue-white patches of illumination. Max turned his head so that the moon was in his peripheral vision. He spat smoke.

"I bet he's managing just fucking fine."

Despite his body's urgings, Theo couldn't settle down. The bedroom pushed him away like magnets with polarities reversed. He found the house claustrophobic and yet empty at the same time. Needing a little more space, he creaked his way through the kitchen, every joint protesting. He opened the back door and carefully eased himself out onto the back step.

He stared up at the moon, felt her light on his skin, and shuddered. It was like tentacles sucking directly at his life force. The cold hit him too hard, getting past his weakened defenses. Even so, he crept down into the backyard. Then his legs gave out and he fell backward into the snow.

It was painfully cold. He wore a button-down shirt, jeans, slippers under his robe, and still the chill came right through. He never looked on Mother Moon naked when she was full like this. At least, he hadn't in years, when he and Ma and Grandmother had slept out here four-legged during hot summer nights.

Theo didn't like pain, but he welcomed the cutting cold and the wicked burn in his body. It was an answer to his irritating restlessness. It reminded him of himself, made him aware of his own body in intimate detail. This hurt him, and only him. It didn't require anybody else.

I don't want anyone here. The longer he lay there, the harder it got to move; numbed hands and legs added to his weakness. If he didn't move soon, he'd be stuck out here.

I could really use a hand. That admission of dependency angered him into action. He rolled onto his side and, cursing steadily under his breath, dragged himself through the snow, up the steps, and inside. That was the limit. Just inside the door, he unfastened everything and let his clothes hit the floor. Then he changed and sank down on top of them. He put his chin on the linoleum and sighed heavily through his nose.

There's no point wishing he was here. He was never supposed to be here. He was never supposed to know.

That produced a new kind of ache. He was really glad to be four-legged, in a body that didn't weep.

CHAPTER SIXTEEN

Tucking his arms behind his head, Adrian sighed as he looked up at the dingy motel room ceiling.

"That's better."

"Mm-hm." Kelsie slid from the bed, her fingers trailing over his bicep. It was one of their traditions: once the moon fully let loose her grip, they'd have a thorough romp in bed to celebrate.

"Why'd we have to come back here, though?"

"We've got some privacy here," she said on her way to the bathroom.

"What? There's doors in Grandmother's house."

"Yeah, like I'd do anything with you under your grandmother's roof—much less with Theo in the house."

"Since when are you shy?"

"It's not being shy, Adrian, it's being normal," she called as she closed the door. He snorted, scratching at his cheek and listening to the shower run. Left without anything specific to do, he got up and pulled on a pair of boxers. He picked his jeans up off the floor, then paused. He inhaled through his nose. "There's that smell again," he muttered, frowning as he got into his jeans. Fastening them, he went to the door; the dense, inky smell grew weaker there. "What the hell is that?"

When he turned back, about to call to Kelsie, a startled yell escaped him instead. Every hair on his body stood up at once and he took a step back from the black figure. Fiercely cold fingers touched his wrist, and he twisted to see another cookie-cutter shadow behind him, and another to his left. All three came at him at the same time.

"Adrian?" Kelsie's muffled voice reached him from the bathroom as he crashed back onto the bed. He struck the lamp off of the bedside table with a flailing arm, crying out again as he felt something go straight through his skin and into him. Layer after layer of alien energy sank into his mind, crushing him, blocking his access to his other body. This body went suddenly numb and still despite his desperate thrashing around inside it.

"Ade? What's wrong?" Kelsie burst from the bathroom, dripping lather from her hair, her robe wrapped haphazardly about her. His gaze went to her, directed by someone else; his body moved jerkily upright. She immediately approached, putting a hand on his stomach and looking up at him. "Baby, what's wrong? Say something—"

He watched in horror as his own right fist swung toward her face; the blow threw her to the side. Before she could regain her balance, his fist caught her in the solar plexus hard enough to take her right off her feet. She was flung like a wet towel against the bathroom door, knocking it aside, and collapsed to the tile floor. *You bastards, I'm gonna tear your fucking throats out, nobody treats my girl like that!* Feeling something rummage around inside his mind, he screamed in frustration and a new kind of pain, and then somebody pulled the plug.

With the notable exception of the time he'd gotten into the liquor cabinet at age fifteen, for which Grandmother had made his life unpleasant for days afterward, Theo had never drunk alone. He'd always thought it would feel lonely and sad, like being an alcoholic. Intellectually, he knew that many sensible adults managed to live perfectly normal lives while enjoying a solitary drink or two at home, but his instincts had always warned him away from it.

They'd been right. He'd done nothing for the past two hours but sit in his living room with a bottle of whiskey, and he was miserable. For a while, he'd felt like he could handle the break-up, but tonight the loneliness and regret grew to unbearable levels. Slumped in the corner of the couch, he pressed his glass to his temple and gazed at nothing. His eyes burned but had no more tears available. His fingers reached up to play with the charm, but then he remembered he'd left it in the kitchen because its scent had started making him nauseous.

I suck. I just totally and completely suck. Some of Max's accusations had sunk in like knives. *He was right. He sees me so clearly, I should have …* No. He closed his eyes. *Stop being so pathetic. You always swore you'd be true to yourself. The first mainstream guy who shows interest, you'll throw that all away? Just for a guy with great skin and a gorgeous smile and a body that plays yours like you play an FPS …*

"I'm not that shallow," he whispered, and tossed back half a glass. The room spun around him when he closed his eyes. "It wasn't just physical for me."

His mind ruthlessly brought up images and sensations: Max apologizing; Max's hand linked with his; Max's look of concern; Max's laughter on so many occasions; Max's gratitude for his help, freely expressed. This assault made him curl up.

"So maybe it wasn't all physical for him, either. He didn't really accept me. Not the real me. I had to." He shuddered as the room dipped and tilted, fumbling the glass onto the table. He ached fiercely, and the whiskey was no longer giving him relief. *Did you really, Theo?*

A sly, nasty whisper in his mind. *Would you really have broken it off, or was it just because he stopped showering you with nice words and attention?* "Shut up," he groaned. More than anything else, what stuck with him was Max's ugly tone and the wounded fury in his eyes. Groping blindly, he grabbed the bottle. After taking a couple of pulls from it, he capped it and held it against his chest. "I'll never find anybody else like him. I don't want anybody else," he mumbled as the whiskey carried him off.

And then he jerked back, too late, as a hand caught him by the hair while another forced a wet cloth over his face. He choked and sputtered, fighting to get his hands to his face but finding them trapped under someone's knee. Arching off the couch, he tried to free himself as he grew rapidly weaker.

It can't be. Only werewolves know about wolfsbane— He was taken away into darkness before he could begin to understand.

This is just getting sad. Max didn't have to be there. He, in fact, shouldn't have been at Jimmy's. Anastasia was running errands in town, so he wasn't leaving her alone, but there were a million things he could be doing at home. Yet Max remained stubbornly at the little plastic table, an empty plate and mug next to his laptop. The afternoon light was warm through the streaked windows. He'd stripped down to shirt sleeves, and when people came in the outside breeze was cold enough to raise gooseflesh on his bare wrists. He'd done all the updating of the kennel webpage that he could. Now he sat, chin propped on one hand, while he scrolled through his inbox. A pair of earphones and some music shut out the sounds of Jimmy's.

Under a cluster of new emails from pet supply stores and dog show organizers, he spotted an email from Theo. For some time he stared at it, startled by its presence, and wondered if he could handle opening it. Then he clenched his teeth.

If he thinks he can just—The email was empty save for a link. Max frowned, then clicked on it. It opened a small, dim, and crackly video file. It had a date stamp on it that read December first—today. Max's eyes didn't immediately make sense of the dim image. He sat up, heart pounding, then turned the laptop away from the window and shifted his chair so he could see better.

It was a narrow view of his own living room—all he could really see was part of his couch. On the couch sat Theo. Blindfolded. Theo sat tilted to one side; even as Max watched, his head drooped.

"Oh my god," Max whispered. "What the hell is this?"

A shoulder blocked the camera, then the rest of the person came into clearer view. Adrian paused before Theo, his expression flat. Max clenched his teeth so hard they squeaked. His hands started to shake.

"You bastard!" He kept the fierce exclamation under his breath.

Theo stirred, lifting his head.

"Max?" The staticky sound of his own name spoken in Theo's nervous voice hit him like a blow to the chest. He slapped his hands down on the table because he needed its support. "Max, this is ... this is kind of—too hardcore for me maybe." His upper lip glistened strangely, and his head lolled forward, then back.

Max clutched at his hair with one hand, leaning heavily on the other. Panic and rage battled it out in his head.

Adrian sat down next to Theo. He slid his right hand up Theo's throat, looking into the camera.

"Seriously ..." Theo's voice was unsteady, uncertain. "This isn't funny. S-say something."

Adrian bent his head. It looked like he was nuzzling Theo's shoulder as his hand slowly glided down over Theo's chest, making him arch his body. Adrian made a sharp motion, so quick it left dark trails behind him, and came away with a piece of fabric in his teeth. He spat it out, giving the camera another of those unblinking looks. His hand came up to awkwardly caress the flesh he'd bared.

Theo, damn it, I'd never do anything like that to you!

Adrian turned again to the camera. Again Max saw a dark shadow behind him. Just barely, a single thought managed to get through the seething fury in his head: the shadows didn't make sense. They were warping around Adrian too unevenly to be a flaw in the video.

"Oh, shit," he whispered, going from very hot to very cold in an instant. Video cameras sometimes picked up spiritual energy. "Oh, hell." He fell silent, watching as Adrian held up a notebook with words scrawled across the page.

Come find us. We're closer than you think.

Behind him, Theo's voice could be heard only faintly.

"Gr—"

Max's hand crept to his own shirt and clenched the fabric as his whole body quivered.

"Grapefruit ..."

Slamming his laptop closed, Max crammed it and his coat under his arm and charged from the coffee shop.

Now that she was out of the house, Anastasia found that she wanted to stay away a little longer. Her sympathy for Max was wearing thin. She'd seen him get down over relationship troubles before, but not this angry about it. His presence in the house was becoming more unsettling than reassuring.

So, even though she was tired from driving all over town to get some long-neglected chores done, Anastasia decided to drop by Theo's.

I really could use a cup of coffee, anyway. She checked her cellphone, then tucked it back into her purse and got out of the car outside of Theo's house. Before she could ring the doorbell, the door abruptly opened and a blonde woman stared at her through the screen door. Anastasia stared back before belatedly recognizing her.

"Kelsie?" she hazarded. Then she noticed the dried blood on Kelsie's chin. "Oh, my god. Are you okay?"

"Do you know where Theofanis is?" Kelsie demanded. Her gaze was very intense.

"No, I was just coming to see him. What's wrong?"

"Ade. My fiancé. Adrian." Kelsie's nostrils flared, and she craned her head to look out into the street. Anastasia noticed the purple bruising all down the side of Kelsie's face. She started to feel very sick.

"I have to go." Kelsie opened the door.

"Where? And where are your clothes?" Anastasia stood her ground, alarmed that Kelsie wore a T-shirt—which looked like one of Theo's—and nothing else.

"I have to get out of here. The stink's making my head spin."

"Kelsie, I think you might have a concussion." Anastasia cautiously reached out to touch Kelsie's shoulders. *One thing at a time. Get her to the hospital, then see if I can get a hold of Theo.*

"No, from wolfsbane." Kelsie fluttered a hand in exasperation. "It puts us out. I don't have time for this. I've got to find Ade."

When Kelsie pushed past her, Anastasia caught her

arm. She found herself getting dragged down the stairs. The slim woman wasn't very steady on her feet, but she was alarmingly strong.

"Whoa! Wait! You don't know where he is."

"I'll find him," Kelsie said curtly. "No matter how long it takes." She lifted her head and sniffed loudly, and Anastasia belatedly understood.

"Maybe you shouldn't. Look what he did to you."

"That wasn't Ade. He was acting funny. Smelled weird." Kelsie didn't even sound defensive; instead, her tone was as distant as her gaze. Her legs looked pale and vulnerable beneath the dark shirt. Anastasia still clung to her arm.

"How about we talk in my car? Maybe I can help."

Kelsie slowly turned to look at her, pale eyes narrowing. Then she slowly nodded.

"Okay. I'll just close Theo's door. You get in and wait for me, okay?" Anastasia pressed her key remote as she jogged up the stairs. When she turned back, she was relieved to see Kelsie sitting in her passenger seat. She hurried around her car, got inside, and glanced through the windshield.

To see Theo's car parked in front of her.

"Was that here when you got here?" she asked Kelsie, pointing.

"Yeah."

"Now that I think about it, I pulled up behind it. So if it's here, where's Theo?" Clenching the steering wheel, she turned to look at Kelsie. "What's wolfsbane? If it puts you out, then why would Theo have any?"

"It looked like he'd been hitting the bottle," Kelsie said. "I thought maybe he was using just a little bit to knock himself out." She shrugged. "He's taking this whole break-up hard."

"Okay. Okay." Anastasia closed her eyes and tried

not to panic. "I don't know what's going on here, but I'm starting to think it might be really, really bad. I still think you should get yourself checked out. If it's a concussion—"

"No doctors. Not ever," Kelsie snapped. "Werewolves don't."

"Even if it's life or death? Believe me, I get the need for privacy, but—wait a minute." A flash of inspiration made her feel a little bit more in control. She put the key in the ignition and gave Kelsie what she hoped was a reassuring smile. It felt tense on her face. "I know just the guy."

Driving south through town, Max ran more than one red light with only cursory glances to see if he was clear. Once he hit the highway, he exceeded the speed limit by reckless amounts. Max gripped the steering wheel so hard it squeaked, or perhaps that sound was the protests of his knuckles. His back teeth refused to separate. Breathing quickly through his nostrils, he sounded to his own ears like a wild animal.

A small part of his consciousness knew he was way out of control, but adrenaline lashed him on down the highway. He also knew he wasn't alone in his car. There were at least three curious spirits in the back seat, and by the way the antenna and windshield wipers kept moving around, he had a poltergeist on the hood.

Something pulled his hair straight up. In his overwrought state, this made him leap in his seat and bat at the playful spirit.

"Piss off, I need to concentrate!" He thumped the steering wheel.

As if in protest, the steering wheel jerked right, and the tires appeared to leave the surface of the road. The world twisted around and blurred until he lost his orientation. The tires on one side hit frozen gravel with a loud crunch, and the tail of the car made a last firm slide to the left.

The car came to rest on the correct side of the road but facing the wrong way. Max shook in the grip of adrenaline that threatened to burn his heart right up. For a moment, he put his face in his hands and tried to make the world stand still. It stubbornly tilted and spun around him, and he was terrified that he would faint.

"Ice. Just hit a patch of ice. Keep it together. Keep it together," he whispered to himself. "Get off!" He turned to glare at the young spirit who leaned over the back of his seat to peer at him. Offended, the pale beige form prodded him in the neck with a cold finger before retreating. The car rocked, the hood flexing, as the poltergeist amused itself. "Jesus." The shock of it all had blown away all his fury. Now he recognized the feelings that fury had hidden. "Hang on, Theo. I'm coming." Glancing up and down the highway, he did a U-turn—at first the tires spun, terrifying him that he might be stuck until the car jerked free. It fishtailed again on the icy highway, but then caught traction and he was off.

To her great relief, Louis was out front shoveling the snow off his steps, when she drove in. Anastasia left the car running as she jumped out so the heater would keep going. She was even more relieved to see that Louis appeared to be alone.

"Louis, I'm sorry, but I really need your help. Can you help me without asking too many questions?"

Louis leaned on his shovel and blinked at her for a while. Anastasia glanced back at the car to make sure Kelsie was still in it. She feared the woman would bolt at any moment.

"That depends. I don't know if I can help or not until you tell me what's going on," Louis finally said.

"I've got a friend in the car. I think she might be hurt worse than she looks, but she won't go to the hospital. She's got her reasons for that, and we don't have a lot of time. Could you take a look at her?" Anastasia rubbed her hands together, twitching with cold and nerves.

"Does this have anything to do with those things?" Louis' voice went just a little unsteady, raising new sympathy in her. She couldn't think about the shadow spirits without fear, either.

"I think it might." She looked him in the eye as she said this. He nodded decisively and set his shovel aside. She explained her concerns as she escorted him to Kelsie. Then she leaned against the hood of her car while she tried calling Theo on her cell. Behind her, Louis was asking Kelsie questions in a businesslike tone. Theo didn't pick up at all. She tried Max, then Theo again, alternating between the two until Louis cleared his throat.

"It's hard to say for sure, but I don't think she has a concussion. Who's the bastard who hit her?"

"Her fiancé," Anastasia said. Louis's expression darkened.

"I told you, it wasn't him!" All at once Kelsie was out of the car and in the conversation. Anastasia opened her mouth to respond, but all at once her mind filled with noise. She looked sharply at Louis, whose face contorted with pain. Kelsie looked from one to the other. "What?"

"The spirit world," Anastasia said, setting her back teeth together. Normally she had to reach out to the spirit world to hear it, and rarely was it this loud. "Something's got it riled up, but I can't hear anybody clearly enough."

"Jesus!" Louis clutched at his head.

"Something about ..." Anastasia closed her eyes, trying desperately to make sense of it all. She could feel the spirits withdrawing, disconnecting from a single place. A place nearby. Her eyes flew open. "I think it's at my house."

"Where's that?" Kelsie demanded. Anastasia instinctively pointed through the trees, then immediately regretted it.

"Kelsie, don't!"

Kelsie stripped off the T-shirt. The flash sent Anastasia and Louis reeling back. A tawny wolf leapt forward through the trees and disappeared. Anastasia stumbled back around the car. She squinted through spots at Louis over the roof to see that he was staring at her. His face had gone pale even despite his cold-reddened cheeks. Moving like an automaton, he ducked into the passenger side and closed the door.

"Louis, what are you doing? I have to go." Anastasia hastily got in the driver's side.

"I don't know what the hell I just saw." He swallowed visibly, his heavy jaw working. "Scratch that. I do. Either way, I think I might be useful."

"I hope you're wrong." Anastasia put the car in reverse. "But I don't think you are."

CHAPTER SEVENTEEN

Max parked in front of Adrian's truck, not surprised to see it. He wasn't alone as he walked toward his trailer. Snow flew upward in small, upside-down tornadoes as the poltergeists he'd gathered couldn't resist the chance to play. The other spirits had fled once he'd gotten too close to home. They were obviously still afraid of the shadow spirits.

He had no plan. His burning anger had been cooled by the near-accident. Max stared at his trailer as he straightened his spine and wished he was still angry. Now he could feel fear both for himself and for Theo. His father had told him there was nothing more frightening than seeing one's loved ones in danger; Ambrose had taught him that most anger comes from fear. Max felt that he now truly understood what they had both been trying to tell him.

Screw fear. I don't care what happens to me, I'm getting Theo out. He marched stiffly toward the trailer. His breath caught in his throat as he drew level with the window and he saw Theo hunched over on the couch. Adrian wasn't in view. Max's heart pounded hard and fast. Yet his hand was steady as he reached for the door knob.

He opened the door and let it fall against the wall of the trailer. Framed by the doorframe was Adrian's tall figure. He stood stiffly in the kitchen, his hands held out from his sides. His expression was completely blank, his dark eyes like stone walls.

Max looked past him to see Theo more clearly. Even from this angle he could see the sweat slowly dripping from Theo's chin and the blue tinge to Theo's lips. His jaw tightened, and he stepped inside. It was cold in the trailer already, but the temperature dropped further as the poltergeists followed him in. Apparently they weren't afraid.

"So." Max hooked his thumbs in his pockets as he glared up at Adrian. "I came. What do you want?"

Adrian's heavy lips moved, slowly and awkwardly.

"You." His voice was thick and slow, like a bad recording. He gestured vaguely at Max's chest. Unsurprised, Max removed the charm and tossed it over his shoulder.

"You've got me. Untie him."

Adrian shook his head. Max broke out in a sweat of fresh rage. He snapped his fingers and pointed to Theo.

Hey, guys? Bet you can't untie him. The two poltergeists who had been hovering near his head pounced on this new game. Adrian's head jerked around to watch as Theo collapsed onto his side, his arms bouncing off his back as the poltergeists tugged at the chain around his wrists.

At the same time, Max felt the pressure of the shadow spirits grow in the back of his mind. He stiffened as icy fingers closed around his wrist. He was flung bodily into the cabinet next to the door. Winded, he tried to pull free. The shadow spirit brought him around to hit the wall face-first. A hard knock to the forehead twisted him around. Dizzy, he fell to his knees. He glanced up blearily to see another shadow peel itself from Adrian's body. It stepped aside as Adrian thudded to the floor. That impact excited the poltergeists, spurring them on; Max winced as Theo slid off the couch.

Then he lost track of Theo, because he was flanked by

two shadow spirits, with a third one fading into view in front of him. His heart tried to jump through his ribcage. He narrowed his eyes to try to stare the newcomer down. For a breath, there was nothing. Theo moaned, and that broke the thread.

"Jesus!" Max snarled, scrambling back. The shadow spirits closed in, grabbing his arms with crystal-hard hands. He pulled against them as they drew him up to his knees. His legs slid out from under him and he fell to his back. As his arms were pinned to the floor, he saw the strange faces of the shadow spirits up close. The vague bumps where features should be unnerved him. "Get off me!" The third one leaned over him, and he saw its pointed fingertips coming toward his face. "You'll have no vessel in me. Let go of me! My mind is my own! Get off!" A poltergeist shot by over him, slicing right through the shadow spirit. It distorted, flickered, and reappeared in the far corner of the room. Apparently other spirits could hurt the shadows. Max thought frantically as the shadow spirit approached again. Both werewolves were out of action. He needed help, spiritual help, but more powerful than poltergeists ... The solution came to him. He hated it. He dreaded the thought of it. Yet he knew it was his best chance.

Max let his head fall back and he gazed at the ceiling, letting himself drift closer to the edge of the spirit world. It was currently a noisy place. That noise guided him in.

I'm here. Come on, Deep Murky. He didn't know what the original inhabitants called this particular earth spirit; as it had never been human, it didn't favor words and had never named itself to him. *Remember me? You took me for a walk when I was small. I'm here. My mother is not. It's just you and me.*

First his fingers, then his wrists went numb from the shadow spirits holding on too hard. He slid further away from his body, distancing himself from that distraction. Making himself easier to possess. The shadow spirit leaned over him again, but the poltergeist got in the way and it jerked back.

This is your land, Deep Murky! Are you going to let these bastards take it? Come to me, this vessel can be yours. Don't you want it? Speaking into the spirit world was like casting a fishing line into a dark ocean. Until he heard a response, he had no idea if he was being heard. *Deep Murky!* And even as he strained to be heard, he felt the familiar creeping dread of being in a hostile place, of blind holes and isolation. The question that came to him was not quite a word.

Conditions?

Hurt no living people. Max felt instant disgust in reply. *Do you want these interlopers here? I'll lend you this vessel. Use it to destroy them.* He waited, then, for an eternity of seconds. The shadow spirit bent down next to him again, reaching out to his chest. Tingles broke out on his skin as those frigid hands touched it through his clothes. He arched his back off the floor, thrashing around desperately as those fingertips sank through his skin. "No! Get off!" In the middle of the pain and growing panic came one more almost-word.

Agreed.

And then decayed earth and tarry despair poured in, and the shadow spirits scattered like birds.

Adrian was stirred from a darkness that hadn't been sleep by the taste of his own blood. Opening his eyes revealed cream-colored linoleum. His back prickled fiercely, the hairs on his arms and neck were standing up, and the ugly smells filling his nostrils made him retch. He got onto all fours as his stomach emptied itself.

"Oh, hell," he croaked, crawling back from the mess he'd made. "I think I just threw up shit I ain't even ate yet." Blessedly back in control, he fell back against some cupboards. "Feels like my head's been flushed with antifreeze."

Looking straight ahead, he saw Max on his back and surrounded by the shadowy monsters that had made him bring Theofanis here. Max was thrashing around. Adrian pushed himself up the cupboards. In the process, he spotted Theofanis lying face-down in the next room, wedged between a couch and a coffee table. Adrian staggered toward him. He could see that Theofanis' wrists were bound with chain. Teeth snapping together, Adrian straddled his cousin's legs and grabbed those chains in both hands.

His hair whipped around his face as first one, then another isolated blast of wind shot by his head. When he pulled at the chain, something else pulled, too. Adrian's eyes widened as he watched a chain link start to open.

Creepy as hell, but it's helping. Adrian ground his teeth as he bore down on the chain, too. The metal bent back, and he pulled harder. The invisible thing with him grabbed the link just above his hand and redoubled its efforts. Then the link gave way abruptly and Adrian fell over into the glass coffee table. His elbow went right through it.

He didn't have time to feel any pain. Something happened behind him. He felt the atmosphere change, grow heavier. His invisible helper shoved past him, apparently fleeing. Adrian's body stiffened with new dread. He snatched Theofanis off the floor. His cousin was dead weight in his arms as Adrian turned to look in the kitchen.

The shadows were retreating as Max got to his feet.

He unfolded slowly like he was eight feet tall. His hair rippled gently, a wheat field on a breezy day, and his eyes were closed. Goosebumps rose on Adrian's arms. Eyes snapping open, Max looked at the shadows. His lips peeled back from his teeth into a smile that didn't fit his face. Adrian shuddered.

This guy looks like he should be in those girly movies Kelsie watches. On him that look just ain't right.

"Ade?" Theo's voice was barely there.

"It's gonna be okay, runt," Adrian said roughly. "I got you."

He jumped as Max made a slashing gesture with his hand. A matching diagonal split appeared in the shadow thing to his right, and in the fridge behind it.

What the—Adrian saw a shadow twist to look at him and threw Theo over his shoulder. Both Max and the shadows blocked the way to the door. "Aw, shit!" He backpedalled until he was up against the bay window. Cornered, he set Theofanis down on the broad windowsill. The shadow was moving his way, although it was clearly keeping an eye on Max as it did. Adrian watched it in turn. Sweat built up on his forehead. In contrast, his mouth was bone-dry.

Fear, for Adrian, was something that happened to other people. He'd been larger than most others all his life. He was comfortable intimidating just about anyone. But he had someone to protect, and that made fear meaningless. Adrian set his feet, keeping himself between his cousin and the shadow. Baring his teeth, Adrian tore at his clothes, and changed.

Every dog on the place was silent. That was the first thing Anastasia noticed as she drove into the yard. The second was the sight of the horses plunging through the snow in the hayfield; they'd obviously broken out of their paddock. As she came around the corner to see Max's trailer, she understood their fear.

The trailer roiled with dark energy. It wasn't just the shadow spirits, either. Whatever was in that trailer, it was powerful and malevolent. She looked at Louis and saw that he'd gone very pale.

"What the hell is going on in there?" he asked, his voice strangled.

"I don't know." She swallowed hard. Her hands had begun to tremble. "I've never seen anything like it. Louis, don't go in there."

"No chance. What are you going to do?" he asked as she left the car.

"I think my brother's in there. I have to go see." She hurried away before she could lose her nerve. She ran a hand along the side of Adrian's pickup truck as she drew close to the trailer. That was when she started to feel the pressure in her skull; the shadow spirits were definitely there. It was the larger spirit broadcasting its presence that she didn't recognize. Her instincts told her it was more frightening than the shadow spirits. It got very hard to keep walking. Finally, she stopped, leaning on a tree trunk.

It was then that she spotted the pale golden wolf. Kelsie was crouched behind a nearby tree, her ears flattened against her skull and her fangs showing.

"I know. I'm scared, too." Anastasia felt a little better with an ally. "Is Max in there?"

Kelsie nodded her head exaggeratedly.

"Theo and your fiancé, too?"

Another nod.

"God. What are we going to do?" Anastasia clenched the protective charm and stared at the trailer. She could see a silhouette in the bay window, but it was very still. She startled at a strange *zark* sound. It was followed by a dry, explosive noise, and then a chunk of trailer wall went spinning into the trees. Another long, thin slice of Max's trailer burst from over the bay window and tangled in the branches over her head. "Oh, god! In the house!" Hunching over as branches cracked alarmingly, Anastasia fled. "Kelsie, come on!" When she looked over her shoulder, she saw Kelsie hesitate, then lope after her. She waved frantically at Louis on her way by her car, too, and they all charged into the house together.

Max remembered this feeling of being thrown into the back of his own mind—Deep Murky was not gentle. Yet he felt his limbs thrumming in a new way, loaded with power, and he watched in awe as Deep Murky made air into blades. Another attack split a shadow spirit in two. It flickered over to another part of the room, but Deep Murky simply hit it again. This attack went through the shadow spirit, exploded the cans of club soda on top of the fridge, and created a plate-sized hole in the wall. The shadow spirit re-formed, but it was now jittering. As Max had guessed, Deep Murky could really hurt them.

The shadow spirits fled into the living room, but Adrian held them off. Beyond him, Theo was lying up against the windowsill. Max wished he had control of his own eyes so he could see Theo better. Seeing him crumpled up like that hurt. However, alarm distracted him as he felt his hand rising again. Deep Murky sent another attack through the living room, gruesomely decapitating one of the shadow spirits. A slice appeared in the wall just above the window; a rectangle of wood paneling dropped next to Theo's foot. Pink insulation dangled from the hole.

Too close! He had no concern to spare for his trailer with Theo in such danger.

Deep Murky ignored him. Adrian had crouched during the attack, but his bass growling didn't cease. Strings of slobber dangled nearly to his knees, and his ears were flattened against his skull. When the reeling, headless shadow spirit got within range, he lunged. He caught it by the leg. It writhed and tugged, but couldn't free itself. Max's elation was echoed by a toxic kind of delight from Deep Murky.

He can hold them! No wonder they're scared of werewolves!

Deep Murky let loose with a new kind of attack. Spheres of dull white light zapped toward the shadow spirit. It danced and jerked with every impact, then spiraled up into itself. Adrian staggered, then spat out a black curl. That curl zipped to the twisted up shadow spirit, which then imploded with a nasty bang.

Holy shit!

Feeling his own vocal cords vibrate with laughter, Max watched Deep Murky let loose a barrage of attacks. The trailer shuddered as the side wall and kitchen window were Swiss-cheesed. The two remaining shadow spirits dodged and skittered. Max watched Adrian's big paws tap dance on the carpet as he apparently tried to dodge without leaving Theo open.

Hey! Deep Murky laughed harder as a shot caught Adrian right in the ribcage. With a startled yip, Adrian was sent tumbling off his feet. *No! He's a person, a living person! Not him!*

Person? Bah. As if to prove his point, Deep Murky swooped an arm up. Adrian was flung into the air. His massive frame smashed right through the window and disappeared from sight. Glass rained down on Theo.

No! Horrified, Max slammed his will against Deep

Murky. *This isn't the deal! Get the shadows, you asshole!*

His body turned before he could get a good look at Theo. Deep Murky marched him down the narrow hallway. One of the shadow spirits lurked in his bathroom. It was flickering, obviously wounded. Its silhouette took on jagged edges as it puffed itself up. When it charged, Deep Murky blasted at it like a machine gun, making it dance wildly. Finally, it had enough and curled up into nothingness as its fellow had done. Max felt Deep Murky's deep satisfaction and found no room left for his own. The angriest he'd ever felt was nothing compared to the peripheral hints he was getting of Deep Murky's rich, endless hunger. Why Deep Murky hated so deeply, Max didn't know, but it shook him badly.

The last shadow spirit was in the bedroom. It had taken the fewest hits but didn't seem to be able to hide from Deep Murky. It looked pale gray yet was still visible. Deep Murky started throwing that lethal energy around again, and hole after hole appeared in the back wall of the bedroom. The window cracked and splintered, and the outside grew increasingly visible. Somehow, the last shadow spirit managed to dodge every shot. Then it made a break for it, leaping through one of the holes in the wall.

Oh, no, you don't! Deep Murky snarled.

Theo had been aware of noises, incomprehensible noises, for some time. The darkness wouldn't let go of him. His body was just in range of his awareness, limp and useless. Yet now something tapped at his cheek, giving him a point of focus. He very slowly came to. His eyelashes reluctantly parted, and he found himself looking at Anastasia. Her cheeks flushed, she was breathing quickly, and her eyes were very wide as she peered into his face.

"Oh, Theo. Oh, thank god. Come on, we have to get you out of here."

"Out of where?" He reluctantly responded to her urgent tugging. He was almost surprised that his legs took his weight. "Wolfsbane must be ... wearing off."

"What? No time to talk. I'm not sure this roof will stay up much longer." Anastasia looked up apprehensively as she put his arm around her shoulder. She was too short to support him, but he was able to use her as a guide. While he could see, nothing he saw made sense to him. The only light appeared to be coming through holes in the walls. Dust roiled through the air and insulation ballooned out of broken wood paneling.

"Max's." He remembered the familiar scents sneaking through the wolfsbane stench earlier. "I'm at Max's."

"That's right. Hurry, now." Anastasia's words remained breathless. His senses were clearing, and he could now detect her sweat.

"Don't worry," he said automatically. She gave a strangled laugh.

"Same old Theo. Here we go, through the door. Easy on the stairs."

Fresh cold hit him in the face and neck. The frigid wood of the stairs against his bare soles shocked some of the fog from his head. He couldn't make sense of the light— it was dim, but he couldn't tell if that meant morning or evening. The clusters of scent that teased his nostrils didn't make much sense, either. He swore he detected Adrian and Kelsie in that tangle of information. And the shadow spirits. And some things he didn't recognize at all.

"What's going on?" He forced himself to focus on Anastasia. Every step in the fresh air seemed to awaken his sluggish brain a little more. His next question was so important, brought so much fresh fear, that just asking it was like a bracing slap to the face. "Where's Max?" He paused at the end of the trailer, frowning at her obvious reluctance to answer. Then a tree trunk snapped, sending sharp echoes across the fields. He turned in that direction, hearing strange whooshing and cracking noises.

"Theo, come on. You'll be safe in the house."

Theo shook his head, yanking off his T-shirt.

"What are you doing?" She grabbed at his arm as if trying to restrain him.

"Four-legged I'm tougher. It won't affect me as bad," he said. "Don't worry."

"Theo, you're in no shape to do anything."

"Max is out there, isn't he?" He looked her in the eye. Her expression crumpled, and she nodded, fingers slipping off of his arm. "Then I have to go." Shoving down his pants, he turned away from her.

"Theo, be careful. Please."

Theo nodded, and changed.

He'd gone through a hole in the wall and somersaulted smoothly to his feet outside, a maneuver he couldn't have managed on his own. Tramping down untouched snow, he followed the shadow spirit. At a wave of his hand, white spirals blasted through the trees, severing the trunk of one. The shadow spirit leapt into the air and whirled around into a knot. Leaves, snow, and twigs battered tree trunks as that dark knot spun faster and faster, then imploded. The release of energy made Max's body stagger back.

And then things went still beyond the shifting and cracking of the broken tree and Deep Murky's sense of satisfaction. Max's body wasn't even out of breath. Seconds went by with nothing but silence from Deep Murky. Max waited impatiently; he wanted desperately to get back to check on Theo.

They're gone. The deal is done.

No done in that deal, Deep Murky scoffed.

No! I never offered you that. I didn't say forever!

You didn't specify. Deep Murky turned his head, surveying his surroundings. Through heightened senses, Max was aware of the life forces in the house. They kept him from total panic.

He's safe. He should be safe now, everybody should be okay, the fuckers are gone. Maybe if it's just me ... Intense resistance crashed over the rest of that thought. *No. I don't want to go. I'll never see my family again, and I'll never*—It shocked him how heavy this blow was, equal to thoughts of his family. *I'll never see Theo again. Never get him back. Never touch him. Never tease him until he gets mad at me but doesn't say anything, just sits there and sulks until I make him smile, and man I love that smile. No, you twisted monster, I'm not letting you do that to me!* His passion was met with contempt as Deep Murky sauntered toward the back of the property. But Deep Murky paused and turned back.

A dark shape shot across the snow, coming to an uneven stop at a cautious distance. Theo shook his head, then focused on him. His muzzle wrinkled, revealing fangs that gave Max a turn to see aimed his way.

No, Theo. You can't. He'll hurt you.

Clearly unsteady on his feet, Theo nevertheless dodged Deep Murky's first attack. He ran in a half-circle, trying to get in behind. Deep Murky whipped around and slapped him with wind. With a yip that tore at Max, Theo tumbled and rolled over several times. He got up again and shook himself, then feinted and lunged. Deep

Murky dodged, imperfectly; Theo's mouth closed around his wrist, and Max was flung off his feet. Now he was glad to be cut off from his sense of touch. Snarling, Deep Murky jabbed his fingers into Theo's sides; Theo yelped, leaping off like he'd been burned. As Deep Murky got up, a golden streak passed in front of him. The wolf next to Theo was smaller, but her snarl was determined.

You can't get them both. Give up. Max got disgust in reply. The wolves leapt in opposite directions as a line of wind tore up the grass. Deep Murky started when Kelsie—Max didn't know who else it could be—leapt at him. Her teeth snapped together right next to his cheek. His hand cut through the air toward her. She snarled wildly as she jumped straight up, twisting in midair and limping out of the landing. At the same time, Deep Murky sent another of those nasty blades winging toward Theo, who'd been creeping up on the other side.

But the two werewolves kept on the move, dodging attack after attack, forcing Deep Murky to twist and turn. Max bore down with his will, frustrated by his own helplessness.

Deep Murky snarled in response; just then, teeth gripped his right calf, and weight hit him in the back. He fell forward. Deep Murky immediately turned his head and tried to get his hands under him, but two pairs of paws stomped on his wrists and shoulders. Kelsie's fangs were right in front of his eyes. Another set of teeth closed around the back of his neck. Max could just barely feel the pressure and the hot saliva dripping onto his nape. He shook off his instinctive fear and focused on Deep Murky again.

They're giving you a choice. This body dies, what happens to you? I bet nothing good.

Only inarticulate anger came back at him. He desperately suppressed the certainty that Theo wasn't going to kill him. That certainty was tested, but not shaken, by the terrible growling that started low in Theo's chest. Kelsie's voice joined in, a lighter echo. The sound grew and grew until it didn't seem very distant to Max, as isolated as he was. Abruptly Theo bit down and gave a shake.

They're serious! Do you want to see what dying's like? He was aware of his heart pounding; it rattled his invisible prison. Knowing intellectually that Theo and Kelsie wouldn't kill him wasn't the same as convincing his adrenal glands. He numbly felt how his body trembled. Theo's teeth broke skin as he worried Max's neck again, and that did it. Deep Murky howled in silent fury, but he went.

Abruptly feeling everything, Max nearly howled, too. He felt himself get thrown from side to side, hitting the restraint of very heavy paws on his arms each way.

"Wait, wait, wait, he's gone!" he yelled, dizzy, cold, and drenched in sweat. Theo whined as he immediately let go. Every muscle and joint protesting, Max pushed himself up out of the snow. He groaned as he got himself to his feet. Disoriented, he just tried to stay upright.

A flash of light later, Theo was right there next to him.

"I'm sorry," he said hoarsely, hands reaching out to Max's neck. "I'm so, so—" Feet tangling, Theo fell against him. They hit the ground together, Theo's weight bending his ribcage painfully. This pain was rather beautiful, making Max laugh on an explosion of breath. He felt a damp nose on his forehead and heard snuffling.

"We'll be okay for a sec," he told Kelsie, tilting his head back to look at her. "Adrian needs you more." She licked his cheek, then trotted out of sight. "Theo?" He turned to look into Theo's face and found his eyes were closed. "Theo? Can you hear me?"

"Wolfsbane," Theo mumbled. "Hits us like anes... aness ..."

"Hang in there," Max said, fully aware of the irony of his words; he'd gone limp, completely drained. "It'd really help if you could walk to the house, because I'm not doing so hot myself, and werewolves are heavy buggers." He saw Theo's mouth quirk slightly and kissed him on the forehead. "How could you think I'd do something like that to you? Ever?

"I didn't," Theo whispered, eyes still closed and chin dropping to his chest. Max ran his hands over his shoulder in a desperate caress, gratified by the response. "I just wanted it to be. Knew you'd stop."

"God, Theo."

Theo made only a tiny noise. As Max held him, he found that he had far too many words, and they had to come out.

"I'd be willing to bet a lot of money we've both had ancestors burned at the stake. And we both had a million times in school when people called us freaks or looked at us and told us even without saying a goddamn thing how weird and unwelcome we were. And maybe that turned us into different people, but ... At some point I just said to hell with it and decided to be who I wanted to be. And I figure you probably did the same, right?

"And you know what? Maybe we both hang on to ourselves a little too hard sometimes because of it. Maybe we should let other people in more. Maybe we should even change what we do once in a while." Tears started to drip from his eyelashes. Theo's head turned, and his eyelids twitched. "So I'm going to admit some stuff that's hard for me right now, Theo. Yeah, when we first met I thought you were a freak. But you were a freak it was so easy to be around, it was like I could finally *breathe*." He gulped in air as if to demonstrate. "But I've never had someone I needed to keep before, and any time you took a step back from me, stuck to being geeky old Theo, it made me nervous. And today, the sight of you ... The thought of what was happening to you was too much. I couldn't handle it. I can't handle the fact that I'm never strong enough to help you, but that's not the worst thing. Never being here to try would be the worst thing."

"Max, I can't understand what you're saying," Theo mumbled. Heart leaping in his chest, Max squeezed Theo against him.

"I think you're it for me, Theo."

When Theo's eyes opened, he was frowning. He dragged his bleary gaze up to Max's face.

"Caught you again," Max said, smiling through tears of relief and so many other things.

"No." Theo's voice was gravelly and slow. "This time I caught you."

Relief and exhaustion and joy swooped down on Max, stealing his ability to speak. They remained slumped against each other, Max's arms locked around Theo's torso, until he heard his sister's frantic voice. In fact, even when she found them, Max had a hard time letting go. But he finally did, because he knew Theo wouldn't run away again.

CHAPTER EIGHTEEN

No! No fucking hospitals!" Adrian's voice rang out in the yard, drawing answering barks from the kennels.

Leaning on each other, Theo and Max made their way around the end of Max's ruined trailer. Theo's head was still reeling, and his knees didn't want to behave, so Max was having to come up with most of the support. He was also a vitally important source of heat.

Below the shattered bay window, more drama was going on. He frowned at Louis Wilson, who came over to throw a blanket around both of their shoulders; Louis' presence didn't make sense. Theo felt too weak to do more than watch as Anastasia gamely hurried over to help Kelsie pin Adrian down. On his back in the snow, covered in a pile of winter coats, Adrian was not cooperating, and the combined weight of the two women wasn't enough.

"Ade, Baby, you're messed up." Kelsie's voice jerked as she shoved his shoulders down.

"You know we can't go to those places! They'll see weird shit in my blood and I'll never get out of there again. Kelsie, you know I can't!" Adrian shook his head wildly. His right arm flailed blindly at Anastasia, sweeping her aside, but the left lay at an awkward angle across his stomach.

"Hey!" Louis Wilson didn't have Adrian's lung power, but his authoritative tone made them all pause. "Cool it!"

"Who the hell are you?" Adrian demanded.

"Just a guy who was a paramedic for twenty years," Louis snapped, kneeling by Adrian's side with a large first-aid kit. "You don't want too many questions asked; I can pull some strings at the hospital." He looked at Kelsie. "Let's get this big dickhead's arm wrapped up, then move him."

Kelsie, wearing nothing but a winter coat, nodded calmly. She helped Anastasia to her feet and they both watched as Louis went to work.

"No hospitals, I said," Adrian muttered.

"Not your call, buddy."

Theo had never seen his cousin so quickly subdued. On the other hand, he could see the tension in Adrian's cheeks; he was obviously in a lot of pain.

"Come on," Max said. "You, too." Theo shook his head.

"No hospitals."

"You sure?"

"Theo," Anastasia said, "are you sure?"

"I just want to ..." Theo bit his lip. The words he wanted to say didn't seem to fit a scene like this. He felt Max's arm tighten around his waist.

"You can be selfish. Right now, you can be whatever you want."

"I just want to rest. Get warm. With you." He spoke quickly before his throat could tighten up; Max's generous words were too much.

"But Theo, you could be really hurt," Anastasia protested as Max escorted Theo toward the house.

"Ana," Max said, escorting Theo past her, "let me take care of my own boyfriend, okay?"

He could no longer feel his feet, his head thudded with the aftereffects of wolfsbane, and his mouth tasted like old garbage. His cousin was injured, Max's trailer was destroyed, and too many people knew the family secret.

Nothing was really settled between him and Max. Yet the smile wouldn't leave Theo's face.

"Okay, you. Let's get you upstairs into a warm tub." Max was still holding Theo up, although he wasn't clear on what was holding *him* up. Possession didn't usually drain him like this, so he suspected it had something to do with Deep Murky's power. He was starting to notice the bruises and aches from being tossed around by the shadow spirits, too.

"Don't worry about me," Theo said. His voice was hoarse, his words slightly slurred.

"Come on, don't pass out on me. I can't carry you." Somehow they made their awkward way up the stairs. Max got Theo sitting on the edge of the tub, leaning against the wall. He fiddled with the taps until he had a tub full of warm water. Theo climbed into the tub unassisted, although once he was in the water he was very still, gazing into the middle distance. Max sat on the edge and caressed his forehead.

"Tell me if anything hurts," he murmured. "Anything at all."

"I'm okay, Max," Theo said, sounding mildly exasperated. Max looked at Theo's hand resting near his knee. He sucked in a breath at the bruises and scrapes on Theo's wrist.

"Jesus."

"I'm fine. You should, should look at yourself. Your face. And your neck's bleeding a bit."

"Eh?" Max got up and went to the mirror. All around his eyes, the skin was puffy and already starting to purple. The skin on his chin was split, and his cheek was a network of blue and brown spots. "Holy crap. I'm surprised you didn't run away when you saw me."

"I wouldn't."

"That was a joke, Theo." Max smiled, which made all kinds of things hurt. He bent down to rummage in the cabinet under the sink to find the first aid kit. After a cursory wipe of his nape, he put on a large patch of gauze as best he could without being able to see it. Then he started putting Band-Aids on his various cuts, feeling the silence. "Don't fall asleep in there. I don't think I can pull you out."

"Max, I'm sorry about the things I said."

"No, you're not." Max turned around and leaned his hips against the counter.

"But ..." Theo gazed at him, brows knitted. "I didn't want to hurt you, or, or make you go away. I just got, y'know, scared."

"It's okay," Max said. "I probably needed a smack-down." He toyed with a small bottle of antiseptic, not quite meeting Theo's gaze. "Fixing behaviors and relationships is kind of what I do for a living, and, well," he shrugged, "I'm not used to serious relationships. I was watching so close for the other shoe to drop that I think I maybe just started throwing shoes instead."

This made Theo snort, and some of the tension leave his cheeks.

"Yeah," he said, smiling. "Maybe I was, too." His smile faded. "What happened in there? I don't really remember."

"Do you really want to talk about that tonight?" Max asked. *I sure don't.* When Theo hesitated, Max straightened and grabbed a towel. "We better get you out of there and dried off before one of us passes out." Theo eased himself out of the tub, biceps visibly trembling. Max stepped in close to wrap the towel around Theo, then found himself unwilling to break the embrace. Theo turned his head to look at him. For a moment, they just looked into each other's eyes. The kiss came naturally and was gentle and warm. Theo made a little noise in his throat, then withdrew, licking his lips.

"You taste like antiseptic."

"Mm. I'm not very sexy right now, am I?" Max patted Theo's forearm. "Let's go collapse." Taking Theo by the hand, he led him toward the main bedroom.

"I don't care if you're sexy," Theo said quietly. Max laughed, startled.

"It's not permanent."

"That's not what I—"

"I get it, Wolf Boy. I get it."

They climbed into bed together. Max pulled his cellphone out of his pocket and began responding to texts from both Anastasia and his mother. Theo leaned his head on Max's shoulder.

"Any news about Ade?"

"Sounds like things are going okay at the hospital."

"Good." Theo sighed heavily. "So are they gone now?"

"I don't know. Just have to wait and see, I guess." This was another thing Max didn't feel up to talking about right now. He leaned over and kissed the top of Theo's head. Theo's eyes were closed, and his own eyelids felt heavy. "Shit."

"What?"

"I have to go see if the horses came back and check on the kennels."

"Maybe I can help."

"Nuh-uh. I didn't drag you to the hospital, and in exchange for that you're staying here and staying warm. Oh, man."

"What now?"

"My trailer's totaled. I don't want to move back into the main house."

"So move in with me." Theo's words were mumbled, barely audible. Max stared at him, but Theo's eyes were closed and his breathing had slowed.

"Are you serious?" Max asked quietly. Theo simply grunted in response. Max lingered there, watching the steady rise and fall of the blankets covering Theo. "You know I'll start cleaning it up on you." When he got no response, Max leaned over to kiss the top of Theo's head, then dragged himself off to deal with his other responsibilities. His life was obviously about to change. But Theo was safe, his family was safe—Fort Rivers might even be safe. Everything else could be figured out later.

Last Quarter

Theo, wrapped in a blanket and bookended by the twins on the couch, took it in good humor as Charli spoon-fed him pudding and Chrissi brushed his hair. Louis stood by the front window with Mom and Dad, discussing the damaged glass. Kelsie and Anastasia chatted in a friendly way while Adrian glowered defensively nearby. Max leaned on the wall that led into the living room, occasionally taking sips of wine as he kept an eye on the proceedings on the couch.

He glanced up when a shadow fell over him; he said nothing, looking at Adrian. Working his jaw from side to side, Adrian glanced into the living room, then jerked his head in the direction of the kitchen and walked past. After a moment, as much to assert his independence as out of concern, Max followed.

Adrian leaned his hips against the sink, toying with a beer bottle. A white sling held his cast-encased arm. It didn't hurt Adrian's thuggishly handsome looks to have the white tape across the bridge of his nose. Max stood near the table and crossed his arms over his chest as he waited. He wasn't going to be the one to speak first.

"I don't like you monkeys," Adrian finally muttered. Max raised his eyebrows, but didn't respond. "The only thing you got on us is numbers, but you still make it real hard for us to live."

"Oh, come on now," Max said, exasperated.

"Just listen, all right?" Adrian snapped, glaring. He took a swig of beer, transferring his glare to the inoffensive garbage can next to fridge. "But when you came for Theo …" His expression softened into something more familiar; it was the expression he'd expect to see in conversations with a buddy, not exactly gentle or even friendly, but honest and steady. "That was pretty badass."

"Thanks." Sensing that Adrian was completely serious, Max resisted the urge to laugh.

Adrian shook himself. It reminded Max of the way dogs would suddenly shake, as if their skins had slipped awry and needed to be thrown back into place.

"That sucked so harsh," he said.

"I can believe it," Max said.

"Can you?" Adrian was glaring again. "How can you possibly know, gay monkey? You know what it feels like hitting your own skinny, little girlfriend and seeing her just—just on the floor, and you can't even see if she's okay, 'cause your own damn body's going somewhere else? And Theofanis." He shook his head, teeth clenched. "Yeah, we wind each other up, but I've known him since he was a baby, man. Seeing my own hands putting him in fucking chains, like some kinda goddamn animal—"

"That wasn't you," Max said, unable to stop himself. He did not like Adrian, but he wasn't going to blame him for being possessed. "That was the shadow spirits, not you."

"I know that," Adrian snapped, but his voice lacked

bite. "I just can't get it outta my head. She's all I got. And I coulda killed her."

"But you didn't. Just like I could've killed you, and I didn't," Max said. "Get over it." He didn't feel guilty letting Adrian think he'd had any control over that. This got him an irritable look, but then Adrian cleared his throat.

"Look, man, stop trying to piss me off. I'm trying to apologize."

"I already told you, that wasn't—"

"For before that." Adrian over-rode him. "I just couldn't see you being good enough for the runt, that's all. I was just trying to scare you off, you know."

It took Max a moment to wrestle his anger down. He looked at the harvest gold fridge, and it seemed to ground him. He walked over to stand in front of Adrian, looking him in the eye. Slouched over, Adrian was just a little smaller today.

"Just so you know," Max said, "you don't throw people you care about into walls. Or treat their houses like your own personal playground. Or mess with their partners. I'm a peaceful guy most of the time, but if you ever get all hyper-macho on Theo again, I'll do my 'badass' thing."

Adrian gave him a disgusted look, then took a long swig of beer. He set down the bottle and held out his hand.

"Deal," he said, smiling his nasty smile. Max shook that hand, which engulfed his own and held on far too tightly. "You hurt him, though, I'll twist your head off."

"Fair enough," Max said. He retrieved his wine glass and left the kitchen. Kelsie passed him on the way back to the living room and gave him one of her what-can-you-do smiles. He smiled back.

"Okay, enough of that," Max told the twins, gesturing

for them to get off the couch. "My boyfriend."

"But—" they said, just slightly off unison.

"Get!" Grumbling, they did so. Theo smiled at him and shifted to make room. Slipping his arm around Theo's shoulders, Max gave him a light kiss on the mouth. "You doing okay with all these people here?"

"People I know are never a problem," Theo said quietly. "And right now it's good." He paused, obviously choosing his words. "I think you never really got this. I like belonging, y'know. Being at cons, it's all people like me, and it's awesome. And it's not like family, where you're always stuck as the same person no matter how much you grow up or change."

"I get that, Theo, I really do."

"But I got to thinking, like, your family's kind of weird." He grinned wryly. "Maybe weird enough even I could ..."

"You think you've got a choice on that one?" Max laughed to hide how moved he was. "The Shevchenkos laid claim on you, Wolf Boy. You belong to us whether you want to or not." *In a matter of months I went from stubbornly single to this. Shit, I could marry him.* Max felt his throat tighten as he gazed at Theo. *Maybe it's too early to think this way, but I think I could seriously take this nerdy werewolf to have and to hold.*

Perhaps sensing how deep things were getting, Theo broke the gaze. He plucked at the blanket rather mournfully. "I'm just a little worn out, you know. It's been five days. I'm fine."

"You should probably know your complexion means it's really obvious when you haven't been sleeping," Max said, relieved for the distraction. "If you'd go outside once in a while when the sun's still shining, you wouldn't look like a panda right now."

Theo bristled for a moment; then he visibly relaxed, rolling his eyes.

"I do go outside. Just not enough to tan."

"With all that Mediterranean blood, shouldn't you tan pretty much instantly?"

"Yeah, well," Theo muttered. Max grinned, bumping his shoulder against Theo's.

"When everything settles down here, I want to take you somewhere sunny." He saw the wariness in those lovely gray eyes, and shook his head. "Not because I want you to be this whole different guy who loves parties on the beach or anything like that, but because I want to see you out in the sun, smiling and happy and gorgeous and just ..." He smiled tightly. "Just plain mine." Then his smile relaxed and spread as he saw the warmth come into Theo's eyes and felt his weight lean his way. As people around them talked about all kinds of worrisome things, most of them in the past tense, they came together at the same moment, hands on each other's cheeks, in a single, discreet, important kiss. They came apart and leaned their shoulders into the couch so they were facing each other.

"So where do you want to go?" Theo asked.

"At this time of year, maybe California? Or Mexico," Max mused. Theo put a hand on his knee, his eyes widening.

"There's a con in San Francisco in, like, a month," he said breathlessly. Max threw his head back and laughed, making everyone look. "No, seriously, we could do both," Theo rallied. He then looked sharply at the door.

Picking up on that signal, Max went to open it. He blinked in surprise as Frankie burst past him, Whitney and Marnie right on his heels.

"Theo, man, you here?" Skidding to a stop, Frankie looked from person to person, then focused on Theo. His face paled. "What? What's wrong? You okay?"

"I'm just—uh, yeah. What's—" Theo started to get to his feet.

"When you didn't show up for lunch, we got worried," Whitney said. Marnie stood behind him, hands on his shoulders, her eyes wide behind her glasses.

"Oh, shit, it's a lunch day." Theo put a hand to his forehead. "God, guys, I'm sorry."

"We called you, like, a thousand times," Frankie said.

"I just haven't, uh, been feeling so hot, and I turned stuff off, y'know, like I do ..."

"How many times have we told you? You have to let us know when you're going to do that," Marnie complained. Theo floundered, looking from one friend to another.

Anastasia made her way to Frankie, smiling and holding out her hand. "Hi, I'm Anastasia Shevchenko. Max's sister. You might know me as the woman Theo pulled out of the river."

"Nice to meet you—no way!" Frankie's eyes widened as he shook her hand. "I'm Frankie."

"Could you help me in the kitchen, Frankie?" She linked arms with him and smoothly guided him down the hall.

"But wait, Theo's clearly lying," Max heard Frankie saying. "He's a crap liar." Snorting into his drink, Max nudged Theo's leg.

"Told you."

As Theo, at a loss, sank back down onto the couch, Max gestured for Whitney and Marnie to go in. They hesitantly entered the living room.

"You really okay, Theo?" Whitney asked.

"Yeah," Theo said with an unfettered smile. "I really, really am." Then the room grew busy with introductions and pleasantries; Whitney filled Theo in on some arcane rundown of a TV show he'd been missing, while Max's parents came over to discuss Christmas plans. The room was warm, golden, and alive with an eclectic mix of personalities.

Max stood a little to the outside of all this, watching Theo grow more animated as he talked to his friends. It no longer bothered him that Theo acted easier with them.

That just means they don't excite him like I do. It just means I have a different place in his life. He couldn't believe they'd ever fought about such things. With things like Deep Murky out there, or the shadow spirits, or natural disasters or car accidents or disease, how could he ever have thought it was important to "normalize" Theo?

I love him. Max slowly smiled, easing himself off the doorframe. *I think I'll go tell him that.* When Marnie and Whitney were drawn into conversation with Max's parents, Max slid in next to Theo on the couch. Theo turned to him, blinking solemnly.

Max leaned over to whisper in his ear.

CPSIA information can be obtained at www.ICGtesting.com
Printed in the USA
LVOW13s0302091213

364369LV00001B/10/P